"You know how to use that thing?"

Kate VanNam swallowed hard as she raised the revolver. "Certainly," she lied. "I'm an excellent—"

Before Kate could finish her sentence, Sheriff Travis McCloud had taken the gun away from her and then pulled her up against him. "Never aim a weapon unless you mean to fire it. You hear me?" he asked.

"Yes."

"Damn it to hell, I knew it."

"Knew what?" she asked, intensely aware that his slim hips and long legs were pressed flush against hers. She could feel the heat radiating from him, making her own body warm.

"That you'd be trouble. You are trouble. You'll cause trouble. For yourself. For me."

"That's a lot of trouble, Sheriff."

"Too much trouble," he said, releasing her before he placed the revolver on the sofa bed. "Why don't you pack up and leave before somebody gets hurt?"

"I am staying in Fortune, and if you don't like it I'd suggest you stay out of my sight."

Both annoyed and amused by Kate's determination, Travis raised his hands in surrender. "Fine, Miss VanNam, but if I catch you anywhere near a saloon or out on the streets after dark, you're going to jail."

"Fair enough, Sheriff," Kate said. "And if I catch you anywhere near this house after dark, I'll be forced to shoot you."

The Sheriff

NAN RYAN

MIRA®

ISBN 0-7394-6244-X

THE SHERIFF

Copyright © 2006 by Nan Ryan.

Printed in U.S.A.

For my fellow classmates with whom
I graduated dear old Bryson High on that
warm Texas night all those summers ago.

Fannie Ainsworth

Rollins Bilby

Vernon Crager

John Denning

Joe Gillespie

Jerry Graybill

Shirley Harrison

Joyce King

LaRue Matlock

Imogene McNear

Bobby Mitchell

Glenda Odom

Delores Shook

Dorothy Sims

Malvin Teague

Betty Lou Wells

Colleen Wolfe

Prologue

In a candlelit hotel room on San Francisco's rowdy Barbary Coast, a handsome man lay on his back upon the bed.

He was naked.

So was the woman astride him.

The pair were making hot, eager love.

They had been at each other from the minute they rushed into the room, locked the door and hurriedly began stripping off their clothes.

Now the lusty pair moved together in a frenzied mating. The voluptuous woman's heavy breasts bounced and swayed with her rapid movements. She gripped the man's ribs and murmured his name repeatedly.

A blue officer's campaign cap bobbed atop the woman's head. A captain's uniform was draped over a bedpost.

And atop the bureau, a pair of golden spurs gleamed on freshly polished black boots.

In minutes, the pair climaxed.

Immediately after the loving, the man anxiously asked, "Did he die?"

"Yes," the woman replied breathlessly, doffing the campaign hat and brushing back her long dark hair to reveal a blue trinity tattoo on the side of her neck.

He nodded. "Did you get the assay?"

"Yes, I did," she confirmed.

"Did the doctor or nurse see you?"

"No one saw me," she assured and leaned down to kiss his doubts away. On the Embarcadero below, drunken miners shouted and fired their guns in the air.

One

Boston, Massachusetts
March 1855

A cold winter afternoon, in a sparsely furnished room in Boston's South End, twenty-two-year-old Kate VanNam read to her elderly, hard-of-hearing uncle. Nelson VanNam was a gentle, caring, life-long bachelor, who had raised Kate and her older brother, Gregory, after their parents had perished in a fire at sea a dozen years earlier.

For a short time, he had been a successful and prosperous businessman who had provided well for his niece and nephew. But in 1849, an unexpected reversal of fortune had changed all that. The once prominent VanNams had fallen on hard times. The grand Chestnut Street mansion in Beacon Hill had been lost, along with the VanNam fortune.

When the fortune disappeared, so did Gregory VanNam. The senior VanNam was now in failing health and eternally grateful to his sweet-natured niece for selflessly tending him.

On this bitter January day, the two sat as close to the fire in the grate as was safe, blankets draped over their knees. As Kate read to her uncle—shouted, actually—she heard a loud knock on the door.

Kate lowered her well-worn copy of the Dickens novel *Oliver Twist,* and gave her uncle a questioning look. He shrugged his thin shoulders. Kate laid the book aside.

"I'll see who it is. Stay right where you are," she said to her uncle.

Nelson nodded.

Kate opened the door. A uniformed messenger stood shivering on the steps. He handed her a sealed envelope on which only her name was written in neat script. She started to speak, but the youth who delivered the message had already turned and left.

Puzzled, Kate closed the door and returned to the fire and her uncle. She held out the envelope to him.

Squinting, he read what was written. "It's addressed to you, my dear. Open it."

Kate tore open the end of the sealed envelope and slipped out the folded velum paper. After reading the brief message quickly, she explained to her uncle that it was a summons for her to come to the law offices of J. J. Clement, the attorney who, like his father before him, had always represented the VanNam family.

"Why on earth would Clement want to see me?" Kate mused aloud, as she handed the message to her uncle.

"I have no idea, child," he stated, reading the missive. "But I'm sure it can wait. No need for you to..."

He stopped speaking, shook his white head and began to smile. The curious Kate was already reaching for her heavy woolen cape hanging on the coat tree beside the front door.

Swirling it around her slender shoulders, she said, "It's time for your afternoon nap, Uncle Nelson. While you rest I'll walk to the law offices and see what this is all about." She smiled at him as she buttoned the cape beneath her chin and drew the hood up over her gleaming golden hair. "I will be back within the hour, the mystery solved."

Nelson VanNam knew it would do no good to argue that it was far too cold for Kate to be walking to the attorney's office. His pretty niece, while as kind and caring as a ministering angel, was also a decisive, strong-willed young woman who discharged duties and met challenges with an immediacy that was admirable, if at times somewhat annoying.

The old man smiled fondly as Kate waved goodbye and stepped out into the cold. He sighed, folded his hands in his blanketed lap and gazed into the fire, recalling the first night the ten-year-old Kate had spent in his home.

"No, Uncle Nelson." She had set him straight when he'd offered to leave her door ajar at bedtime. "Please close it. I do not fear the dark, sir."

Nelson VanNam was warmed by the memory. He had learned in the years since that the dauntless Kate was not afraid of much.

His smile abruptly fled. *He* was afraid for her. What, he wondered worriedly, would become of his dear sweet Kate once he was gone?

Teeth chattering, shoulders hunched, Kate briskly walked the eight blocks to the law offices of J. J. Clement. Hurrying across the narrow cobblestone street, she dashed up the steps of the two-story red-brick building and entered the wide central corridor.

Sweeping the hood off her head and smoothing her hair, she knocked politely before entering the attorney's private chambers. A warming fire blazed in a large hearth.

"Why, there you are already, Miss VanNam," said J. J. Clement, rising from his chair. "I had no idea you'd come in this afternoon. Please, have a seat." He gestured to one of two straight-backed chairs pulled up before his desk.

Kate frowned as she sat down. "Your message summoned me, Mr. Clement, did it not?"

The attorney smiled. "So it did. Your prompt response is admirable, but I hope you didn't freeze on your long walk." He sat back down across from her. "It was thoughtless of me to have you come in. I should have paid you a visit at your—"

"Never mind that." Kate waved her hand. "What's this all about?"

The attorney smiled at the impatient young woman. He leaned toward his desk, picked up a legal document and informed Kate, "My dear, I believe I've a bit of good news."

"You do?" She shrugged out of her heavy cape. Unlike the drafty rooms of home, this handsomely appointed office was comfortably warm. "For me?"

"Indeed. The firm has been informed that Mrs. Arielle VanNam Colfax—Nelson's aged aunt and therefore your great-aunt—has passed away in San Francisco. She has left all that was hers to you."

Stunned, Kate said, "Why? I didn't know her. Never corresponded. I never even met her, so why…?"

"The elderly widow had no children. With the exception of Nelson, you are her next of kin. You and your brother, Gregory. However, Arielle made no provision for Gregory. Now, to tell the truth, I don't know if you've inherited anything of real value. The old lady was quite secretive." The attorney shrugged.

Kate nodded.

"However—" he shoved a printed handbill across the polished desk "—as you probably know, a great deal of gold has been brought out of the Sierra Nevadas of California in the last five years."

"Yes, I've heard about the gold rush. Who hasn't?"

J. J. Clement said, "You have fallen heir to a house of sorts. I understand it has not been lived in for the past five years. And there is a claim to a California gold mine that may or may not be worthless." He handed Kate a map indicating the mine's location.

"The house? It's in the mountains of California?"

"Yes, the house and the mine are both high up in the Sierra Nevadas in a mining camp called Fortune," said the attorney. "I've no idea what Fortune, California, is like, but I would imagine it's one of those primitive tent cities populated by hardscrabble miners hoping to strike it rich." He shook his head.

"But if my great-aunt built a house there, then surely—"

Interrupting, he said, "As I told you, Kate, it has been abandoned for years. Obviously, your great-aunt deserted the house and the camp for a good reason."

"I suppose so," Kate grudgingly conceded.

"Child," said the kindly attorney, "I'm aware of your financial woes. Your uncle has been a friend as well as a client for many years. I'd like to be of help."

Lips parted, Kate stared at him. "That's very kind, Mr. Clement."

"Tell you what, I'll have our California agent, Harry Conlin, take the claim and the property off your hands and—"

"No," she interrupted. "It is not for sale. I'll just hold on to it for the time being."

She rose to leave, fastening her cape under her chin. J. J. Clement came to his feet.

Kate said, "When I lose my dear uncle Nelson, there'll be nothing holding me here. Who knows?" She picked up the printed handbill. "I might just head West."

Two

Kate hurried home with the plat map and the will rolled up and tucked under her arm. She could hardly wait to show both to her uncle Nelson. No doubt he would be as surprised as she that a woman whom Kate had never met had left everything to her.

She smiled as she envisioned her uncle putting on his spectacles and studying the documents while she knelt beside his easy chair and stretched her hands out to the warmth of the small fire.

Nose cold, cheeks red, Kate reached the rented rooms and hurried inside, calling her uncle's name.

"Uncle Nelson, you are not going to believe this!" she exclaimed loudly as she removed her woolen cape, hung it on the coat tree and rushed across the room toward his chair. Mildly annoyed that he hadn't bothered to turn around when she'd come in, she continued, "My great-aunt—that mysterious lady you have told me about, Mrs. Arielle VanNam Colfax—has passed away out in San Francisco and left me a…I have her will here and…and…" Kate stopped speaking.

She was beginning to frown when she reached Uncle Nelson's chair and the old man still had not responded.

"Uncle, what is it? What's wrong?" she asked, and gently touched his shoulder. He fell forward in his chair. Kate immediately dropped the documents and sank to her knees before him, grabbing hold of his upper arms. "You're ill," she said, "that's it. You're not feeling well. I'll just run and get Dr. Barnes and he'll fix you right up. You'll be good as new and…no… No, Uncle Nelson, no!" Kate murmured, not wanting to believe that the kind man who had been mother and father, friend and protector, was dead. Gently, she leaned him back in his chair and closed his sightless eyes as tears filled her own.

When finally she dried her eyes, she saw that her uncle was clutching a piece of neatly folded bond paper in his right hand. She carefully removed the document and laid it aside without looking at it.

Long minutes passed while she sat on the floor with her forehead on her uncle's knee. Finally, eyes red from weeping, Kate rose to her feet, took a deep breath, and immediately went about the unpleasant task of seeing to it that her beloved relative was taken to the undertaker's parlor around the corner.

Afterward, when she returned home alone, Kate paced the chilly room, wondering how she could possibly give her uncle the kind of funeral he deserved. She had no money. And she had too much pride to ask for help from her uncle's few close friends.

Despairing, Kate sat down in her uncle's chair and leaned her head back. The fire in the grate had died. It was cold in the room. She shivered and rubbed her arms. It seemed she could never get warm.

Kate turned to look for the blanket she'd had earlier, and suddenly noticed the folded sheet of heavy bond stationery her uncle had been clutching when she'd found him.

She reached for it and carefully unfolded it.

She read and reread the message. In his neat, distinctive hand, Nelson VanNam had told his niece where the last of his cash was hidden, along with a pearl-handled Navy Colt pistol he treasured.

Kate refolded the letter and put it in the pocket of her dress. She went into the tiny alcove where her uncle had slept, and removed a battered tin box from beneath a loose floorboard at the foot of his bed. When she opened the box, Kate's eyes widened. The heavy pistol rested atop neat stacks of cash.

Kate hurried to the dining table and placed the box

there. She lifted out the pearl-handled Colt revolver and gently laid it down. Then she took the stacks of bills from the box and carefully counted them.

Immediately, Kate felt as if an unbearably heavy load had been lifted from her shoulders. There was more than enough money to give her uncle a proper burial.

And to get her all the way to Fortune, California.

"You simply cannot do this," warned Kate's best friend, Alexandra Wharton. "A woman does not go alone across the country from Boston to California. It isn't safe. No telling what might happen to you."

"I'm not going across the country, Alex," Kate said, and affectionately hugged the frowning Alexandra.

The two women had been friends since the days both had attended the Willingham Academy, an expensive private school for young ladies where they had learned the difference between a lemon fork and an oyster fork and how to converse in French. While Alexandra still enjoyed a privileged life with wealthy parents, she continued to count Kate as her best friend and an equal in every way.

"But, Kate," Alexandra said now, "California is on the other side of America. You will *have* to travel across the country."

"No, I won't," Kate merrily corrected. "I'm going by ship!"

"Oh, you know very well what I mean," scolded Alexandra.

"Yes, of course I do. Ah, Alex, don't look so grim. No terrible fate will befall me." Kate pulled back and smiled reassuringly at her friend.

"You don't know that to be true. Even if you travel by ship, the horn is treacherous and—"

Interrupting, Kate shook her head and said, "Did you know that the route via Cape Horn is a journey of thirteen thousand nautical miles and takes four to eight months to complete?"

"Well, there you have it. You can't possibly—"

"I'm not going via the horn. I'm taking the short-cut across the Isthmus of Panama." Kate snapped her fingers. "Nothing to it! I'll be in California in no time at all."

Alexandra frowned. "Even so, it's uncivilized out there, Kate. There are bandits and Indians and…"

"I appreciate your concern and I will miss you terribly, but this could be my golden chance, don't you see? Maybe there's actually gold in the mine my great-aunt has left me. Wouldn't that be something? And maybe the house is a solid, well-built mansion where I'll be warm for once in my life."

Continuing to frown, Alexandra said, "I've told you a dozen times you can come to live with us. Father and Mother would welcome you and—"

"It's a kind offer and I'm truly grateful to you and your parents. But I cannot accept. My mind's made up. You know how I love the idea of embarking on a great new adventure. I am going to California to seek my fortune!"

"What about Samuel? Will you just leave him behind with no regrets?"

Kate shook her head. Alexandra was referring to Sam Bradford, a fine young man who had shown an unflagging interest in courting Kate. But the attraction was not mutual. While Kate genuinely respected Sam and realized he had a bright future ahead in his father's flourishing ship brokerage firm, she was not interested in him romantically. Nor was she interested in anyone else. While Alexandra dreamed of marriage and children, Kate yearned for excitement and travel.

She laughed now and said, "Tell the truth, Alex. Wouldn't you like to console Sam in my absence?"

Alexandra flushed guiltily, then smiled. "I can't deny that I find Sam incredibly appealing." She frowned again. "But it's you he likes, not me."

"So he thinks. But I predict that a week—two at the most—after I'm gone, Samuel T. Bradford will come calling on you."

Alexandra's eyes sparkled. "You really think so?"

Kate laughed. "I do, yes. And in a year or so, I'll expect a wedding invitation." Her well-arched eyebrows lifted.

"Where shall I send it?"

"Soon as I'm settled, I'll write," promised Kate.

Then, with a sly grin, she affected brittle, privileged, lady-of-the-manner diction, and teased, "My dear Miss Wharton, I shall see to it my personal secretary drops you a note with the return address of my California mansion."

Both young women laughed and hugged once more.

At the Boston harbor, on the bitter cold morning of March 27, 1855, the two young women hugged again.

But neither laughed.

"I'll miss you so," said a teary-eyed Alexandra.

"And I you," Kate replied, swallowing the lump that had formed in her throat.

She turned away and hurried up the gangway of the clipper ship *Star of Gold*.

Three

May 1, 1855
San Francisco, California

"Conlin. Harry Conlin, California representative for Clement and Clement." A smiling, expensively dressed man with salt-and-pepper hair stepped forward to meet Kate when she disembarked at the busy harbor early on that May morning. "From J.J.'s description, you must be Miss Kate VanNam, heir to Mrs. Arielle VanNam Colfax's estate."

Kate shook his offered hand. "Yes, sir, I am Kate VanNam. Thank you for meeting me, Mr. Conlin."

"Welcome to San Francisco," he said with a friendly smile, "port of entry and financial center for the mining camps of the mother lode. Here, let me take that."

Harry Conlin quickly relieved Kate of her heavy valise. He took her arm and guided her through the swarms of merchants, shippers and passengers packing the Vallejo Street wharf. Dodging handcarts and wagons, coaches and cabs, Conlin and Kate carefully threaded their way through the crowd.

When they reached the berth where the steam packet *Lady Luck* was moored, Harry Conlin explained, "Miss VanNam, I've engaged a stateroom for you on board."

"No, Mr. Conlin, I won't be needing a stateroom for such a short journey. I'll just—"

Interrupting, he said, "Miss VanNam, Fortune is a hundred and fifty miles from San Francisco."

Kate frowned, disappointed. "That far? I thought surely I'd be there this by afternoon."

"I'm sorry. I know you must be terribly exhausted. Perhaps you'd prefer to spend the night here in San Francisco and leave tomorrow or the next day?"

"No, I'm quite anxious to reach Fortune."

"Very well. You'll spend a couple of nights on the *Lady Luck* before reaching the river settlement of Golden Quest and transferring to a much smaller steamer for the shorter trip to Fortune." Kate nodded, trying to smile. Conlin ushered her up the gangway.

Once on board, Harry Conlin said, "Now, tell me about your long journey from Boston. Was it terribly harrowing?"

"Not at all," Kate replied and meant it. "It was an

unforgettable adventure." Though weaker than when she had set out, Kate had lost none of her enthusiasm. "I can't imagine why anyone would complain about such an incredible experience."

"No seasickness, no ocean storms?"

"Well, I was a bit seasick, but only for a day or two. And there were a couple of storms with high winds that pitched the ship around, but I wasn't all that frightened." She smiled then and declared, "It took us only eleven days—with an overnight call in Havana—to reach the Caribbean port city of Aspinwall. There all the passengers disembarked and we were transferred to open-air railcars for the forty-eight miles across the isthmus to Panama. There, we embarked on the *Sonora* and steamed north for fifteen days. And here we are!"

"Here you are indeed," said Conlin, charmed and amazed that this spirited young woman registered no complaints whatsoever regarding a route most found extremely difficult.

"I'm so glad to be in California," she said. "And I can hardly wait to reach Fortune."

"Well, the *Lady Luck* will be getting under way very shortly," he stated. "Time for me to disembark. You'll be okay? You don't need anything or…"

"You've been most kind, Mr. Conlin." Kate thanked him warmly.

"My pleasure, Miss VanNam," he said with a smile. "Should you decide you've had enough of Fortune, just hop the steamer coming downriver and return to San Francisco. Our firm will work something out with you, take the Fortune property off your hands."

"I'll remember that," Kate said, and bade him goodbye.

In minutes the *Lady Luck* left the harbor. Soon it was steaming its way up the American River toward the towering Sierra Nevadas to the east.

Within an hour the vessel left the coastal hills behind and rode a rising tide up the long, winding waterway.

Two days later as Kate boarded the much smaller steamer at Golden Quest that would take her the rest of the way to Fortune, she entered the main cabin and looked curiously around. It was empty. There were rows of wooden seats. She chose one by a porthole, lowered her valise and sat down. She hoped against hope that no one would sit beside her. She wanted the opportunity to doze. She hadn't slept well on the *Lady Luck* and was tired.

She started in alarm when she spotted coming down the aisle an unshaven, mean-looking man whose wrists were clamped in irons.

Kate tensed, then released her held breath when a skinny, sandy-haired fellow shoved the bearded character down into a seat across the aisle and two rows up. He then sat down beside him.

The man in irons looked back over his shoulder.

His gap-toothed, leering grin sent a chill of distaste
darting up her spine. Quickly, she turned her head
and looked out the porthole.

"Would you mind if I sit beside you, miss?" a
friendly voice asked. Kate looked up and saw a
white-haired, well-dressed gentleman with a craggy,
but kindly face smiling down at her. "Allow me to introduce myself," the elderly gentleman said, thrusting out his hand. "I'm Dr. Milton Ledet and I'm on
my way up to Fortune, just as you are."

The steamer began to slowly move away from the
levee as Kate nodded. "Kate VanNam, Dr. Ledet,"
she replied, shaking the offered hand. "Yes, by all
means, please join me."

"Thank you, child." The elderly physician took the
seat beside her. "I so enjoy having a bit of company
on long journeys, don't you?" Not waiting for an answer, he added, "Have I seen you in Fortune before,
Miss VanNam? Or is it Mrs. VanNam?"

"Miss. And no, you have not," she replied. "I've
never been there."

The doctor's white eyebrows lifted. "Then I suppose you live in San Francisco and you're going up
to visit a...?"

"No, sir. I am moving to Fortune from Boston, Massachusetts. I intend to make Fortune my new home."

"Oh, my dear Miss VanNam," Doc Ledet exclaimed impulsively, "I'm afraid you'll find For-

tune quite different from the charming old city of Boston."

"I am well aware of that, Doctor," she said with conviction. "No doubt there will be a degree of adjustment, but I don't mind. The truth is I look forward to the challenges ahead."

Dr. Ledet was instantly curious. Why would this beautiful young woman move to a mountain mining community she had never seen before? Not for a minute did the doctor entertain the possibility that she might be aiming to join the ranks of numerous "ladies of the evening" servicing the lonely miners. There was an innate dignity about her that spoke of good breeding and background. But why was this beautiful, golden-haired girl moving to Fortune, where the males outnumbered the females fifty to one?

Dr. Ledet longed to question her, but was wise enough to wait until she was ready to tell him.

"You probably know my reason for moving to Fortune," Kate said, as though she'd read his mind.

"Let me guess," he said, and rubbed his chin. "You have a sweetheart that came out to the goldfields, got settled in, sent for you and now you're joining him to get married?"

"Heavens, no!" She waved a hand in the air as though it was a preposterous idea. Proudly, she stated, "I have inherited a gold mine."

"You don't say," he replied. "Why, that's wonderful! Is the mine...?"

"The Cavalry Blue," Kate interrupted. "You may have heard of it?"

The physician exhaled heavily. "The Cavalry Blue," he repeated, his brows knitted. "Arielle Colfax's old diggings."

"Yes, my dear great-aunt. You knew her?"

"Yes, I did. I knew Arielle, albeit briefly, and her husband, Benjamin. He was a geologist who came out West with Freemont." Dr. Ledet shook his head. "Miss VanNam, I hate to tell you this, but the Cavalry Blue has been boarded up for years. Ever since your aunt left Fortune." He paused, then as gently as possible said, "My dear, there's never been a single ounce of gold brought out of that mine."

Kate smiled, undeterred. "That's excellent, Dr. Ledet."

"It is?"

"Why, yes. Obviously all the gold is still inside, just waiting for me to bring it out."

Charmed by her childlike exuberance, the elderly doctor had no wish to burst her bubble. That would happen soon enough. He said, "Could well be, child. Could well be."

Kate kept glancing out at the changing scenery. The banks bordering the ever narrowing river had become lofty cliffs forested with tall, fragrant pines. She was enchanted.

And all the while she conversed with her congenial companion. Kate learned that the doctor was a

childless widower who had left his San Francisco
practice after Mary, his cherished wife of thirty-three
years, contracted scarlet fever from one of his patients. She had died three days later.

Dr. Ledet had been in Fortune for the past six
years, and Kate had plenty of questions about the
community she planned to call home. He had all the
answers and was glad to share them. Enjoying his
captive audience, Milton Ledet regaled Kate with
tales of the wild and woolly town where he practiced
medicine. He knew just about everyone who lived in
Fortune and had a story to tell about most of them.

Kate was fascinated by the colorful yarns, which
made the time pass quickly. As morning turned to afternoon, Kate noticed that the air thinned so dramatically she was having a little difficulty breathing.

She heard the physician say calmly, "Take a deep,
slow breath, Miss VanNam."

Kate nodded and obeyed.

"They say it's the air the angels breathe," he
stated. "We're getting close to Fortune." He rubbed
his chin. "Now where was I?"

He continued by telling her that at one time or another, he had cared for just about every citizen in town.

The steamer rounded a bend in the narrowing
fork of the river and the buildings of Fortune loomed
just ahead.

Laughing, Dr. Ledet said, "All but one, that is. The
sheriff."

"The sheriff has never been sick or injured?"

"No doubt he has, but he's never sought my services," said the doctor. "He patches himself up and goes on with business. He's one tough son of a gun, begging your pardon for my crude language, Miss VanNam. He was hired by the Committee of Vigilance—of which I myself am a senior member—to keep the peace, and Travis McCloud rules Fortune with fast fists and faster guns," he declared, his eyes twinkling. "Step out of line and you have to deal with the fearless Marshal McCloud." He paused, then smiled at Kate.

Feeling as if she were expected to comment, but not knowing what to say, she said, "And this courageous sheriff, is he from San Francisco or…?"

"No, no. McCloud's a native Virginian. Came from an aristocratic Tidewater family." The steamer was sliding slowly toward Fortune's levee. "McCloud was educated to be a physician like me, but he—"

"He's a murderer!" muttered the man in irons from across the aisle. He was then roughly urged to his feet. "Killed a man back in—"

"Move it!" ordered the armed, sandy-haired guard, prodding the prisoner up the narrow aisle.

Kate gasped at the startling accusation. She immediately turned questioning eyes on her companion. "Can that be?"

The steamer's whistle blasted loudly in the thin mountain air, silencing her.

"We're here," Doc Ledet announced as the vessel came to a stop, its hull slapping gently up against the wooden dock. Smiling, he pointed and said, "There's our sheriff now."

Curious, Kate looked out the porthole.

A tall, broad-shouldered man in a black hat with the brim pulled low over his eyes stepped up to the lowering gangway. He wore a white, long-sleeved shirt, black leather vest and black trousers. A gun belt with a brace of Colt revolvers rode low on his slim hips.

As Kate stared, he lifted a hand and with the tip of his long index finger, he pushed up the brim of his hat, releasing a shock of coal black hair onto his high fore-head. The move afforded Kate a good look at his face.

She quickly sucked in her breath.

Fortune's fearless sheriff was a ruggedly hand-some man with smooth olive skin, soaring cheek-bones, a straight nose, sensual lips and eyes of a color she couldn't quite determine, shaded as they were by long, curling lashes.

"That's him, sure enough," said the physician. "Marshal Travis McCloud. He's here to take posses-sion of that foul-mouthed prisoner that came up on the steamer with us."

Kate continued staring at the imposing sheriff. There was a strong masculinity about him in the set of his lean, hard body, the way his broad shoulders moved. He came forward to meet his skinny, sandy-haired deputy and the man in irons as they stepped down from the gangplank.

"I'll take over, Jiggs," Kate heard the marshal say in a surprisingly soft voice with a slight Southern accent.

"He...the sheriff looks...he looks mean," Kate murmured over her shoulder, unable to take her eyes off the most compelling man she had ever seen.

"I doubt he'll be mean to you, Miss VanNam," the doctor said, adding with a chuckle, "that is, unless you misbehave. Then he'll have to throw you in jail."

"I'll be very careful," she answered with a laugh, but felt a shiver skip her up spine at the prospect.

"Here, let me help you with that," said Dr. Ledet when Kate lifted her heavy valise and started down the gangway.

"No, thank you." She turned down his kind offer of assistance. "I can manage. It's been a genuine pleasure visiting with you, Doctor."

The man beamed. "I look forward to seeing you again soon, although not as a patient. You take care of yourself and stay well. You need anything, Kate, you let me know. My office is two doors down from the Eldorado Hotel. You can't miss it."

Kate smiled, nodded and left him. She carried her belongings from the riverfront to Main Street. The hotel that the doctor had mentioned was the first one she saw. Kate entered the Eldorado, checked into a third-floor room, glanced around and immediately focused on the big double bed.

She smiled and hurried to examine the mattress and bedding, turning back the covers and admiring the clean white sheets. She sighed with pleasure. The two things she wanted most in life were hers to be had in this hotel room.

A bath and a bed.

Soon Kate, fresh from her hot, relaxing bath, climbed into that soft, clean bed and smiled.

She fell asleep at sundown.

Four

At sundown Fortune came alive.

Thirsty miners hit the town's many saloons the minute they laid down their picks and shovels. Tired and dirty, the men swarmed into the bars, eager for their first bracing shot of rotgut whiskey.

In Fortune's most favored saloon, the Golden Nugget, the long polished bar, faro wheels and poker tables filled up as the sun slipped fully behind the western mountain peaks. Loud piano music resounded up and down the busy streets as the shrill feminine laughter of painted women in gaudy gowns mingled with the voices of lusty miners.

The man who single-handedly saw to it that trouble stayed away from his town was presently at the Golden Nugget.

But he wasn't downstairs.

Sheriff Travis McCloud was enjoying a hot bath in a plush upstairs suite at the soft hands of Miss Valentina Knight, the Golden Nugget's beautiful songbird owner and Travis's favorite female companion.

With his clothes neatly draped across a blue brocade-covered chaise longue, and his black hat hooked on the newel of a high-backed rocker, the six-foot-three-inch Travis sat in a suds-filled tub with his knees and torso sticking up out of the steaming water.

Feeling relaxed and enjoying himself, he smoked a fine Cuban cigar and drank Kentucky bourbon from a lead crystal glass, while the prettiest woman in Fortune gently scrubbed his broad shoulders with a soft-bristled, long-handled brush.

"Feel good, Marshal?" Valentina asked as she drew the brush back and forth over his gleaming back.

"Mmm," he replied lazily, his eyes half-closed, his even white teeth clamped firmly on his lit cigar.

Valentina smiled, pleased. She loved giving this big handsome sheriff a soapy, sensuous bath. She loved even more the moment when he stepped out of the tub, allowed her to dry him off, and then spent the next hour in her soft bed while she cuddled in his strong arms.

Those fleeting golden moments were as much of Travis McCloud as she would ever have.

So she made the most of his visits.

Valentina Knight was a clever woman. She knew that she couldn't hem Travis in, so she never tried. She realized that the reason she, and she alone, was allowed to entertain the handsome marshal was because she was convenient and made no demands on him.

Valentina Knight was a beautiful, porcelain-skinned Creole who had come out West from her New Orleans home to seek her fortune. She had wisely surmised that the goldfields of California offered an opportunity to make lots of money without ever going near a mine. There were, she had read, literally thousands of men pouring into the many mining camps springing up across the Sierra Nevadas. They were willing to part with their precious gold dust for a drink and a smile from a pretty woman.

Valentina had guessed correctly.

In this male-dominated world with very few women and little semblance of customary society, she had become very wealthy during the four years she had owned the Nugget.

She was a respected citizen of Fortune who turned heads wherever she went, but it was more than her raven hair and magnolia skin that made her so desirable. Her generosity, charm and wit secured her position as the object of affection to Fortune's many menfolk.

When she came downstairs to sing for the miners, they immediately fell silent. They gazed worshipfully at the sweet-voiced vision in the stunning gowns that accentuated her voluptuous figure, in the diamonds that sparkled at her throat and ears.

It was a whispered, well-known secret that in her plush upstairs suite, she drank—from fragile stemmed glasses—vintage French champagne delivered by Wells Fargo. And fresh cut flowers, that rarest of all luxuries, were delivered daily.

The lovely Creole had a French maid, a must for the most prosperous of the frontier madams. Gigi responded to the summons of the richly brocaded bell-pulls, then prudently disappeared when her mistress was entertaining the town sheriff.

When Valentina went out, she rode behind matched blacks in a Brewster carriage imported across the Isthmus of Panama at great expense. Sable muff, scarf and lap robe kept her warm on exhilarating winter rides. Gloves, straw hat and silk parasol protected her porcelain skin on summer jaunts.

Valentina Knight had everything.

Except the man she loved.

Travis McCloud.

The lawman's heart would never belong to her even though hers belonged to him. Valentina never so much as batted a flirtatious eyelash at any other man, nor would she allow another to make to love to her.

Now, as she rinsed the soap off of the most magnificent male chest she'd ever laid eyes on, Valentina shivered with sweet anticipation of the lovemaking ahead.

"We have two whole hours before I must go downstairs to sing," she said as Travis gently moved

her hand away and rose to his feet, water sluicing
down his body.

Valentina picked up a large white towel and began blotting moisture from his clean, wet flesh.
"Promise you'll spend those two hours right here
with me?"

"You talked me into it, darlin'," said Travis with
a smile.

He motioned for her to back away, and stepped out
of the tub. Valentina rose to her feet before him. He
took the towel from her and finished drying off. She
stayed where she was as Travis dropped the damp
towel, turned and padded across the patterned Per-
sian carpet to the bed. He stretched out on his back
atop the satin sheet and laid his dark head on an
abundance of soft feather pillows resting against the
ornately carved headboard.

Valentina shivered deliciously.

If ever there was a sight that was pleasing to her,
it was that of the lean lawman lying naked on her bed.
The darkness of his skin against the whiteness of the
sheets never failed to delight her senses. His fierce
masculine power, unclothed and unprotected, was
for the moment hers and hers alone.

Valentina began to sway seductively toward the
bed. A subtle but purposeful movement of her shoulders made the shimmering satin lapels of her long,
ice blue robe part, revealing to her naked lover tempting glimpses of her full breasts. She raised a hand,

took the diamond pins from her hair and allowed her dark, lustrous locks to spill down around her shoulders.

She laid the pins on the marble-topped night table, then leaned over and gave the sheriff's tight belly a wet, warm kiss.

Travis sucked in his breath. His hand came down to clasp a handful of her hair and gently pull her head up. "Get in bed, baby," he gently commanded, and she obeyed.

Valentina didn't take off her tightly sashed robe, but left it on as she stretched out beside Travis and snuggled close against his bare torso. He kissed her, then urged her over onto her back. He moved atop her, supporting his weight on stiffened arms.

The satin of Valentina's robe lay between them. For a time they left it there, a sensuous slippery barrier to the pleasure of penetration.

Travis found it incredibly erotic to feel the summoning heat of Valentina's feminine softness just out of reach beneath the fabric. For Valentina it was tremendously exciting to feel the insistent power of his masculine hardness thwarted by the sleek obstruction of satin.

It was a thrilling game.

But short-lived.

Soon he levered himself up, reached between them and swept the robe out of his way. Valentina eagerly parted her legs and sighed in approval as he slid into her. She raised her knees, gripped his ribs and clung to him as they made leisurely, lusty love.

But just at the instant of climax, a gunshot rang out.

Valentina's eyes flew open and she blinked in stunned surprise. "You got me, Sheriff!" she proclaimed, and pretended to fall over dead. Then she laughed throatily and teased, "Any ammunition left in that...?"

"Afraid not," said Travis, and laughed with her.

Then, with a quick kiss, he pulled out, fell over onto his back, took a couple of deep, quick breaths, and got out of bed.

"No," she protested, raising up on an elbow, "don't go, Travis."

"I have to, Val," he said, pulling on his trousers. "Somebody's firing a weapon downstairs. I'm the sheriff, remember? Hired to keep the peace."

Five

Kate awoke at dawn feeling rested and ready to start her new life. She hummed happily as she donned a simple blue-and-white gingham dress and brushed her blond hair. Optimistic, tingling with excitement, she left the hotel with map in hand. She was eager to explore the town, but first she wanted to locate her newly inherited property and inspect the house her aunt had left her. She planned to return to the hotel for her belongings later and then move in. She was sure there would be no reason to stay another night in the hotel. She would spend it in her own home.

Kate passed—two doors down from the hotel—the offices of Dr. Milton Ledet, the kindly white-haired physician she had met on the steamer ride to Fortune. She dashed past his office windows in case he was inside. She had no time to visit this morning.

Kate walked to the very end of the sidewalk and soon left Fortune behind. Her breathing grew short from the altitude, and her legs quickly grew weak, but she climbed an ill-defined lane up through the towering green conifers and white-trunked aspens, swatting low, leafy limbs out of her way.

When she'd gone no more than a half mile, Kate stepped out into a broad, lush clearing and saw a large white house looming in the distance.

She had, she knew, located the real estate she now owned.

Set amid the tall sheltering pines, the property bordered a breathtakingly beautiful deep turquoise lake no more than a hundred yards from the front door of the house. The lake was fed by a clear, crystalline stream flowing out of the mountains on the north side of the estate. Swift waters poured down from the melting Sierra snowpack. Kate could hear the crystal water gurgling and splashing over the rocks.

With her lips parted in awe at the spectacular scenery surrounding her, Kate skirted the grassy banks of the placid turquoise lake and headed toward the house. When she stood directly before the large, two-story structure, she clucked her tongue against the roof of her mouth.

Before even going inside she could see that the once splendid Victorian mansion was uninhabitable.

Kate despaired. Like it or not, she would *have* to live in this badly neglected house. She had no choice.

If she were to have enough money to hire men to work her mine, she could ill afford to live at the hotel, even for a brief period of time.

Kate exhaled heavily and made her way across the weed choked grounds to the mansion's broad front steps. The second step was missing. Kate grimaced, lifted her skirts and cautiously stepped over the gaping hole.

She crossed the broad veranda and paused at the entrance. There was no front door. It had been removed from its hinges and carried away. Kate shook her head and went inside.

The mansion had been ransacked. Most of the furniture had been carted off; only a few odd pieces remained. A French gilt chair with a broken leg lay on its side before a magnificent black marble fireplace. A gigantic crystal chandelier that had been carelessly pried from the ceiling was on the floor, its fragile prisms shattered. There were blank spaces on the faded, silk-covered walls where massive mirrors and oil paintings had undoubtedly hung. Remnants of an elegant silk shade dangled from an open window.

Kate quickly realized that more than half of the solid wooden doors had been carried away. Most of the windows had been broken.

Kate climbed the stairs to the second floor. She jumped, startled, when she stepped into the spacious master suite and a bird flew in through an open window.

"Shoo! Fly away!" she shouted, chasing the winged intruder, flapping her skirts to scare it. "It's bad luck to have a bird fly into one's house. Get out, get out!"

The bird circled the room, then sailed away.

Kate shuddered with the dawning knowledge that the bird might not be the only creature that had the run of the place. No doubt there were black bears and sleek bobcats and all manner of dangerous animals roaming these rugged mountains. How would she stop them from taking up residence in the mansion? And how on earth could she survive the coming winter with no windows and doors to shut out the cold?

Kate shook her head again as she slowly went back down the grand staircase, whose steps sported only remnants of the fine carpet that had once covered them.

Kate had been in Fortune for less than twenty-four hours when Sheriff Travis McCloud heard about her arrival. His deputy, Jiggs Gillespie, had been the first to mention it. Dr. Ledet, the second. The newcomer quickly became the topic of conversation all over town as word spread that the young woman from Boston who had inherited the old Colfax mansion and the abandoned Cavalry Blue Mine intended to make Fortune her home.

They were all certain she was in for a big disappointment. There was no gold in the Cavalry Blue. Travis knew that. Everyone knew that. Which meant, mercifully, she wouldn't be staying long in Fortune. That suited Travis fine. The sooner she gave up and left, the better.

But that could take awhile. Gold fever was a sickness from which it was hard to recover. She might stay weeks, even months in the vain search of a treasure that did not exist.

Travis ground his teeth at the possibility. He hoped to hell she was homely. Protecting a young, single woman from a townful of lonely, lusty miners would be anything but easy.

Kate returned to the Eldorado, collected her belongings, paid her bill and trudged back to the ruined mansion. She deposited her things in the drawing room at the very front of the mansion. She looked around, sighed, then turned away. She'd see to making the room livable later.

First things first.

By noon she was back in town to visit the Federal Land Office. When she stepped down into the street, she encountered a dirty, drunken man weaving dizzily toward her. Kate shook her finger in his face and warned him off, threatening him within an inch of his life. The drunk anxiously backed away.

Chin raised, Kate stepped past him and into the land office. Deed in hand, she introduced herself and handed the document to the balding clerk. He studied it for only a minute. Then he looked up and shook his head pityingly.

"Miss VanNam, I'm sorry you've traveled all this way for nothing."

"I beg your pardon?"

"You're wasting your time," he informed her. "All the placer gold is gone from the stream on your property. Has been for years now."

"Placer gold?" she repeated, having no idea what he meant.

"Placer. The pebbles containing particles of gold that wash down the stream from the mountains. It's all long since been panned and sold. There is no more."

"No, of course not," she said. "I knew that. But the mine…"

"Miss VanNam, I hate to be the one to tell you this, but the Cavalry Blue has been abandoned for years. All boarded up. And with good reason. There has never been a single speck of gold brought out of that mine."

Kate said calmly, "I know."

"You do?" He frowned and scratched his gleaming pate.

"Yes. I came up on the steamer from Golden Quest with Dr. Milton Ledet. He mentioned that the Cavalry Blue has never produced any gold."

The man nodded.

Shoulders squared, Kate continued, "I informed the good doctor and now I'll tell you. The gold obviously remains inside. I will bring it out."

* * *

Travis got his first glimpse of Kate VanNam at noontime.

He was alone in the front office of the city jail, doing nothing. Leaning back in his chair, booted feet propped up on his desk, hands folded behind his head. He yawned and exhaled slowly, enjoying the peace and quiet that came all too infrequently in this wild mining community.

He looked out the window at nothing in particular and his eyes immediately widened.

He spotted her sunlit hair, shining as brightly as the gold she sought.

Kate VanNam.

He knew it was her.

Travis swore under his breath. He was instantly reminded of another golden-haired Jezebel whose memory was still vivid after all these years.

Travis scowled as Kate encountered the weaving, drunken Zeke Daniels, but his frown quickly turned into a grudging smile when the delicate young woman shook a finger in Zeke's liquor-veined face and rebuked him.

Zeke backed away as if he had encountered a bobcat.

As the sheriff studied the woman, he noted that her gleaming golden hair was not her only attribute. She was tall and appealingly slender. Her lithe, willowy body was draped in a girlish blue-and-white gingham dress with flounces and bows that made her look all too young and innocent. Her fine-boned face was exquisite, her ivory skin flawless. She was very pretty, very feminine, very desirable.

She did not belong in Fortune, California.

Six

Map in hand, sunbonnet on her head, Kate went up into the mountains alone the very next morning and easily located the Cavalry Blue claim. The entrance was boarded up, just as she'd heard. She peered curiously through wide cracks in the weathered timber, foolishly hoping she might detect a vein of gold winking at her from deep inside the dark cavern.

She saw nothing.

It would take further exploration to uncover the treasure. She was undeterred. Gold was likely buried in the floor and the walls of the mine. The solid granite would have to be hammered and chiseled, and the crushed rock that fell away carefully probed and sifted and picked through. She couldn't possibly do it by herself. She would, she realized, need to hire at least a couple of strong-backed men to work the claim.

Kate returned to the mansion and decided she would wait no longer to begin the daunting task of making a home of sorts in the downstairs drawing room. For the time being, she would leave all the other rooms untouched.

In a back room, Kate located a sofa that had once been a grand piece of furniture. Elaborate mahogany trim on the couch's arms and high back was artistically carved. The once plush rose velvet covering was faded and torn, but the sofa was long and comfortable, ideal for a bed. She would move the heavy sofa once she'd thoroughly cleaned the drawing room.

The sun had already reached its zenith as Kate made a short list of necessities and walked back to town. Once there, she took the opportunity to fully explore Fortune, strolling leisurely up and down Main Street.

The bustling alpine community was spectacularly framed by the pine covered peaks of the high Sierras, and it was larger than she had realized. There were a half-dozen hotels—the Bonanza, the Eldorado, the Alpine, the Sierra, the Frontier and the Mint. There were at least twenty-five or thirty saloons. The Glitter Gulch. The Bloody Bucket. The Quartz. The Mother Lode. The Golden Nugget. The Amber Lantern. And many more.

Fortune had five general stores, the largest of which was Barton's Emporium and Dry Goods. She also found one doctor's office, four banks, an elaborate two-story opera house, a stationery store, a bakery, three express offices, two barbershops, four blacksmith shops, five livery stables, three assay offices, two fire companies, two undertakers, a newspaper and a city surveyor.

And, of course, the city jail.

When Kate had reached the southernmost end of town she saw a large tent city that stretched for a half mile down a gentle incline. As she gazed at row upon row of small canvas shelters placed very close to each other, she wondered who was unfortunate enough to live in the tents.

When she reached Barton's Emporium and Dry Goods, she walked among its display tables looking at the varied merchandise while Clifton T. Barton, owner and proprietor, pointed her toward her requests. He never moved from his cane-bottomed stool behind the counter.

A big man with droopy eyelids and large ears, Barton paid little attention to Kate as she gathered up a broom, a mop, a large pail and a coal oil lamp. She came over to place the items on the counter.

"That it?" he asked, continuing to sit.

"Not quite."

While Cliff Barton scratched his chin, Kate turned away and went in search of sheets, a blanket and a pillow.

"All right, I guess that's all for now," she announced, and placed everything on the counter. She reached for her reticule. "How much do I owe you?"

The store owner finally got off his stool and totaled up her purchases. Kate was stunned when he informed her she owed him $28.75.

"That can't be. You've surely made a mistake in addition," she said. "These few items can't possibly cost—"

"Everything's expensive up here, miss," he interrupted. "You're in a gold camp high in the Sierras. Everything has to be transported up from San Francisco." He grinned then and added, "Just wait till you want to buy a mincemeat pie from Mrs. Hester down the street at her bakery. A dollar and a half is how much it'll set you back."

Kate shook her head in disbelief. "I can live without mincemeat pie and…" She sighed, took the blanket and pillow from the stack of merchandise she'd chosen, and pushed both back at him. "I can sleep without a pillow. It's almost summer, so I need no blanket."

"You can say that again. Gets hotter than the hell up here in the summertime."

Kate nodded, paid for her merchandise and left.

Out of breath by the time she reached the mansion, she allowed herself only a few short minutes to rest. Then, covering her hair with a cloth, she rolled up her sleeves and went to work. She spent the remainder of the day making the large front parlor as livable as possible. She swept the hardwood floor, sneezing and coughing from the dirt she stirred up. She mopped with water brought up in a pail from the lake. She cleaned the marble fireplace.

Kate returned to the back room where she'd found the faded sofa. She batted the dust from it and polished the wooden trim. Then, puffing and groaning, she dragged the heavy sofa through the wide center hallway and into the spotless drawing room.

Come nightfall an exhausted Kate blew out the coal oil lamp. She tiredly climbed onto the sofa, which was now made up with the newly purchased sheets. Wishing she had a pillow, she folded an arm beneath her head and turned her face toward the tall front windows looking out on the untended yard and turquoise lake beyond.

Kate was grateful for the full moon that shone with an almost day-bright radiance. The light made her feel safe and secure. No one could possibly slip in and surprise her.

Kate lowered a hand and touched her uncle Nelson's Navy Colt revolver where she had placed it on the floor. Then she laid her arm across her waist and closed her eyes.

She was almost asleep when a noise from the back of the house shattered the silence. Kate snatched the gun and sat up. She lit the coal oil lamp with shaking fingers, and then, gun in one hand, lamp in the other, she moved down the wide hallway in search of the intruder.

"Who's there?" she called out, expecting to encounter a bear or man any minute. "Show yourself or I'll shoot!"

No response.

After a thorough inspection of all the downstairs rooms turned up nothing, Kate began to relax. She told herself the noise she'd heard had probably been nothing more menacing than a field mouse. Laughing at herself for being so easily frightened, she went back to bed.

She returned the revolver to its place beneath the sofa. She exhaled tiredly, yawned, and again gazed out the windows to the placid lake beyond.

The moon was full.

The gun was loaded.

Kate was soon fast asleep.

After spending several fruitless days trying to hire help to work her mountainside diggings, Kate was becoming exasperated.

She had thoroughly combed the community for laborers, finally realizing that she was looking in the wrong places. She knew exactly where she had to go. There was no use delaying any longer. She needed to go where men congregated.

In the saloons.

Kate waited until well after sunset.

Then, making sure the loaded Colt revolver was in her reticule, she walked the short half mile to town. Once there, she headed directly to the largest, liveliest saloon on Main Street.

The Golden Nugget.

As she approached she heard loud music, men's voices, thunderous laughter, and what could only be a fierce fistfight in progress.

Kate slowed her steps. Then blinked in astonishment when a man with a bloody nose and a bruised face came flying out the saloon doors and landed flat on his back in the middle of the street.

She gasped and put a hand to her mouth. Hesitating, she strongly considered abandoning her mission. She knew she should just turn around and go right back home.

But she couldn't do that.

Kate squared her shoulders and marched forward. She had never been inside a saloon, but she had to go in and find men willing to work the Cavalry Blue.

Kate reached the saloon.

She drew a quick breath, stiffened her spine and placed a hand atop the slatted bat-wing doors.

But before she could push them open, a low, masculine voice warned, "Hold it right there."

Seven

Kate's head snapped around.

She found herself looking squarely at a shiny silver badge resting on a man's broad chest.

Kate tipped her head back and looked up.

Sheriff Travis McCloud stood with his booted feet apart and his thumbs hooked into his low-riding gun belt. His facial muscles were drawn tight and his dark eyes cold.

"You're not going in there, miss," he informed her in soft, low tones.

"And why ever not?" she retorted. "There are ladies inside. I hear feminine laughter."

He looked at her and his expression changed. His lips widened in a slow smile and his dark, daring eyes held the probing scrutiny of a highly virile man. Kate was instantly unnerved by him.

After a pause that seemed interminable, he said, "They are not exactly ladies. I imagine you are." There was another pause. "So you're not going inside."

"You know nothing about me, so how…?"

"I know a great deal about you," he said, taking hold of her upper arm and firmly turning her away from the saloon's swinging doors. "You are Miss Kate VanNam from Boston and you've come to take up residence in the house your late great-aunt Arielle VanNam Colfax left you."

"The house is the least of it, Sheriff." Kate attempted to pull her arm free of his encircling fingers.

He refused to let her go. "Ah, yes. So you've seen the elephant."

"Seen the elephant?"

"Never mind. You're here for gold," he said, shaking his head.

His air of egotism was offensive. Kate gave him a sharp look. "Why, yes, if you must know, I intend to bring gold out of the Cavalry Blue. Which is why I was going into the Golden Nugget. I need to find laborers to work my claim."

Travis quickly set her straight. "That's not going to happen, Miss VanNam. You won't find anybody willing to work at the Cavalry Blue."

"Why not?"

"The people in Fortune are dreamers, just as you are. They work at their own small claims and diggings, hoping to strike it rich. That's why they came to California, the 'land of second chances'."

"Does that include you, Marshal?" She smiled when she saw the slight narrowing of his eyes, then told him, "It really shouldn't matter to you why I'm here. My presence in Fortune is none of your concern and I—"

"You're wrong there, Miss VanNam. It is very much my concern," Travis said. "I've been hired by the Committee of Vigilance to keep the peace in Fortune. That's exactly what I aim to do."

"Well, I should hope so," she retorted. Glancing up at his handsome face, she immediately felt the same frightening tingle she'd experienced when she'd looked out from the riverboat's porthole upon arriving in Fortune. She mentally shook herself, and then flippantly teased, "I promise not to cheat at cards or get into fistfights or shoot up the saloons."

She laughed.

He didn't.

Stopping in midstride, he yanked her to such an abrupt halt her head rocked on her shoulders. Drawing her close, he fixed her with his dark eyes. "Listen to me, Miss VanNam, and listen well. In case you've failed to notice, there are at least fifty men to every woman in this community. Any idea what that could mean to you?"

"No, I—"

"Word has already spread that you are to be liv-

ing alone up there in the Colfax mansion. How safe
do you suppose you are?"

"I don't see—"

"No, you don't see. If you did you'd climb right
back on the steamer and head downriver to—"

"Listen to me, Marshal, and listen well," Kate interrupted. "I'm going nowhere. I am staying in Fortune until I find the gold in the Cavalry Blue. You
don't want me here? Too bad. This is now my
home. I have no other and nothing to go back to
Boston for."

Travis frowned. "Your family?"

"I have no family left," she declared, no longer
counting her brother, Gregory, as family. "But I'm
made of rather stern stuff, Sheriff. One of my an-
cestors, Ebenezer Stevens, participated in the Boston Tea Party. Like him, I don't back down or
frighten easily. Now if you'll kindly unhand me, I
am going home."

"I'll see to it you do." He finally released his hold
on her arm. "I'll walk you there."

"Not necessary." Kate was swift to turn down his
offer. "You surely have troublemakers to apprehend."

"I'd say you're presently the biggest troublemaker
in Fortune," Travis gently teased.

Kate was not amused. "There is no need for you
to escort me home. Good night to you, Marshal Mc-
Cloud," she repeated, and walked away.

Travis stayed where he was, crossed his arms over

his chest and shook his head in annoyance. Then he easily caught up with her.

"It will be a good night once I've seen you safe inside behind locked doors."

Kate sighed irritably. She didn't want him to go with her. She knew what would happen. He would see what bad shape the house was in and insist she couldn't live there. She didn't like this big, bullying marshal. She didn't trust him. He was too decisive, too commanding, too cocksure.

The thought struck her that this tall, hard-faced sheriff was nothing like her gentle companion and friend, the boyish, soft-spoken Sam Bradford, half a world away back in Boston. Instinctively, she knew no one would dare boss this handsome Virginian around, as she had so often done with the good-natured Sam.

The pair reached the end of the wooden sidewalk. As she stepped down onto the ground, Kate glanced up at Travis and made a misstep. He reached out to steady her, and she found herself leaning against him.

The moonlight struck his face fully. He was even more handsome than she had thought. For a moment they stayed as they were—she pressed against his side, her hand lying on his hard abdomen, he holding her until she could regain her balance, his eyes focused on her upturned face.

Travis wanted to lift a hand and run his fingers through her long golden locks, which gleamed silver in the moonlight. He was tempted to bend his head and kiss her cherry red lips as they parted over her perfect, small white teeth.

"Sorry, Sheriff," Kate said finally, and pushed away, shaken by the contact with his lean, hard body. "I lost my footing. How clumsy of me."

"Quite all right, Miss VanNam," Travis said, his eyes glinting as he spoke.

Kate realized she would only waste her breath if she again told him she could walk home alone.

The moonlight disappeared as they left town and climbed through the dense pine forest. After walking only a few yards they were forced to continue single file, Travis falling in behind Kate.

Over her shoulder, she explained that the house was in need of a bit of repair, but that she had already fixed it up some. She would have to keep him far from the mansion so he wouldn't notice the missing front door, among other defects.

When they stepped out into the broad clearing by the sparkling lake, Kate turned to face Travis. She put out her hand for him to shake and said sweetly, "I do appreciate you walking me home, Sheriff. It was most kind of you. Good night."

Travis didn't take her offered hand.

His eyes were on the darkened mansion. Without a word he left Kate standing there, and moved along the curving bank of the lake, headed directly toward the house. Kate gritted her teeth and followed.

"As I mentioned, the place needs a little work and—"

"Jesus Christ." Travis swore as they reached the overgrown yard. "There's no front door."

"Well, no, but...that's...wait...wait! Where are you going?"

Travis had crossed the yard, climbed the front steps and walked right into the house. He took a sulphur match from the breast pocket of his white shirt, struck it on his thumbnail and looked around the wide central corridor.

He glanced into the large front parlor and spotted the coal oil lamp on the floor beside a long sofa. He went inside, sank down into a crouching position and lifted the glass globe. He touched the match to the wick and the lamp blazed to life.

Kate entered the room as he was replacing the globe. She gave him an apologetic little smile and said, "I told you the house..."

"I had no idea this place had fallen into such bad repair," he said, shaking out the match. He rose to his feet. "Are you out of your mind? You can't stay in this house. I can't leave you here alone and unprotected. Get some things together and I'll take you back to town. You can sleep in a vacant cell at the city jail."

"Thank you, no."

"I don't want to argue, Miss VanNam. Get your clothes. You're coming with me. You'll be safe at the jail."

Travis stood with his feet apart, his hands at his sides. The lamplight cast eerie shadows on the mansion's walls. And on the marshal's scowling face. He looked angry.

"What an absurd proposal." Kate swiftly vetoed the idea, uncaring how angry it made him. "Have I done something illegal? You don't own me, Marshal. You can't tell me what to do."

Travis exhaled heavily. "I'm trying to help you here."

"I don't need or want your help, Marshal. All I want is for you to leave. *Now.* And in the future, if you'll kindly stay out of my way, I promise I'll stay out of yours."

Travis gazed at the gorgeous golden-haired girl standing there with her hands on her hips and her chin raised, speaking to him as no one else dared.

"Do you have a gun, Miss VanNam?"

Kate raised her right arm. From the drawstring reticule dangling from her wrist, she withdrew her Colt revolver. "I am armed, Sheriff."

"You know how to use that thing?"

"Certainly," she lied. "I'm an excellent shot."

"Fine, you hear anything moving, shoot and ask questions later. Anything comes around here, be it bear or panther or man, shoot to kill."

"Does that include you, Sheriff?" The minute she'd said it, Kate wished she could take it back.

His dark eyes blazed and he took a menacing step toward her. "Try it, sweetheart."

Kate swallowed hard. She started raising the revolver. In a flash he was next to her and had taken the gun away from her. He grabbed the sashed waistband of her dress and yanked her up against him. His face was now inches from her own. "*Never* aim a weapon unless you mean to fire it. You hear me?"

"Yes."

"Damn it to hell, I knew it."

"Knew what?" she asked, intensely aware that his slim hips and long legs were pressed flush against hers. She could feel the power and heat radiating from him.

"That you'd be trouble. You *are* trouble. You'll have trouble. You'll cause trouble. For yourself. And for me."

"That's a lot of trouble, Sheriff."

"Too much trouble." He released her, stepped back and placed the revolver on the sofa. "Why don't you be a good girl, pack up and leave before anybody gets hurt?"

"You must have a hearing disorder, Marshal," Kate said acidly. "My uncle Nelson was hard of hearing, so I'm used to having to raise my voice to be heard." She then shouted loudly, "I am staying in Fortune, and if you don't like it I'd suggest you stay out of my sight."

Both annoyed and amused by her determination, Travis raised his hands in surrender. "Fine, Miss Van-

Nam, but I catch you anywhere near a saloon or out on the streets after dark and you're going to jail."

"Fair enough, Marshal," Kate said. "And if I catch you anywhere near this house after dark, I'll be forced to shoot you."

Eight

Travis muttered to himself as he walked back to Fortune.

Damn her to hell!

Of all the gold camps in all the mountains in all the world, why did she have to wind up in his? Protecting Kate VanNam would be a twenty-four-hour-a-day job, and just himself and his deputy, Jiggs, wouldn't be enough manpower to keep ten thousand desperate miners at bay.

Impossible.

He'd be damned if he'd spend all his time worrying about a woman who didn't have enough sense to know what she was in for. She'd confront all sorts of problems up there all alone in that run-down mansion where she didn't even have a door to lock.

By the time Travis reached the sidewalks of town,

he was in a black mood. He would have to forget about Miss Kate VanNam.

It had been a long day. Travis was tired and thirsty.

But when he heard the piano music coming from the Golden Nugget, he finally smiled. He walked into the saloon and immediately felt better. All was as it should be.

In a corner was Big Maude, the muscular, six-foot-plus Amazon who was a fixture at the Golden Nugget, presiding nightly over the roulette wheel. With a smile, she called for him to come join her.

In the most crowded part of the room, Rosalita, a strikingly pretty Spaniard, sat behind the monte table, a cigarillo dangling from her painted red lips. Players flocked to Rosalita's table, their hard-earned money going across the green baize and into her small deft hands.

Travis walked inside just as the beautiful, dark-haired Valentina, garbed in a dazzling gown of bronze satin, climbed up on the square piano, smiled down at the piano player and crossed her shapely legs.

Whistles and applause from the roomful of men was deafening.

Valentina caught sight of Travis and threw him a kiss. He nodded and headed for the bar. She turned her attention on her adoring audience. Raising her hands for silence, she waited until they had calmed a bit before she placed a palm on the skirt of her shimmering gown, raised it a trifle, opened her mouth and began to sing.

"Ring, ring de banjo,
I love that good old song,
Come again my true love,
Oh where you been so long?"

Travis stood at the bar. He tossed down a straight whiskey and motioned the barkeep to pour another. As the liquor burned its way down into his chest, he relaxed and stopped worrying about the strong-willed, golden-haired Kate VanNam. Instead he looked at Valentina perched atop the piano, singing to the miners in her sweet, clear voice.

She was both a temptress and a tease. Her gown was cut so low and the waist was so tight that the tops of her full breasts swelled above the bronze silk. Travis grinned. He could see the twin nipples pushing against the shimmering fabric and a shapely gartered knee of her crossed legs.

"...Come again my true love," she sang, and looked directly at Travis.

He lifted a hand, pointed a finger at the ceiling. She smiled and nodded, knowing exactly what he meant.

Travis turned and walked out of the saloon. For a time he stood just outside in the cool mountain air, listening to Valentina sing. Then he walked away. When he reached the alley, he turned and went to the back of the two-story building that housed the rollicking Golden Nugget. He climbed the outside stairs, fished in his trousers pocket for the key and turned the lock.

When he entered Valentina's private quarters Gigi bowed and quickly took her leave. She had been told that anytime—day or night—Travis McCloud came to visit, she was to leave and stay in her quarters until Valentina summoned her.

Travis stripped down to his skin and sat down on Valentina's bed. From the silver box on the night table that Valentina kept filled for him, he took a fragrant cigar and lit it. Next to the silver box was a cut-crystal decanter filled with Kentucky bourbon that was also for him. Valentina drank only French champagne.

Travis poured himself a drink, then sank back onto the soft bed. He knew he'd have to wait at least an hour for Valentina to finish entertaining, but he didn't mind. He'd enjoy a smoke and a drink and unwind so he'd be completely rested and ready to make love to the beautiful Creole when she arrived.

When an hour finally passed and Valentina walked through the door, she smiled seductively at Travis. Yanking the covering sheet down, she glanced at his flaccid groin and said, "Well, now, I can't allow this."

Travis grinned. "No? Then what are you going to do about it?"

Valentina assured him she could fix it. She laid a warm hand on him and felt him immediately stir against her palm. She leaned down, kissed his bare chest, nipped playfully at his flat brown nipple, then raised her head.

"That's better, my love," she said. "I like my man with a drink, a smile and a hard cock." She laughed musically. "And not necessarily in that order."

Travis laughed, too, then surged upward when she ran her long-nailed forefinger the length of his erection and around its thrusting head.

"Don't torture me tonight, Valentina," he said, ready for her to come into his arms.

"My impatient darling," she murmured as she hastily shed her shimmering satin gown and climbed astride her lover. She wore nothing but her long silk stockings and a necklace of glittering jewels.

Hands folded beneath his head, Travis watched approvingly as Valentina reached out to the bedside table, stuck her fingers in his shot glass of bourbon, rubbed up and down the length of his straining masculinity, then guided him up inside her. She moved her hands away, loosened her swept-up hair from its restraints and allowed the dark locks to fall down around her bare ivory shoulders.

"I'm gonna give you some extra special loving tonight, my darling," she promised, rolling her pelvis and setting her heavy breasts to swaying. "And I will not allow you to get out of this bed before morning," she whispered, using her lush body to excite him in ways she had been taught in New Orleans. There she had learned how to please a man so completely he'd become a helpless slave to the unique sexual pleasures she could provide. Valentina practiced everything she knew to keep Travis satisfied and coming back for more. She wanted only to please this darkly handsome lawman, with whom she was madly in love.

She was extremely disappointed when Travis said, not an hour later, that he couldn't stay the night.

"What is it?" Valentina asked, when he rose and hunched into his trousers. "What's bothering you, Travis?" She sat up in the bed and wrapped her arms around her raised knees.

"Not a thing. But you know that I can't lie around here all night making love. I'm the sheriff, hired by the Committee of Vigilance to keep the peace."

Left unsaid was that he couldn't forget about a young, foolish woman who was living alone and un-protected in a run-down mansion. Or that he felt compelled to walk half a mile and check on her.

With his white shirt back on but unbuttoned, Travis shoved his arms into his black leather vest and strapped on his gun belt.

"Thanks for a great evening, Val."

"It wasn't an evening," she huffed, "it was one short hour."

He grinned. "You sure made that hour count, baby."

"Go! Get out of here," she said, and threw a pil-low at him.

After the sheriff had gone, it had taken Kate awhile to calm herself. She was upset and it was his fault. She didn't like Travis McCloud. She didn't like the conflicting emotions he aroused in her. She'd met him only tonight and yet he was keeping her awake. One minute she was seething with anger at him for his high-handed audacity, and the next she was squirming at the vivid recollection of being momentarily pressed against his lean, powerful body.

Finally, after a couple of hours had passed, Kate was just about to fall asleep when a noise came from the back of the house. It was the same sound she had heard every night for the five nights she had been here! Her heart racing, Kate reached for her loaded revolver. She lit her lamp and crossed the room to the wide corridor.

Cautioning herself to stay calm, but remembering the sheriff's advice to "shoot first and ask questions later," she crept down the long hall, not knowing if she would encounter a bear or a bandit. She was halfway to the back of the house when she saw something move in the shadows.

She lifted the revolver and took aim.

"I...I've got a gun," she threatened. "I know how to use it!"

Her eyes widened when she heard a distinctive hiss. Kate lifted the lamp high and saw, crouched against a wall, its back arched, a big fat calico cat, its golden eyes gleaming in the darkness. Relief flooding through her, Kate sank to her knees.

"Here kitty, kitty," she called, not really expecting the overweight feline to come to her. "So it was you," she said in soft, low tones. "You've been making all the noise and I thought it was a bear. Come here, let's be friends."

The cat made a low rattling sound in the back of its throat and stared at Kate with slitted golden eyes. It didn't budge.

She laughed softly. "You know, I wondered why there were no rats in this old house. From the looks of you, I'd say there's not a rodent within a mile of the place. What do you say?"

The rattling stopped. The calico finally meowed.

"That's better. Now come over here. Please. I'm all alone and I need a friend."

To Kate's surprise, the cat padded slowly closer, stopping just beyond her reach. "I'm Kate, Cal. If this is your home, that's fine with me. We can live here together. Okay?" Kate reached out and tried to touch the cat. It backed away.

But when she'd sat there unmoving for a minute, the cat cautiously came closer. It reached her and, when she didn't make a move to touch it, rubbed its furry side against her knees. Then it slowly walked around her, rubbing up against Kate as it went.

When the cat was again facing her, Kate said, "I'm going back to bed now. You're welcome to come sleep at the foot of my bed. It's up to you."

She lifted the lamp and gun, rose to her feet,

turned and walked away. She was disappointed to see that the cat hadn't followed. Still, just knowing it was there made her feel less lonely and afraid.

She lay back down, but sleep still would not come. Kate again got up.

She left the lamp and gun where they were and went out onto the porch. She yanked up the tail of her long gown, sat down on the first step and tucked the fabric between her knees. She gazed up at the deep cobalt sky overhead. The heavens were brilliant with stars. They glittered like diamonds in the still, thin mountain air.

She smiled when she felt something warm and furry press against her hip. She looked down at the big calico cat and knew she'd found a much needed companion. Very slowly, very carefully, she lifted a hand and laid two fingers lightly atop its head. When the cat looked up at her, she slipped her hand beneath its throat and began to gently stroke it. The cat purred contentedly and was soon catnapping.

Neither the girl nor the cat were aware that someone was watching.

When Travis had reached the clearing, he'd seen a lamp flickering inside the house. From afar, he'd watched as the light moved from the front room and down the hall to the back of the mansion. Minutes later it returned to the front and soon went out.

The girl had, he supposed, gone to sleep.

Travis had started to turn away. Then he hesitated, deciding to stay just a few more minutes.

He'd moved closer to the mansion and took up a post beneath a towering pine at the edge of the yard, where he had an unobstructed view of the house and its surrounding grounds. He sat down and leaned back against the solid trunk.

Less than ten minutes later the girl came out of the house dressed in her long nightgown. She stood on the porch for a couple of heartbeats while the night winds pressed the thin white garment against her tall, slender body, and her unbound hair whipped around her head.

His eyes dry from not daring to blink, Travis stared at the vision in white and lost his breath entirely when she impetuously yanked the long skirt of her nightgown up around her thighs and sank down on the front step, shoving the fabric between her legs and pressing her knees together.

Travis ground his teeth so hard his jaws ached.

Damn her beautiful hide!

All the warning in the world hadn't made one bit of difference. He had a good mind to march up there and haul her back inside.

Just then a big calico cat sauntered out of the house and over to her. Travis watched, disbelieving, as Kate stroked the cat's raised throat.

That cat had been left behind when Mrs. Colfax moved away. He'd seen the creature running wild through the woods. Apparently it had taken up residence in the empty mansion.

The animal had turned feral years ago. Yet already this Boston blonde had made an obedient pet of it.

Travis's eyes narrowed.

He stared at Miss VanNam, remembering how another golden-haired beauty had made a pet—and a fool—out of him.

Silently he vowed that would never happen again.

Nine

As Sheriff McCloud had suspected, Kate VanNam's presence in Fortune caused quite a stir. In mining regions, men would travel a great distance for a glance at a newly arrived female, since, aside from the girls working in the bordellos, very few unattached women lived in gold camps, and none were as young and as pretty as Kate VanNam. She was, fortunately, such a novelty that most of the hard-bitten miners treated her with awed respect. She represented their mothers, sisters, daughters, wives and sweethearts back home.

But not all.

There were a number of dirty, foul-mouthed curs who would have loved to get their hands on a genteel woman like Kate VanNam. Sheriff McCloud put the word out that if anyone trifled with her, he would have to answer to him. Still, Travis worried for her safety. She was, he knew, too much of a temptation to the lonely miners.

Travis enlisted the help of his deputy, Jiggs Gillespie.

"I need a hand, Jiggs," Travis said early one morning as the two were drinking coffee at the jail.

"What can I do?" asked the always congenial Jiggs.

Travis took a sip of the steaming black brew. "The young woman up at—"

"Kate VanNam?"

"Yes, Kate VanNam. Jiggs, she's up there by herself in that run-down mansion. Jesus, there's not even a front door and—"

"Why don't we take turns checking on her?" said Jiggs, anticipating Travis's request.

"You wouldn't mind?"

The skinny deputy smiled, rose to his feet and hitched up his trousers. "Lordy, no. It's not like I have a wife and family to go home to at night."

"I'd be much obliged to you, Jiggs." Travis frowned when he added, "God knows she's a royal pain in the ass, but I don't look for her to be staying long in Fortune."

"I do, Trav."

Travis blinked, taken aback. "Why would you say a thing like that?"

He shrugged narrow shoulders. "I heard her talking to Doc Ledet on the steamer up from San Francisco. She told him she was going to stay here until

she found gold in the Cavalry Blue. I'd say that
should take about…um, well, put it this way. You and
I will be dead and gone, and she'll be a withered old
woman, before an ounce of gold is brought out of the
worthless Cavalry Blue."

Travis nodded. "I'm betting she'll tire of the futile undertaking." He took another drink of coffee.
"But until that happy day, we'll have to keep an eye
on the pretty Easterner."

"I'll wander on up two or three times tonight."

"Thanks, Jiggs. Once you're up there, stay safely
out of sight. She's got a gun and I told her to shoot
and ask questions later."

"She'll never know I'm within a hundred miles of
the place."

There were no respondents to her "Miners
Wanted" ad in the weekly *Fortune Teller.* Kate was
disappointed. She was becoming increasingly frustrated by the fact that she couldn't find anyone to
work her mine. Obviously Sheriff McCloud had been
right when he'd predicted she wouldn't be able to
hire any laborers. It seemed that all the men in Fortune were working their own claims.

Since she had been warned by the inflexible sheriff not to step foot inside one of the many saloons,
Kate had to limit her hunt to placing the advertisement
in the weekly newspaper and to checking at the Wells
Fargo office when the mail carrier delivered the post.

After sending a letter to Alexandra Wharton, her dear friend back in Boston, Kate made an inquiry at Wells Fargo. No takers. Discouraged, she left and was heading down the sidewalk when she heard loud thudding sounds and muffled groans.

She stopped, turned her head and listened.

She heard the unmistakable moaning of an animal in pain. Kate hurried and peered down the shadowy alley between two buildings.

She gasped in horror.

Two big, rough looking men, the taller one with a black patch over one eye, the other sporting a bushy red beard, were mercilessly beating a helpless little Chinaman. The one-eyed man had his knife out, trying to cut off the Chinaman's queue.

Kate didn't hesitate.

She reached into her reticule, drew her uncle's Navy Colt revolver, hurried into the alley, raised her arm above her head and fired into the air.

"Hit him one more time and I'll blow your heads off!" she warned, lowering the gun and at the same time taking close notice of their faces and clothes so that she could describe them to the sheriff and help identify them.

The startled ruffians instantly released their victim and fled out the back of the alley. Kate put the weapon away and hurried to the suffering Chinaman, who lay crumpled on the ground.

"You speak English?" she asked, taking a hand-

kerchief from her reticule to dab some of the blood
from his pummeled face.

He grimaced, but nodded.

"Good. We'll get you across the street to Dr. Ledet's and he'll—"

"No…no," said the man through clenched teeth.
"No doctor. Not need one."

"Yes, you do! You're badly hurt and—"

"Do not need doctor," the Chinaman said again.

"You are going to the doctor!" Kate stated firmly.
"Now, we'll carefully sit you up and let you lean back
against the building. Once we've accomplished that,"
she told him, "I'm going to drape your arm around
my shoulder and put my arm around your waist. You
understand?"

He grimaced, his eyes glazed with pain. Kate
slipped her arm around him and very carefully, very
gently positioned him beside her.

"That's good. You ready to give walking a try?"

"Ready," he muttered, then groaned in agony
when she moved him.

"I'm so sorry," Kate murmured, supporting the little man's weight as she half dragged, half carried him
across the street.

"Can I help?" asked a toothless old sourdough
with a miner's pallor who looked as if a puff of wind
would blow him away. "Want me to carry him?"

"We can manage," Kate said with a smile of gratitude, "but thank you, Mr.…."

"H. Q. Blankenship," the man said, and backed away.

Dr. Ledet, seated at the desk in his front office, looked out the window, saw the pair and came running out to meet them.

"Chang Li, who did this to you?" asked the white-haired physician. The battered Chinaman gave no reply. Dr. Ledet instructed Kate, "Let's get him into the back room, Miss VanNam."

Once there, they carefully lifted the suffering man up onto the examining table. While the doctor turned away to wash his hands, Kate stood gently patting Chang Li's shoulder while she stated, "Two bullies, Doctor. Both very large, very dirty men. One had a black eye patch, the other a full red beard."

Over his shoulder as he soaped his hands, Ledet said, "Titus Kelton is the one-eyed man. The red-bearded fellow is Jim Spears. Miscreants both. Always trouble, they are. Mean as snakes and—"

"I must go, Dr. Ledet," Kate interrupted, then smiled down at Chang Li. "The doctor will care for you."

"Yes, yes, you go on, child. I'll take over," Dr. Ledet said as he dried his hands on a clean white cloth.

Once outside she took a deep breath but quickly lifted her skirts and hurried across the dusty street. The few men who were loitering about noted the set of her jaw and the flash of her eyes. Everyone wisely stayed out of her way.

She marched two blocks up the sidewalk to the city jail.

Blinking as her eyes adjusted to the light inside the office, Kate saw Fortune's fearless sheriff, his feet propped up on his desk, his hands laced across his stomach. He was dozing in his chair.

Her anger immediately flared.

While a poor, defenseless little Chinaman was being brutally beaten in an alley two blocks away, the town marshal was asleep at his desk. Unforgivable! Seething, Kate swept over to Travis. Peaceful as a baby he was, shiny star moving up and down on his chest with his slow, rhythmic breathing.

She reached out and shoved his booted feet to the floor.

"What the devil!" he snarled.

"I'll tell you what the devil!" Kate said, leaning close. "You! You're the devil! The big, bad sheriff who's supposed to be some kind of legend. Everybody talks about your he-man prowess, your pistol-packing, rifle-toting, frontier-taming...your unsurpassed greatness. You think you're tough. You're not so tough. Dear Lord, here you are sleeping on the job! You're supposed to keep the peace in this town, Sheriff! Do it!"

She turned to leave. Travis's hand caught hold of her flowing skirts.

"You let me go!" she ordered, trying desperately to free herself.

"Go? You came here to make a complaint, didn't you?" He reeled her in by her skirt. To her chagrin, he plunked her down hard on his left knee. "Make it. Tell me what has happened to bring you here in such a state of agitation."

"I am not agitated and you are not awake. I'll come back later to—"

"You're going nowhere until you tell me what this is all about."

"Let me up this minute or I will scream," she warned.

"No you won't," said Travis, clamping a long arm around her trim waist.

Kate stiffened. "I will, so help me."

"You do and I'll arrest you for disturbing the peace," he said, unsmiling. "Toss you right into a cell and lock you up. Now what's on your mind, Miss VanNam?"

Leaning away from his muscular chest as far as she possibly could, Kate stated, "Two of your town bullies—Titus Kelton and Jim Spears—have beaten a poor, helpless man within an inch of his life while you were sitting here sound asleep!"

Travis said nothing. Looking directly into his dark eyes, she continued, "They attempted to cut off his queue, but I got there in time! Swear to me you'll make them pay."

"I swear," Travis said. He yawned, pushed her to her feet and rose to his own. "Anything else I can do for you?"

Kate took a step back. "What are you going to do to them?"

"Find 'em first," he said with slow smile that made her want to smack his smug face.

"And then?"

Travis shrugged broad shoulders, "Perhaps a dose of their own medicine."

Kate was appalled. "For heaven's sake, are you saying that you intend to beat them?"

"What would you suggest I do with them?" he asked, running a hand through his thick raven hair. He reached for his hat.

"Why, that's barbaric! You simply cannot behave like an animal, Sheriff. You're supposed to be an officer of the law and—"

"I *am* the law, Miss VanNam. And you have just reported a criminal act, one that calls for harsh punishment. This is not Boston. It's Fortune, California. If you don't like the way things are done here, may I suggest you return to the civilized East." He picked up his gun belt, slung it around his hips and buckled it. "You come in here and tell me that Kelton and Spears beat up a defenseless man. Fine, I believe you. Now believe me when I tell you that they will pay."

Travis stepped around her, headed for the door.

"Marshal McCloud."

He turned back to look at her. "Yes, Miss VanNam?"

"Don't ever do that again."

"What's that, Miss VanNam?"

"Sit me on your knee." Her face flushed as she said the words.

Travis put his hat on his head and adjusted the brim. "Wake me like that again and you'll be lucky if I don't turn you *over* my knee."

He tipped his hat and left Kate glaring after him. She watched him unhurriedly cross the street, and felt again the heat of his arm around her waist when he'd sat her on his knee. She shivered inwardly. There was an air of mystery and power about the town sheriff that both repelled and excited her. He was handsome in a ruthless way and she had no doubt there were women who looked upon him with favor.

Kate shook herself out of her foolish reveries and hurried back to Dr. Ledet's office to check on the patient.

For the next hour she stayed at the physician's elbow, assisting in any way she could while he worked on Chang Li. Dr. Ledet had given the suffering man a liberal dose of laudanum, and Chang Li was now sleeping soundly.

When finally the doctor was finished with the task, and both he and Kate had washed their hands, he quietly motioned her to precede him out of the room.

Once they were in the front office, Kate reached for her reticule. "How much does he owe you, Doctor? I want to pay."

"Not a thing, Kate." He smiled as he rolled his

sleeves down. She tried again, but he refused to take any money. He said, "Chang Li is resting well, so we'll leave him here in my office for a couple of days. He's going to be fine. Sore for a while, but no permanent damage was done."

Kate nodded. "Thanks to you."

"No, I'd say it's thanks to you, child." He chuckled and said, "You faced down the town bullies. I don't know of many men, much less a woman, who would…."

A disturbance outside caused the doctor to stop speaking. He and Kate exchanged glances, then quickly turned to look out the window.

Marshal Travis McCloud, mounted atop a snorting Appaloosa stallion, came riding down the center of the Main Street with two big, dirty prisoners—one with a black eye patch, the other with a full red beard—stumbling behind him. A long length of rope was wrapped around their bound hands and tied to the sheriff's gun belt.

Bordello girls, bartenders, hotel clerks, store proprietors and anybody else who happened to be in town spilled out into the street. The spectators pointed at the humiliated pair and laughed merrily. They shouted and whistled and applauded.

"Dr. Ledet," Kate said, aghast at the sight of the men's bloody noses and blackened eyes. "Those prisoners have been beaten. Did the marshal…?"

"Indeed he did. Found them and fought them both

and brought them in to jail. And look at Travis—not a scratch on him," the doctor said admiringly.

Kate's jaw dropped. "You approve?"

"Absolutely," he declared with a smile. "Street fighting, stabbing, shooting and claim jumping. You name it, Travis handles it with ease. He's the bravest, finest sheriff in all California."

Ten

"**D**on't shoot!" shouted a strapping, ruddy-faced man in dirty overalls, raising his big hands in the air.

"I surrender!" called another, pretending to be frightened.

"Take me prisoner, please!" pleaded a grinning young boy as he fell to his knees on the sidewalk and offered up his wrists.

Everyone guffawed and whistled.

The teasing was directed at Kate.

And she could thank Doc Ledet.

The miners had learned from the physician that the pretty newcomer had boldly stepped into an alley, fired her big Colt in the air and threatened Kelton and Spears.

Now when Kate went to check on Chang Li, the miners clowned with her as she walked down the street. Unconcerned with their childish ribbing, she headed directly to Dr. Ledet's office two doors past the Eldorado Hotel.

"Dr. Ledet?" Kate called softly as she stepped into the front office. "Are you here, Doctor?"

The physician came through the back room's curtained door and placed a finger to his lips. Kate nodded in understanding.

In low tones, the doctor said, "Chang Li is resting. He awakened earlier this afternoon and ate a little broth. He told me the whole story of how you saved his life."

Kate narrowed her eyes. "And you promptly informed the rest of Fortune."

Looking sheepish, Doc Ledet said, "I might have mentioned it to a couple of people." When she didn't scold him, he smiled, offered her a chair and said, "Some of the miners are saying maybe Marshal Mc-Cloud should deputize you."

At the mention of the marshal, Kate frowned, but made no comment. She sat down and carefully spread her billowing skirts around her feet. "Doctor, why were those men beating Chang Li? What had he done to deserve such brutality?"

"He did nothing to provoke them," the doctor said, stepping behind the desk and dropping wearily into his high-backed chair. "Coolies are hated and reviled because they will work harder and longer for less, and that brings wages down."

The doctor knew a great deal about Chang Li, as

he did about everyone in Fortune. And he was more than happy to share the information. Kate listened attentively.

"Chang Li has been in Fortune for three years while his family is back in China. He's longing for a better life, hoping to make enough money in California to bring his wife and children here one day.

"He lives alone in the tent city at the southern edge of town."

"Those two bullies must be properly punished," Kate replied. "They should stand trial. Chang Li must testify against them and—"

The doctor interrupted. "Kate, Chang Li can't testify. And even if he could, no one would believe his word against theirs."

"But why? Surely…"

"The Foreign Miners License Tax Law of 1850 prohibits Indians and Chinamen from testifying in court."

"That's unfair."

"It's the law," said Doc Ledet.

Kate sighed wearily. "It's getting late, Doctor. I'd better go."

"Yes, you shouldn't be out on the streets after dark," he stated, rising from his chair. "The sheriff wouldn't like it."

Kate frowned. "I don't give a fig what the sheriff would like."

"Now, now, you don't want to get crossways with Marshal McCloud."

Kate bit her tongue, but did not reply. She rose and moved toward the door, then stopped and turned back. "Dr. Ledet, have you ever heard the expression 'seeing the elephant'?"

He chuckled. "Where'd you hear it?"

"Sheriff McCloud accused me of that."

"Child, it's a well-known term that best characterizes the forty-niners and the gold rush."

"It makes no sense."

"Yes, it does. When gold was found in these mountains, people planning to come out West announced they were 'going to see the elephant.' Those who turned back claimed they had seen the 'elephant's tracks' or the 'elephant's tail' and swore they'd seen more than enough of the animal." Eyes twinkling, he rubbed his chin, warming to the story, one he'd told many times before.

"But what does seeing an elephant have to do with hunting for gold?" she asked.

"It's a phrase that arose from the time circus parades first featured the giant elephants. A farmer, so the story goes, hearing that the circus was in town, loaded his wagon with vegetables for the market. He had never seen an elephant and very much wished to do so. On the way to town, he encountered the circus parade, which was led by the elephant.

"The farmer was thrilled to death. But his horses were terrified, so they bolted, overturned the wagon and ruined all the vegetables. 'I don't give a hang,' the farmer said, 'for I have seen the elephant!'"

Dr. Ledet laughed then, a deep belly laugh that brought tears to his eyes and caused his face to grow beet-red.

Kate frowned. "Perhaps a metaphor."

"Kate, Kate," he continued, wiping his eyes, "don't you see? For gold rushers, the elephant symbolized the high cost of their endeavor—the myriad possibilities for misfortune along the way or once they got out here. But, like the farmer's circus elephant, it's an unequaled experience, the grand adventure of a lifetime."

"It's the journey, not the destination."

"You've got it, my girl."

"Well, I hate to admit it, but the sheriff was right. I have come to 'see the elephant.'" She smiled then, and added, "And should I never find my gold, I will have had the grand adventure of a lifetime!"

When Chang Li was able to leave Dr. Ledet's office, less than seventy-two hours after Kate had taken him there badly injured, he told her that he would repay her the only way he knew how. He would work for her.

Kate was delighted. She explained that she had looked for—with no success—men to help her work the Cavalry Blue Mine.

"I understand the going rate for miners is $3.00 a day," she said. "Is that satisfactory?"

"Most satisfactory," he said, happily bobbing his head and setting his plaited queue to dancing. "I help Missy find her gold!"

That same afternoon, while Kate waited just outside, Chang Li quit his job in Mrs. Reno's laundry, where for the past year he had been slaving twelve hours a day, seven days a week for a pittance.

"You know anything about working a mine?" Kate asked when he came out of the laundry.

"Know plenty," he said as they fell into step on the sidewalk. "I work mine while you look for placer."

"No. The placer is gone," Kate stated.

"Not know that for sure. Stream that run across your property changes with every rain. You have good batea?"

"Batea?" Her eyebrows lifted.

"Is pan with…grooves…corrugations in bottom. You will need good one to wash the gravel."

"I'll get one. What else will we need?"

"Pick and shovel and sturdy bucket for me to work inside the mine," he said. "Later we get lumber and build good rocker, handle more volume that way."

"All right. Let's go on over to Barton's and pick out the tools we'll need to get started," Kate said. "Can you be at my house bright and early in the morning?"

"I be there at sunup!" he promised.

Eleven

Just as promised, a smiling Chang Li showed up just
as the sun was beginning to rise.

Within the hour he and Kate stood barefooted in
the clear, sparkling stream that ran past her house.
Chang Li had his loose white trousers rolled up, and
Kate ignored the fact that the hem of her long skirt
was saturated and sticking to her ankles.

She didn't care. She was eager to learn all that she
could from her willing teacher. Patiently Chang Li
instructed her in the fine art of placer mining. She
quickly caught on and delighted in dipping the large
pan into the shallow water, then swishing it slowly
around to wash the gravel in hopes of seeing the unmistakable flash of gold.

Panning for the precious metal was hard physical
labor. By noon Kate's back was breaking and her

arms felt as if they would fall off. But she didn't complain.

At her insistence, Chang Li spent the entire day with her in the shallow stream, teaching her to identify and wash the grains that might yield specks of gold.

"That's enough for today, Chang Li," an exhausted Kate finally said late that afternoon as the sun was westering behind the tallest mountain peaks. "I'm dead tired and you must be as well. Go home now."

The little man nodded and said, "I be back tomorrow. Go on up mountain to Cavalry Brue Mine while Missy pan down here."

"Yes, I believe I can handle it now, thanks to you."

From that day on the unlikely pair worked as a team. Kate panned in the stream and Chang Li hacked at the rock inside the Cavalry Blue. The loyal Chinaman quickly became her trusted right hand.

Kate had become the talk of the town.

The single men in Fortune wanted to court her, and the married men wished they were single so they could court her.

Only one man in Fortune showed no interest in courting Kate.

Sheriff Travis McCloud.

Kate's presence was nothing but a headache for Travis. He heard about the invitations she received daily from would-be beaux, and was relieved when she declined. He hoped she had enough sense to continue saying no to all the amorous young fools.

Travis had also heard that Kate had employed Chang Li and that together they were working her worthless claim. He was certain she would now quickly tire of the futile project and get out of his town.

Nevertheless, Travis loaded a small cart with a saw, a hammer and nails, lumber and a newly purchased heavy wooden door. He'd do his duty and make sure she was safe until she left. He hitched the loaded cart to a strong-backed burro and led the struggling animal up to Kate's place.

Travis parked the donkey cart on the south side of the house. He went around to the front and knocked loudly on the door frame. No one answered. He supposed she was up at the mine with her Chinese helper. Travis unloaded the cart and went to work.

He pried the ruined gold-plated hinges from the old frame and bolted in new ones. Then he hung the massive door and stood back to admire his handiwork. He tried the key in the lock and heard it click.

Nodding to himself, he shoved the key into the pocket of his snug trousers and went back out to the cart to unload some short pieces of lumber. He began nailing boards over broken glass panes in windows of the room where she slept, as a temporary barrier to intruders.

It was nearing three o'clock and the alpine sun was high and hot. Travis was soon perspiring.

He shrugged out of his leather vest as well as his white shirt.

Kate, panning for gold on that warm June afternoon, felt the hot sun beating down on her bare head, and scolded herself for forgetting her bonnet. Knowing her fair face would blister, she waded out of the stream and laid her batea on the bank.

She decided to run down to the mansion, grab a bonnet and come back.

She saw no need to put on her shoes or lower the skirts she had tied up around her thighs. Kate carefully picked her way down the mountainside and around the mansion to the overgrown front yard.

When she reached the front gate, she saw him.

Sheriff Travis McCloud.

His back was to her, and he was unaware of her presence.

At that moment he stripped off his white shirt and dropped it. Kate stood stock-still and stared, her lips parted, her heart racing. Feeling as if she were smothering, she watched the handsome, dark-haired lawman labor in the hot California sun, his smooth bronzed back gleaming with perspiration.

He bent from the waist, picked up a hammer and began working on a broken windowpane. The muscles in his long right arm bunched and strained as he rhythmically swung the hammer. His shoulder blades slipped and slid beneath the smooth, glistening skin of his beautiful back.

Her throat dry, Kate forgot that she was barefoot and that her skirts were tied up high around her legs. She was, for the moment, mesmerized by the sight of the tall, lean, half-naked sheriff. Aware that she should let him knew she was there, yet reluctant to do so, she guiltily lowered her eyes to the snug black trousers that clung to his slim hips and long legs.

She wondered if all of his body was as bronzed and as magnificent as his bare shoulders and deeply clefted back.

She shivered at the thought.

Travis felt someone's eyes on him.

He lowered the hammer and slowly turned around. He immediately saw her framed in the open front gate.

Kate did not make a sound.

She couldn't.

She helplessly stared at the broad torso of this handsome man who possessed an almost animal-like masculinity. Kate had no doubt, as her eyes slipped down to where his belt was buckled just below his naval, that he was a highly virile male who'd had scores of conquests.

Travis was as silent as Kate.

He stood there with the hammer in his hand looking at her, appraising her, admiring her. Never had he seen a woman more desirable than this young, willowy, barefooted vision in gingham. Her wide-set blue eyes were locked on him, and in their depths was unmistakable attraction. Her glorious golden hair was blazing in the sun. Teasing glimpses of her soft, rounded breasts were revealed in her half-unbuttoned bodice. Her pale, shapely thighs, appealingly exposed by the bunched-up dress, were almost his undoing.

Travis found himself longing to fall to his knees before her and kiss her exquisite thighs. The prospect made his belly tighten, but he quickly bit the inside of his cheek to regain his usual control.

He dropped the hammer, picked up his vest and shirt, slung them over his shoulder and walked slowly toward her. Kate held her breath, wondering what he was going to do.

She tensed and waited for him to reach her.

When he did, he stood gazing unblinkingly at her, then lowered his hand.

She anxiously looked down to see what he was doing. He slipped his fingers inside the pocket of his tight black trousers and produced a shiny brass key.

"Lock the front door," he said, holding it up before her face. His dark, liquid eyes smoldered, his lean jaw ridged. "To everyone."

Under his spell, swaying toward him, Kate said, "Even to you, Marshal?"

His eyes dilated. "Especially to me, Kate."

"If you say so," she breathlessly replied. She was

tempted to reach out and spread one hand across the sculptured muscles of his chest. She resisted.

"I say so." Then he took her by surprise when, continuing to look directly into her eyes, he slowly reached out and yanked on her skirts, causing them to come untied and fall down around her ankles.

"Oh, my Lord!" she lamented, mortified. "I had forgotten about my skirts being—"

"Don't forget again."

Twelve

On a blistering hot afternoon in early June, a month after Kate's arrival, a mysterious stranger appeared in Fortune, California.

The tall, slim, fair-haired Winn DeLaney, looking neat as a bandbox despite the withering summertime heat, swung down from the steamer's gangway, looked around, smiled and headed directly to the Bonanza Hotel, nodding politely to anyone he encountered.

He was good-looking, well groomed and wore smartly tailored clothes. A pair of golden spurs flashed on his freshly polished black boots. Winn DeLaney was aware that he looked nothing like the rough-hewn denizens who inhabited this mountain mining community.

Suppressing his amusement at the speculation his presence in Fortune was sure to stir, DeLaney crossed

the street and walked into the three-story brick Bonanza Hotel.

"Your most elegant suite," he informed the short,
squat man behind the marble counter, and reached for
the guest register.

Signing his name with a flourish that called attention to his artistic hands, he placed the pen back in
the ink well and looked up at the curious desk clerk.

"You ain't from around these parts, are you…"
Dwayne, the day clerk, glanced down at the signed
register "…Mr. Winn Delaney."

"No. I'm from San Francisco."

"Just in off the steamer? What brings you up here
to Fortune? By the looks of your hands, you're not
aimin' to work the mines." Dwayne grinned.

"Hardly," Winn DeLaney said with a good-
natured laugh, but volunteered no further information. "If you'll kindly have my bags brought up…"
He accepted the key to the top floor corner suite,
number 312.

"Certainly, sir. Right away."

Delaney nodded, turned and headed for the stairs.
He stopped, slowly pivoted and said in casual com-
mand, "I'll be requiring a hot bath drawn at seven
sharp, followed by dinner in my suite at eight. Beef-
steak rare, potatoes, salad and a bottle of your finest
champagne. May I count on it?"

"Yes, sir, Mr. Delaney," said Dwayne, bobbing
his head, obviously pleased that such an illustrious

guest, a man so wealthy he wore spurs of gold, had chosen the Bonanza.

Upstairs, Winn Delaney looked around the suite, walked directly into the bedroom and crossed to the front windows. He glanced across the street at McNeil's Barbershop. On one side of the shop was the Brass Rail Saloon. On the other side the Bloody Bucket. He closed the heavy curtains and shrugged out of the finely tailored frock coat.

He did not venture out of his hotel room that evening. He luxuriated in the hot tub, then, clad only in a black silk dressing gown, enjoyed his evening meal. When he'd finished dinner, he dropped the robe, picked up the bottle and crossed to the bed.

He poured himself another glass of the bubbly and stretched out atop the soft feather mattress. He leaned back against the stacked pillows and sipped the champagne. A sly smile soon stretched along his lips. A tingle of building excitement surged through his body.

The heat of the summer night and the potency of the chilled champagne made his face flush and his chest and long arms perspire.

Winn ran a hand over his damp torso and down his flat belly. He sighed with a mixture of satisfaction and exhaustion. Half-tipsy, he finished the bottle of champagne, blew out the lamp, and fell asleep.

By the next day everyone in Fortune had heard that a handsome, wealthy gentleman from San Francisco was in town and staying at the Bonanza Hotel in its most expensive suite.

Sheriff Travis McCloud heard about Winn DeLaney and idly wondered what he was doing in Fortune. He didn't really care one way or the other why a rich, cultured gentleman was in town. Winn DeLaney was hardly the type to cause mischief in Fortune.

Three days after arriving in Fortune, Winn DeLaney, dressed for the warm summer weather in smartly creased buff trousers and a freshly laundered white shirt, sat in the lobby of the Bonanza Hotel reading a yellowing copy of the *San Francisco Chronicle*. When he finished the paper, he carefully refolded it and laid it aside.

He was bored and restless.

And then he saw her.

Through the tall front windows of the hotel, he spotted a pretty young woman with gleaming golden hair rapidly approaching. DeLaney rose to his feet and crossed the lobby to the open front doors. He stepped out onto the sidewalk and collided with the young woman, startling her.

"A thousand pardons, miss." He politely apologized, and gently clasped her upper arms to steady her. "I'm so terribly sorry. Are you hurt? Have I injured you?"

"No. No, I'm fine, really," Kate assured him, waving a hand in the air.

Winn DeLaney flashed her a warm smile. He

looked into her dazzling blue eyes and said, "Allow me to introduce myself." He stepped back and clicked his heels together. "Winn DeLaney, at your service, miss."

"Mr. DeLaney," Kate acknowledged, taking notice of his striking good looks and impeccably tailored clothes.

"And I'm addressing…?" said DeLaney.

"Kate," she told him. "Kate VanNam. Now if you'll excuse me, I've errands to run."

She stepped past him, but he quickly turned and followed. "I find myself at loose ends this morning. May I be of help with your errands, Miss VanNam?"

"You're kind, but I need no help."

Undeterred, Winn DeLaney fell into step beside Kate, explaining that he had recently arrived in Fortune and therefore knew no one.

"It's quite bleak being alone in a new place, don't you agree?"

Kate could sympathize on that score. She, too, had often been lonely since arriving in Fortune. But she had no intention of sharing that information with this fair, handsome stranger.

"I'm sure you'll soon have friends," she said, wondering why he had come to Fortune if he knew no one.

"Would I be out of line to say I hope you'll be my first friend?" Kate gave no reply, so he pressed on. "Miss VanNam, may I call on you one evening? Take you to one of the hotels for dinner? Or perhaps to the opera?"

"No, thank you, Mr. DeLaney," Kate said. "Now, I really am in a hurry, so good day to you, sir."

Sheriff Travis McCloud was getting a haircut in McNeil's Barbershop directly across the street from the Bonanza Hotel when he spotted Kate VanNam charging down the wooden sidewalk. Travis was staring at her when a tall blond man stepped out of the hotel and bumped squarely into her.

"Hold it a minute, Mac," Travis said to the barber.

Clippers in hand, Cotton McNeil stopped trimming Travis's raven locks and looked up to see what had captured the sheriff's attention.

"Ah, that there's the wealthy San Francisco gentleman that wears them fancy golden spurs." Cotton laughed then. "I don't see no horse, so why's he wearing spurs?"

"DeLaney?" Travis asked. "That fellow is DeLaney?"

"That's him, all right. Since he arrived, I've seen him sitting in that hotel lobby hour upon hour. It's like he was waiting for somebody," Cotton said thoughtfully. "But who could it be?"

Travis's dark eyes narrowed. He watched as the slim blond man spoke to Kate, smiled at her and then walked along beside her until she stopped abruptly, shook her head dismissively and left him staring after her.

Cotton McNeil, watching the exchange between Kate and Winn Delaney, chuckled and said, "Looks to me like the pretty Miss VanNam has caught the eye of this wealthy DeLaney. I wouldn't be a bit surprised if next thing we know, he's courting her. Would you, Travis?"

"Finish my haircut, Mac. I've got to take 'Monte' Jim downriver to the Committee of Vigilance in Quartzville to stand judgment for claim jumping."

Thirteen

Winn DeLaney possessed a gambler's instinct and a seducer's charm. He would need both in his unflagging pursuit of Kate VanNam. And he was, from the moment he'd bumped into her, a patient, persistent suitor.

"I'll never give up, Miss VanNam," he warned her each time they met. "If it takes a week, a month or a year, the day will come when you will say yes to me." He grinned when he added, "And you'll be glad you did."

Kate was flattered by the attention of such a handsome, sophisticated gentleman. And impressed with his determination. But time after time she continued to decline his invitations.

Until at last DeLaney persuasively argued away all of her objections and she agreed to have dinner with him at the Bonanza Hotel.

Kate looked forward to the evening. She felt sure Winn DeLaney would be entertaining company, and even more inviting was the prospect of enjoying a hot, delicious meal. She had heard that the finest food to be had in Fortune was served in the Bonanza dining room.

Now, as the hour rapidly approached for the agreed upon engagement, Kate stood before a cracked mirror that she had leaned against the wall in the downstairs drawing room. For this evening's momentous occasion, Kate donned the last good dress she owned, one she had not worn since arriving in Fortune.

She carefully drew on the pale blue silk gown with its low-cut neckline, tight waist and billowing skirts. Hands behind her, she struggled to get the garment closed down the back, hoping she didn't miss any of the tiny buttons.

Beneath the dress she wore her fullest lace-trimmed petticoat, and wished that she had some hoops to make her skirts stand fully out as was the fashion of the day. But she had brought neither whalebone corset nor hoops with her. She couldn't cinch in her waist or expand her skirts as she would have liked. Kate fretted over her appearance. She was sure a cultured gentleman like Winn DeLaney was accustomed to courting only rich ladies who wore the latest of fashions.

Kate sighed. Then she bent forward before the mirror and frowned. Too much of her bare bosom was showing above the gown's low-cut bodice. She yanked at the fabric, determined to modestly cover herself. Satisfied at last that there was not too much flesh showing, she stopped fussing over the dress and turned her attention to her hair.

She effortlessly swept her long golden locks atop her head and secured them with an oyster shell clasp. She again studied herself in the cracked mirror, pinched her cheeks and bit her lips. Then she turned around.

"So...how do I look, Cal?" she asked the overweight calico cat. The furry male feline lay sprawled on the rose velvet sofa-bed, stretching his paws out. The cat's reply to her question was a wide yawn and the closing of his golden eyes. Kate laughed and shook her head. "You're a big help."

She came over and scratched Cal's head until he purred deep in his throat. Then Kate blew out the coal oil lamp and said to the dozing cat, "Don't let anyone near the place while I'm gone."

She crossed to the front window and saw Winn DeLaney come into the yard. Right on time. She picked up her reticule and walked out of the room and out of the house. She closed the heavy front door, put the key in the lock, turned it and silently, grudgingly, thanked the town sheriff for making her home more secure.

She walked out onto the porch to meet Winn, unwilling to let him come inside the ruined mansion. Slightly nervous, she stood and watched him approach. He was elegantly dressed in an expensively tailored brown linen frock coat and matching trousers. His starched shirt was snowy white and his cravat was of shimmering bronze silk. His handsome face was smoothly shaved and his pale hair neatly brushed back from his temples.

"Miss VanNam, how lovely you look this evening," he said, resting one foot on the bottom step.

"Thank you, Mr. DeLaney."

"Winn," he said, "please, call me Winn."

Kate nodded. "And you may call me Kate, Winn."

"Kate," he repeated. "Lovely Kate."

Dinner was delightful.

Just as she'd supposed, Winn DeLaney was good company. He was courteous, intelligent and sophisticated. And just as she'd heard, the food at the Bonanza was superb. Closely observing his companion, DeLaney took note of Kate's ravenous appetite and smiled, amused.

Kate looked up, caught his indulgent smile and flushed, embarrassed. She lifted her damask napkin, patted her mouth and said, "You must excuse me, Winn. The truth is that since arriving in Fortune, this is the very first time I've eaten a meal in a restaurant or hotel. The food is so delicious, I'm afraid I've made a terrible glutton of myself."

He laughed approvingly and his gray eyes were warm when he replied, "My dear, I love to see a woman with a healthy appetite." He leaned up to the table. "Now tell me what you'd like for dessert?"

Kate was dying for a slice of hot apple pie, but felt she should decline. "Nothing for me, thanks. I couldn't possibly eat another bite," she said.

Winn DeLaney simply smiled and signaled the white-jacketed waiter.

"May I get you something else, sir?" asked the beaming man.

"The lady will have a piece of pie," Winn said, and looked at Kate. "Mince? Cherry? Apple?" At the mention of apple, her eyes lit and Winn nodded. To the waiter he said, "Hot apple pie and fresh coffee for both of us."

When the exquisite meal was over, the sated pair left the dining room, causing turning heads and whispers just as when they'd entered. They crossed the spacious hotel lobby and stepped out onto the sidewalk.

It was a lovely evening and neither was anxious to end it. As they leisurely strolled up the mountain toward her home, Winn let his hand slip slowly down Kate's arm until he clasped her fingers warmly.

Kate immediately noticed that his hand was as soft as her own. Clearly this was a man who had never done any manual labor.

"I don't believe you've mentioned what your profession is, Mr. DeLaney," she said.

"Winn," he again corrected. He smiled then and told her, "I speculate in gold, Kate. I buy and sell claims throughout the goldfields." He laughed then and said, "Have a claim you'd like to sell?"

"I do have a claim," she said proudly. "But it's not for sale."

"I was only teasing," he assured her.

"I inherited a mine called the Cavalry Blue from my great-aunt Arielle VanNam Colfax."

"That explains what a genteel young lady is doing in Fortune. I had wondered."

Kate smiled. "And I had wondered what a sophisticated gentleman was doing here."

Both laughed.

Kate found Winn DeLaney to be intelligent, congenial and easy to talk to. With little prompting she explained that she had left her Boston home after the death of her dear uncle, he being her only family. She said she had taken the cash inheritance he'd left her, and come to California. She was hoping to find gold in the Cavalry Blue, and fully intended to stay in Fortune until she did.

Winn listened attentively and asked tactful questions, subtly encouraging her to talk about herself.

At last Kate said, "That's quite enough about me. I know next to nothing about you, Winn."

"Not much to tell," he said.

"Ah, that isn't fair. I want to know all about you."

Winn DeLaney smiled. Then he told Kate that he was thirty-one years old, had never been married, lived permanently in San Francisco where he had an aging mother and a younger sister who was married to a doctor. He said he had been fortunate in business and that his successful ventures had brought him to Fortune, though he couldn't predict how long he might be here.

"I hope," he concluded, "I'll be staying long enough to get better acquainted with you, Kate."

She smiled, pleased, and said, as they stepped into the clearing by the lake, "I do as well."

Once they reached the front porch of the darkened mansion, Kate stopped and turned to face her tall, blond companion.

The moonlight striking her full in the face, she said, "Thank you for a lovely evening, Winn."

"The pleasure was all mine, Kate," he said. "Promise we'll do this again soon."

"I promise."

"Next Saturday night?" he quickly suggested. "An early dinner and afterward perhaps the theater?"

"The theater?" Kate repeated, unable to keep the excitement out of her voice.

"Haven't you seen the bill posters around town announcing the arrival of Lola Montez?"

"Lola Montez in Fortune?" Kate's eyes grew wide.

He nodded. "Yes. She's appearing at the opera house next Saturday night. Shall we go?"

"Oh, yes, I'd love to."

"Then let's plan on it. Now, I mustn't keep you any longer. Thanks again for an enchanting evening, Kate." He paused as he gazed down at her upturned face. Then he asked politely, "May I kiss you good night?"

"Yes you may, Winn."

"Sweet Kate," DeLaney said softly as he took her chin in his hand, slowly lowered his head and brushed a chaste kiss to her lips. Then he turned and walked away. Kate watched until he left the moonlit clearing and disappeared into the darkness of the forest.

"You call that a kiss?" asked a low masculine voice that Kate immediately recognized.

She whirled around to see Travis McCloud pushing away from the shadowed porch pillar he'd been leaning against.

Her temper immediately flared. Her hands went to her hips as she snapped, "I will not allow..."

The sentence was never finished, because Travis was at her side in a heartbeat. He took hold of her upper arms, drew her to him and kissed her.

Really kissed her.

He pressed her head back against his supporting arm, and his insistent mouth masterfully parted her trembling lips. His tongue slid between her teeth to touch and toy with hers, and Kate involuntarily shuddered. She pressed a hand against his broad chest, trying to push him away.

Only she didn't.

She swayed into him as though his lean body was a powerful magnet, pulling her against him. His fiery, forceful kiss was unlike anything she'd ever experienced, and it evoked frightening sensations in her.

Suddenly Kate realized that she was kissing Travis back. She was sighing and squirming and eagerly molding her lips to his. She was clinging to him and shaking like a leaf and growing faint and dizzy with delight.

Abruptly he released her.

Kate's eyes flew open in puzzlement and surprise. Travis turned and left without a word or a backward glance. With her brows knitted and one of her hands on her throbbing heart, she watched him walk away in the moonlight.

Both dazzled and aggravated, she called after him, "You call *that* a kiss?"

She seethed with anger when she heard his deep laughter.

Fourteen

Kate hoped Chang Li knew what he was doing.

She watched as the wiry little man thrust a shovel into the packed earth and began digging a large hole directly behind the mansion. He was building her a cistern.

Chang Li had observed Kate hauling water up from the lake, and he told her she needed a nice large cistern to collect rainwater. And today, a Saturday, he had begun work on the new project.

Since hiring the sweet-natured Chang Li, Kate was more than pleased with the way he diligently worked the Cavalry Blue. He had also worked tirelessly to help her make the mansion more livable.

Thanks to him, the wood stove in the kitchen was working properly again and the fireplace chimney in the drawing room had been cleaned and was ready for use as soon as the first chill of autumn arrived in the high country. Cordwood had been cut and neatly stacked by the marble hearth.

And it was Chang Li who had brought up, from Barton's Emporium and Dry Goods, a brand-new zinc tub for Kate's baths. He had carried the tub up on his head, and she had laughed when she saw him coming. He'd laughed with her, then asked where she wanted it.

"Right there in the drawing room," she had instructed, and ushered him into the house. Chang Li had carefully placed the tub to the left of the fireplace and nodded when she'd said, "This will do nicely for now. When we strike gold, I shall have a huge Carrara marble tub imported from Italy."

He grinned, bowed and handed over her little drawstring bag of gold dust, with which she had paid for the tub. Kate had been as thrilled as a child when she found her first traces of placer in the stream that flowed by the house. Each and every day she carefully collected tiny flecks of gold dust and used the precious placer to purchase necessities.

Kate was grateful to Chang Li for all he'd done. She had never seen a harder worker than this slight man, who didn't complain and seemed to never tire.

She was touched when, out of the blue one morning, he arrived for work and said, "Need big favor, Missy Kate."

"Name it," she had replied.

From his loose-fitting white trousers, he withdrew a small leather pouch with a drawstring pulled tight. "All my money inside," he explained. "Live in tent city with thieves and pickpockets."

"I know, and I'm sorry you can't—"

"Is okay. Not afraid. But afraid money be stolen. Can I leave here with you?"

"Well, of course you can, Chang Li. I'll stay right here on the porch. Go inside and hide your stash anywhere you choose. I promise it will not be disturbed."

A smile spread over his thin little face. "Missy Kate most kind, most kind." He indicated the leather pouch. "I save money to bring wife and girl child to America."

"I hope you soon have enough," she said.

"I will." His grin broadened. "Make much more since I work for you."

Now, as he labored to excavate a crater for the new cistern, Chang Li hummed happily. Cal, the calico cat, had wandered out to see what was going on. He ambled up onto the newly turned earth and peered at Kate's assistant, making a low rumbling sound in his throat. Then he hissed his displeasure when Chang Li, rhythmically tossing dirt out of the hole, harmlessly sprinkled him.

Kate laughed as the angry cat raced toward the house, leaped up onto a windowsill and disappeared inside.

"Chang Li, I need to go into town, so I'm leaving you to your project."

The industrious Chinaman continued shoveling as he said over his shoulder, "Yes, you go, Missy Kate. I be right here."

"I need to purchase a pair of kid gloves," she said, eager to share the news that she was going to the theater. "Mr. Winn DeLaney is taking me to see Miss Lola Montez this evening."

Chang Li's shovel stilled in midair. He lowered it, leaned on it, swept his long queue back over his shoulder, wiped the sweat from his brow and squinted at her. "Who is this Mr. Winn DeLaney? Not know him."

"He recently arrived in Fortune," she said. "He's a wealthy gentleman from San Francisco."

Chang Li frowned. "What he doing in Fortune? You sure you safe with him?"

Kate laughed merrily. "He has business dealings here. And I told you, he is a gentleman with sterling manners. I am completely safe in his company."

"Very well." Chang Li nodded and went back to work.

Smiling, Kate turned and went inside.

She *was* safe with the refined gentleman, Winn DeLaney.

The same could not be said, however, for Fortune's cocksure lawman. Travis McCloud was certainly no gentleman. A gentleman did not kiss a lady the way he had kissed her.

But oh what a kiss it had been. A kiss Kate couldn't seem to forget, no matter how hard she tried. Over and over she had guiltily relived the heart-stopping moment when the darkly handsome sheriff had pulled her into his arms and kissed her. She recalled how the heat from his lips had reached all the way down to her toes. She was inexperienced, but she needed no one to tell her that the kiss they'd shared was rawly sexual. It had been downright frightening in its intimacy.

She was not naive enough to suppose the moment had meant anything to him. She didn't care. It hadn't meant anything to her, either. Not a thing. Travis Mc-Cloud was an ill-mannered, cynical, egotistical man who'd had no right to grab her up and kiss as if she were one of the loose women from the saloons.

Doc Ledet had said that McCloud had been raised in a proper Virginia home by aristocratic parents, though Kate now concluded that he had since shed any patina of grace he'd once possessed. He was as rough and rugged as the community he policed, and he was undoubtedly a threat to any decent woman.

Kate suddenly wondered if the sheriff had a sweetheart. Was there one special woman who willingly shared his heart-stopping kisses? And even his bed? Kate frowned, distressed at the thought. She'd be fooling herself if she supposed that the lusty sheriff never made love to anyone. She realized that Travis McCloud was the kind of man women—all women—found exciting. There was an alarming prospect of danger surrounding him that was highly erotic.

Then she scolded herself soundly. She would not waste one more minute thinking about the arrogant sheriff.

As she began to get changed for her trip to town, Cal meowed plaintively from somewhere in the house.

"What is it?" she called, and stepped out into the hall.

She saw no sign of the cat, but followed the sound of his continued meowing. Kate walked the length of the hall to the back of the house. She went into the large kitchen, looked around, but still did not see the cat.

"Cal, where are you?" she called, then went back into the corridor, following his meows. She found him in one of the many back rooms, seated in front of a closed door, one she had never bothered opening, supposing it was nothing more than an empty linen closet.

Cal's curiosity sparked her own. "All right, all right," she said, "we'll have a look inside." Cal made a low rattling sound in the back of his throat and rubbed against Kate's skirts.

She carefully opened the door and peered inside. A set of wooden stairs led down into darkness. Cal raced down the steps and disappeared. Kate shook her head, turned and went for the coal oil lamp. She returned, lit the wick, held the lamp aloft and cautiously descended the creaking wooden stairwell into a gigantic basement.

As curious as the cat, Kate looked around. Odds and ends of furniture were scattered about in a haphazard manner. Wooden cartons and barrels were stacked along the walls. She ventured forward, opened a box, sneezed from the dust she'd stirred, and looked inside. Dishes. Fine bone china dishes banded in gold. She held up a fragile plate, blew the dust from it and admired it. Then she carefully lowered it back to the carton.

She was opening another box when Cal's furious scratching and mewling commanded her attention. She turned to see the cat vigorously clawing at a covering of heavy burlap that was draped over a large gilded frame holding a painting or mirror. Cal's sharp claws snagged in the rough burlap and he yanked at it until the burlap fell away and pooled on the floor.

Kate went over to investigate.

"Oh my," she murmured aloud.

A portrait of a grand old lady with a gaunt, pale face, dark hair and deep-set, penetrating eyes sat looking back at her. The woman wore an elegant gown of shimmering taffeta, and diamonds and rubies graced her throat and sparkled on her fingers.

Arielle VanNam Colfax.

Kate stared, transfixed, feeling as though she was being watched from beyond the grave.

"Where's the gold, Auntie?" Kate asked aloud.

"It's me, Kate. Your great-niece. The one to whom you left your inheritance."

The lady in the portrait continued to hold her regal pose and fix Kate with those piercing eyes.

Kate said, "Aunt Arielle, you belong upstairs."

Warning Cal to stay out of her way, Kate struggled to get the heavy oil painting up the stairs and into the drawing room. There she leaned it against the wall beside the black marble fireplace, and carefully cleaned the dust and cobwebs away from the portrait and its heavy frame.

"Soon as I get the mansion restored," she promised the lady in the painting, "I'll hang your portrait above the fireplace where it belongs." Then she said, "You believed there was gold in the Cavalry Blue, didn't you, Aunt Arielle?"

The lady in the portrait revealed nothing.

Fifteen

As Kate prepared to go into town on that warm Saturday morning, she told herself she hoped to high heaven she wouldn't be unlucky enough to encounter the overbearing town sheriff. Nonetheless, she chose one of her better dresses and brushed her hair until it shone. After all, she might see her handsome new suitor, the charming Winn DeLaney.

Wishing she had a parasol so she didn't have to conceal her hair, one of her best features, Kate reluctantly drew on her straw bonnet, picked up her reticule, waved goodbye to the lady in the portrait and walked out the front door, with Cal trailing after her.

"No, you are not going with me, you bad cat. Stay here!" she commanded, and the cat stopped, glared at her, then stretched out on the porch. Kate smiled and said, "I'll be back soon." Cal pointedly ignored her. "Be a good boy while I'm gone."

On the short walk through the pine forest, she planned how she would go directly to Barton's Emporium and pick out a pair of dainty white kid gloves to wear to the theater that evening. The gloves were an extravagance she couldn't really afford, but she wanted look like a refined lady for this special evening.

Once she'd purchased the gloves, perhaps she would stop in and say hello to Dr. Ledet.

When Kate reached the buildings of town, her breath grew short. She assumed it was the high altitude combined with the growing heat of the day. She stopped where the wooden sidewalk began, took off her bonnet and carefully smoothed her hair.

Barton's Emporium and Dry Goods was three blocks away. If she stayed on this side of the street and walked directly to Barton's, she would have to pass the city jail. She considered crossing the street in an effort to avoid a possible brush with the sheriff, but she immediately checked herself. She was anything but timid or submissive, and she had no intention of allowing the marshal to influence her behavior. She wasn't about to slink around Fortune in constant fear of bumping into Travis McCloud.

Kate lifted her chin and set out down the sidewalk. But as she neared the city jail, she could feel her heart beating erratically. Would she see him? Was he just inside? Would he venture out when he caught sight of her? Would he step into her path so that she would have to stop? Would she get a glimpse of those sensual lips and that powerful physique?

Kate was a few short feet away when the sheriff did indeed step out of the jail. She stopped abruptly and caught her breath.

Travis's dark head slowly swung around. He saw her, glanced at her with bored indifference and barely nodded. Then he unhurriedly crossed to the other side of the street.

Kate paled at the slight. She felt her face grow warm and her stomach clench. She hurried on her way, vowing she would in future stay as far away from the city jail—and the brooding Sheriff Travis McCloud—as she could possibly get.

She would give all her attention and all her kisses to the attentive Winn DeLaney.

Kate hurried the remainder of the three blocks to Barton's Emporium. Inside the cavernous establishment, Clifton Barton sat on his stool behind the counter. As usual.

"Good morning, Mr. Barton," Kate said in greeting. "Nice day, isn't it?" She knew he would have a comment on the weather. He always did.

"Nice? Why, it's so damn hot even the lizards are looking for shade!"

Kate smiled and went about her shopping. She moved among the large tables stacked high with various merchandise. There were dishes and fabrics and pots and pans. Hats and hammers, saddles and salt, cradles and crackers, bread and bibles. Anything a customer might want or need could be found at Barton's.

Except kid gloves.

After a thorough search, Kate returned to the counter. "Mr. Barton, I'm looking for a pair of white kid gloves. Could you point me in the right direction?"

He chuckled and didn't move. "Miss VanNam, where do you think you are? New York City?" He shook his head. "Only gloves we have are men's work gloves."

"Not a single pair of ladies kid gloves?" she asked.

"Now what did I just say?"

Kate nodded. "How foolish of me."

She was disappointed, but she doubted that the other ladies who would be attending the theater would be wearing gloves. If Barton's didn't carry gloves, then gloves could not be found in Fortune.

Kate went back out into the blistering sunshine and hurried toward Dr. Ledet's office. She was still a couple of doors away when a woman stepped out of the doctor's office. She was a beautiful, curvaceous woman with incredibly white skin and gleaming midnight hair. She was dressed elegantly in the latest fashion. Her waist was cinched, her bosom was generous and the flowing skirts of her pastel summer dress stood out in the shape of a perfect bell, indicating there were hoops and lacy petticoats beneath.

And on her small hands were pristine white kid gloves.

The beautiful lady looked up, saw Kate and smiled warmly. Then she raised a silk parasol and walked away, with Kate staring after her.

"You going to stand out there in the hot sun all morning?" the white-maned physician said from the doorway.

"No...I...no." Kate, frowning, came inside. "Who was that lady, Dr. Ledet?"

"Valentina Knight," said the doctor, then changed the subject. "What brings you to town this morning, child?"

As if he hadn't spoken, Kate said, "Why didn't you introduce me to Miss Knight? Or is it Mrs. Knight?"

"It's Miss. I don't think you two would have a great deal in common." His eyebrows lifted.

"Why not? Miss Knight looks patrician and prosperous. Does she own a gold mine? Is that why she's here in Fortune?"

Dr. Ledet chuckled. "She owns a gold mine, all right, one that's made her a very wealthy woman. It's called the Golden Nugget."

Kate made a face. "But that's... The Golden Nugget, why, it's a saloon, isn't it?"

"The most successful saloon in Fortune," said the doctor. "And you know why?"

"No, why?"

"The lovely Valentina sings at the Golden Nugget nightly. The miners adore her."

"I'm sure they do," Kate said.

Dr. Ledet studied her and easily read her thoughts. "Bless your heart," he said kindly, "you're lonely. Lonely for female friends. Aren't you, Kate?"

"Yes, I am, Doctor. That's why when I saw Miss Knight I immediately hoped that..." Her words trailed away and she shrugged slender shoulders.

The physician rubbed his chin thoughtfully. "Women are scarce as hen's teeth in Fortune. Young ladies like yourself are nonexistent. We've had a few young wives come to Fortune with their husbands, but most didn't stay long."

"Doesn't matter," Kate assured him. "I have you and Chang Li for my friends." She smiled then and added, "And I have a handsome suitor."

The doctor frowned. "How much do you know about Winn DeLaney?"

"Enough. I know that he's a wealthy gentleman and that he is mannerly and charming and likable. He's kind and gentle and good-natured." Kate made a face. "Which is more than I can say for some people in this town."

"Aren't I good-natured?"

"Yes, of course. I didn't mean you, Doctor."

"Who then?"

Kate's delicate jaw grew tense. "Travis McCloud. He's bossy and cold and sullen. I don't like him."

"Now, now, Trav's all right. You don't know him

like I do. The sheriff is a man who has lived." Dr. Ledet paused as if in deep thought. "He's been disappointed. He understands the reality of the world." A slight smile lit up the physician's craggy face when he added, "And he's still in the game."

"Disappointed? How?" Kate's blue eyes were wide with interest.

The doctor shook his head. "Never mind that, child. I talk too much. Pay me no attention."

But Kate wouldn't let it go. She said, "Remember that prisoner on the steamer calling Sheriff McCloud a murderer? Is it true?"

"No. The sheriff's no murderer," the doctor said. Kate gave him a questioning look. Finally, he admitted, "All right. Travis killed a man in a duel back in Virginia. Shot him dead."

"No! What were they fighting the duel over?"

"Doesn't matter. The incident happened more than ten years ago, when Travis was quite young. Now that's enough about it. He wouldn't like me gossiping about him."

"But I want to know why…."

"And I want to know more about this new beau of yours."

Kate knew she could get no more out of him. At least not now. Smiling, she said, "Winn's taking me out to dinner this evening. And then to the theater to see Miss Lola Montez."

Sixteen

The Bird Cage was Fortune's newly built opera house. It was an imposing three-story brick structure with wide swinging doors opening into a spacious antechamber with a floor made of gleaming white marble. A lush carpet of deep turquoise covered the grand staircases at each side of the vestibule.

All stairs led up into the large audience room, where row upon row of adjustable seats afforded patrons an unobstructed view of the stage. Turquoise velvet curtains trimmed in gold were yet to be raised as an eager assembly predominantly of men scrambled into their seats on this hot Saturday night.

Directly below the curtained stage, an eight-piece pit orchestra tuned their instruments.

Half a dozen private boxes flanked the walls on either side of the stage. They, too, were upholstered in turquoise velvet, and featured gold lace curtains that allowed the occupants a degree of privacy.

It was to one of these private boxes that Winn DeLaney and Kate VanNam were directed by a helpful usher. Kate was aglow with excitement as she sat down upon a gilt-and-turquoise chair. Her escort, handsome in his dark evening clothes, motioned for the usher to draw the curtains at the back of the box.

Leaning forward on the gilt-painted railing, Kate eagerly looked all around the impressive theater. Below, on the main floor, every seat was taken, but there was not a woman in the crowd. She wondered if she was to be the only female present.

Then she noticed that in a private box on the wall directly across the auditorium, the beautiful Valentina Knight sat alone. Valentina was stunning in a low-cut gown of ice blue taffeta. Sapphires and diamonds flashed on her pale throat, and a snow white gardenia was placed in her dark hair.

"You're much lovelier than she," Winn DeLaney whispered.

"I beg your pardon?"

He smiled and nodded to the dark-haired woman in the box across from them. "You were staring at that lady."

Kate flushed. "Yes, I suppose I was."

Winn reached for her hand. "She's pretty. But not nearly as pretty as you."

"You know her?"

"She sings at the Golden Nugget," Winn stated matter-of-factly. "I stopped in there on my second night in Fortune." His fingers closed around Kate's and gently squeezed. "Before I met you. I haven't been back since."

"Did I ask?"

"No, but I wish you had." He turned his most dazzling smile on Kate. "I'd like you to be a little jealous."

Just then the heavy turquoise curtain began to slowly rise. The whistles and applause were deafening.

The celebrated Lola Montez sang and danced to the delight of her captive audience. Kate accepted the opera glasses Winn magically produced, and gazed at the woman on stage. She had read about the celebrated entertainer's three marriages and numerous love affairs, so she was surprised to see that Miss Montez was not particularly beautiful. Nor was she all that talented.

But the lusty miners whistled and stomped and were soon chanting, "Do the spider dance! Do the spider dance!"

Leaning close, Kate said in Winn's ear, "What do they mean? What's the spider dance?"

"I don't know, but I imagine we're about to find out."

The dark-haired Lola gave the miners what they wanted, though Kate found the performance startling, almost laughable. Montez engaged in a series of whirling motions, during which spiders made of cork, rubber and whalebone were shaken out of her full skirts.

Kate looked at Winn.

He winked at her.

"Silly, isn't it?" he whispered. And before Kate could answer, he raised an arm, laid it along the back of her chair and said, "I'm not interested in Lola Montez. I'm only interested in you. Kiss me, Miss VanNam."

"Winn DeLaney! We're in a crowd of people."

"Ah, but no one's looking at us," he pointed out. "They're all watching Lola."

The prospect of being kissed in a roomful of people was, for some reason, incredibly exciting to Kate. Suddenly she wanted to be kissed.

"Yes," she whispered, and closed her eyes. "Yes, kiss me, please."

Winn smiled, laid a hand on her cheek, turned her face more fully toward his and kissed her. His lips were warm and smooth on hers, but the kiss was as chaste and as brief as the others they had shared. In the blink of an eye it was over.

You call that a kiss? The sheriff's taunting words instantly flashed into her mind, and she had to agree that Travis had been right.

Kate felt disappointed. And guilty.

The kiss had not been thrilling. It did not send a flush to her cheeks.

It wasn't remotely like the one time Travis Mc-Cloud had kissed her, and he hadn't even asked if he could. He had just reached out and hauled her into his arms. The vivid recollection of that dazzling kiss still had the power to make her tingle and squirm.

And to want more.

Kate nervously glanced at Winn. He was looking directly at her. She stiffened. Had he read her guilty thoughts? She hoped not. She didn't want him ever to know that she fantasized about the brash, seductive sheriff.

Winn DeLaney was the consummate gentleman and she was grateful that he was. He could have kissed her the way McCloud had, but he had too much respect for her.

"A penny for your thoughts, Kate," Winn whispered.

"I was thinking," she lied, "that I wish you'd kiss me again."

"Ah, Kate, sweet Kate," he said, and brushed his lips to hers.

The pair held hands through the rest of the performance and whispered to each other. Kate was pleased by Winn's interest in her. He asked dozens of questions. He wanted to know all about her, including her previous life back in Boston. He teased her about her search for gold, then seemed truly engrossed when she declared that she believed there was gold in the Cavalry Blue.

"I'm convinced there's gold in the mine," Kate said. "It's not just some pipe dream. My great-aunt's husband, Benjamin Colfax, was given the claim by Colonel Freemont himself for charting and mapping the Sierras in 1844. Uncle Benjamin was an educated geologist with mining experience, and on his deathbed he told Aunt Arielle that there was gold, lots of gold, in the Cavalry Blue. He told her to keep it in the family, to never give it up. She kept the promise, but she returned to San Francisco and an easier life." Kate abruptly stopped speaking, embarrassed by her fervor.

But Winn had not missed a word. "Go on, my dear, I'm fascinated."

"It's there, I know the gold is there, and I intend to bring it out one day."

Kate told Winn about Chang Li, disclosed the location of the mine and said that she and Chang Li were about to give up on finding any more placer. They were now focused on quartz—or hard rock—mining.

Kate talked and talked, and the attentive Winn hung on every word. He looked directly into her eyes and made her feel as though she were the most entertaining company he had ever enjoyed.

When Lola Montez's performance ended, they wisely waited until the thirsty miners had exited the auditorium and headed for the saloons.

The crowds had dispersed when Kate and Winn came out of the Bird Cage. The sidewalk in front of the opera house was nearly deserted.

But not quite.

Marshall Travis McCloud stood just outside, leaning back against the wall, his thumbs hooked in his gun belt, one of his knees bent, his foot raised so the sole of his boot rested against the building's rough brick facade. The sheriff glanced at the pair and nodded.

"Evening, Miss VanNam, Mr. DeLaney."

Winn laid a proprietary hand on Kate's arm and drew her closer. "Sheriff," he acknowledged. "Did you catch Miss Montez's performance?"

Travis grinned and lowered his foot to the sidewalk. "I was inside," he said. "But I didn't see much of her act."

"Late to arrive, Sheriff?" Winn asked politely.

Travis shook his head. "I was there the whole time."

"Oh?"

"In an official capacity. Watching the crowd." Travis looked directly at Kate. "Making sure everyone behaved themselves."

Seventeen

Kate had given up on finding any more placer.

She now joined Chang Li in the Cavalry Blue, working alongside him, hacking at the stubborn rock, hoping to find the illusive vein of color. She quickly realized what a monumental task lay before them.

As good as his word, Chang Li knew a great deal about mining for gold. He had already built a rocker, which was a necessity to the quartz mining they were undertaking. The sturdy, oblong wooden box was three feet in length and mounted on curved wooden rockers.

Chang Li had nailed wooden bars that he called "riffles" along the cradle's open end. He'd stretched a piece of canvas over the wooden frame and placed it at a slant inside the upper end of the rocker. He had then fitted a handle on a metal screen called a hopper, and placed it at the top of the cradle above the canvas.

"Just tell me what we're supposed to do with this contraption," Kate said on her first morning at the mine, when a beaming Chang Li proudly showed her the hopper.

She was dressed for the undertaking in a pair of britches and rubber knee boots she'd bought at Barton's Emporium. She looked from Chang Li to the hopper and said, "Together we're going to find gold in the rock, aren't we?"

Chang Li bobbed his head and demonstrated how the hopper worked. Kate quickly learned that this phase involved hard, backbreaking work.

First, they would hack at the stubborn stone. Once they had filled a couple of big buckets with the loosened rock, they carried the buckets out of the shaft and dumped the ore into the cradle.

Then they had to trudge all the way down to the lake, fill the buckets with water and return to the hopper. Kate poured water over the rock and gravel while Chang Li rocked the hopper. The rocking motion caused the water to wash over the gravel, which strained through the hopper and canvas screen, allowing any gold sediment to gather in the riffles below.

Nothing gathered in the riffles.

There was no gold in the rock.

The tedious exercise had to be repeated over and over again. At day's end, Kate was more tired than she'd ever been in her life.

As she and Chang Li walked down the mountain,

she said, "Chang Li, I'm beginning to think they're right. There's no gold in the Cavalry Blue."

The little man frowned and shook his head. "Not give up! Not quit! Will find gold. Just take a while."

Kate tried to rally. "You're right. We can't give up, can we?"

"No, not ever. If give up, then Missy have to leave Fortune. And I never bring wife and child to America."

Kate smiled and said, "I'll meet you at the mine bright and early tomorrow."

"I be there," he said, and left her.

When she got home that evening, Kate was so bone tired she wanted to do nothing but lie down and rest.

Cal greeted her when she came into the yard, but it was not the "I'm glad to see you" sweet meow. Instead it was the "I'm starving, where's my food" mewling as he rubbed up against her aching legs.

"Okay, okay," Kate said to the whining feline, and went inside with him close on her heels. "Why don't you get out and hunt food like you did before I moved in?"

Cal ignored the question and raced toward the kitchen. He devoured the leftover pork she gave him, while Kate stood at the cabinet and ate a cold supper of bread and cheese and jerked beef. After only a few bites, she made a face and tossed the beef to Cal. He pounced on it, ate it quickly, licked his chops and then begged for more.

"It's all gone," she said, then turned and walked toward the drawing room.

Cal passed her in the corridor. He raced toward the open front door, shot out onto the porch and disappeared as the last light of day cast long shadows throughout the silent mansion.

Kate lit the coal oil lamp and sank tiredly down onto the rose sofa. She bent forward, drew off the rubber boots and stockings, then leaned back and sighed. She was dirty. She badly needed a bath. But she was tired. Dead tired.

She yawned, rose from the sofa, walked out into the corridor and closed the heavy front door against the gathering night. She went back into the drawing room, blew out the lamp, stripped down to her skin and drew on her nightgown.

She stretched out on her back, sighed and closed her eyes. In minutes she was sound asleep.

Much later that night, Kate awakened.

Bright moonlight streamed in through the windows and fell across the sofa where she lay. Reaching for the small clock she kept on the floor beneath the sofa next to her pistol, she saw that it was ten past two in the morning.

Kate put the clock back in its place, sat up and swung her legs to the floor. It was a miserably hot night. She was perspiring, her face was shiny, her gown was sticking to her skin. Knowing she wouldn't be able to get back to sleep, she rose from the sofa.

* * *

On that sweltering June night Travis lay in bed in his private quarters behind the city jail, wide awake as usual. He was worrying about Kate VanNam up there all alone in that secluded mansion. At least he supposed she was alone. Travis frowned. Maybe not. Maybe Winn DeLaney was...

"Damnation!" Travis swore and got out of bed. He drew on his trousers, tugged on his boots and grabbed a shirt. He reached for his gun belt and went out the rear door.

Travis skirted the backs of the buildings and disappeared into the forest. Muttering under his breath, he trudged up to Kate's place. When he reached the clearing he saw that the house was dark. Satisfied she was alone and sound asleep, Travis considered returning immediately to his quarters, but instead he chose a towering pine and sat down beneath it. Reaching inside his breast pocket for a cigar, he suddenly stopped, blinked and then squinted.

Kate had come out onto the porch wearing nothing but a nightgown.

Travis stared, entranced, as she skipped barefooted down the front steps and crossed the yard. She was headed for the lake. Hardly daring to breathe, Travis watched as she paused at the water's edge, looked warily around and, seeing no one, lifted her gown over her head and dropped it to the ground.

Naked, she stood unmoving for a fleeting moment—just long enough for Travis to get a good look at her beautiful, unclothed body. Then she waded out into the moon-silvered lake and began to swim.

It was all Travis could do to keep from stripping and joining her in the cool, clear water. Perspiring, burning up, he became unreasonably angry as he watched her slicing gracefully through the water. Damn her! What if someone other than him was watching?

Travis rose to his feet.

When Kate began to tire and swam back to shore, she was horrified to see the sheriff standing there holding her nightgown. She screamed and ordered him off her property.

"I'll go," he told her, "but not before you get back inside that house and stay there."

Arms crossed over her breasts, Kate sank down into the waist-high water and shouted at him, "I am *not* getting out of this water until you are gone."

"Yes, you are," he stated firmly, and started to come in after her.

"All right, all right, I'll get out, but you have to turn your back."

It took every bit of willpower he possessed to not look at her, but he obeyed. He held the nightgown behind him. Scowling, Kate stalked out of the water and grabbed the gown away from him.

"Don't you dare turn around," she warned, and anxiously drew the gown over her head and stuck her arms through the sleeves. She yanked the long tails down past her knees and grimaced when she saw how the thin batiste fabric stuck to her wet flesh.

Travis stood facing away from her, knowing she was naked, wanting to turn and look at her. He was coiled as tightly as a watch spring. His jaw was clenched and his heart was hammering. Perspiration beaded his hairline and dampened his shirt.

"Now," she said, "you may leave!"

Travis didn't leave.

Instead he turned to face her and then reached for her.

"What do you think you're doing!" she protested, pushing against his broad chest.

He yanked her up into his arms and carried her, kicking and screaming, back up to the house.

He deposited her on the front porch and said, "Get inside that house and lock the door, which, as you may recall, I hung to keep you safe. And stay there, Miss VanNam."

"You go to blazes, Marshal. You don't own me. You can't make me do anything."

"You'd be surprised what I can make you do," he said with a soft drawl as he reached out and plucked at the wet nightgown clinging to her breasts.

Kate slapped his hand away, looked down and was mortified to see her tightened nipples stood out and were as visible as if she wore nothing at all. "Get off my property! You're trespassing, Sheriff."

"I'm going," he said, "but you keep running around here naked and the Vigilance Committee will have me throw you in jail for indecent exposure."

"Leave!" she shrieked, trembling despite the heat of the night.

Eighteen

It seemed the most normal thing in the world, so right and wonderful in every way.

The two of them were alone together in the mansion in the middle of that sultry summer night.

The darkly handsome sheriff sat comfortably on her sofa and she, in her damp nightgown, was seated on his left knee.

She sighed with bliss when his warm face settled gently into her gown's open bodice and his heated lips pressed lingering kisses over the swell of her breasts.

Kate squirmed on Travis's knee and arched her back. Her arm wound around his neck, her hand clutched at his shirt collar. As his lips brushed her tingling flesh, she moved her fingers up into his hair and clasped a handful of the thick raven locks.

"Travis," she whispered. "We shouldn't, Travis."

"You're a very desirable woman, Kate VanNam," he said softly, as he lifted his head and gazed into her flashing eyes. "You want me to stay here with you, don't you?"

"You know I do," she told him frankly. "I want to spend the whole night here in your arms."

"And wake up with me at sunrise."

"Yes. We'll watch the sun come up, then go back to sleep."

"But before we sleep tonight," he said in the drawl she loved so much, "we'll make love here in the moonlight."

"Yes, oh yes." Kate laid her hand on his chest. She smiled dreamily and said, "Travis, your heart is beating awfully fast. Almost as fast as my own."

"Show me," he coaxed.

Kate turned more fully to him and leaned close to press her left breast against his chest.

"No, wait. Not good enough," he said. "Unbutton my shirt, Kate."

Nodding, she complied. When his shirt was open, she needed no persuading to push it apart and fully uncover his broad chest. Catching her bottom lip between her teeth, she ran her hand over the perfect symmetry of his steely sculpted torso, eagerly raking her fingertips through the dense dark hair that grew in an appealing fanlike pattern. She thrilled to the heavy rhythmic pounding she felt against her palm.

Travis reached up and opened the bodice of her

nightgown. "Now," he said, "let me feel your heart beating against mine."

At once her bare breasts were against his naked torso and both their hearts were wildly racing.

Breathless, she told him, "Travis, the way you make me feel, it frightens me."

"Don't be afraid, Kate," he whispered. "I'll never do anything you don't want me to do."

"I know, it's just… Kiss me, Travis." She brushed her tingling nipples back and forth against his chest. "Kiss me and keep on kissing me, forever and ever."

The sheriff laid his head against the sofa's tall back and drew Kate's flushed face down to his. With his hand in her flowing hair, he cupped the back of her head and drew her toward him, molding her lips to his. Then he opened his mouth and kissed her the way she wanted to be kissed. The kiss was at once tender and passionate, sweet and aggressive, subdued and sexual.

It was thrilling beyond belief.

Kate clung to Travis and gloried in his kiss, a kiss she could feel throughout her body. While his tongue met and mastered hers, it was as though she could feel it circling her aching nipples and licking a path down her contracting belly.

Travis kept kissing her until she was as breathless, weak and limp as a rag doll. She finally tore her swollen lips from his.

"I love the way you kiss me," she sighed, then added truthfully, "but it makes me quite dizzy."

"Then perhaps we should lie down," he said, as he gently laid her on the long sofa. Standing just above, Travis took off his shirt, dropped it and kicked off his boots. He stretched out beside her, drew her into his arms and kissed her again.

"Mmm," she murmured, quickly realizing that kissing was even more enjoyable while lying down.

Kate was glad the sofa was narrow so that they had to lie on their sides facing each other, their hearts beating as one. The stirring kisses continued as Travis's burning lips stayed pressed to hers. He gently eased her over onto her back.

When the prolonged caress finally ended, his handsome face hovered above hers, his dark eyes flashing with ardor as he gazed at her. When she felt the warmth of his hand on her breast, Kate trembled with pleasure. She continued to look into his smoldering eyes as his hand moved down her waist to her hip.

She felt the fabric of her nightgown sliding up her legs. She tensed with anticipation and excitement.

"Let me, Kate. Let me make sweet love to you," he murmured as he gathered the gown and slowly drew it up her trembling thighs.

"I will, Travis, I will, " she murmured, her body vibrating with expectation. "Yes, oh, darling, yes... I...Travis, no, no don't...don't...don't leave me. Please don't leave me. Come back! Come back to me!"

"Come back, come back to me," Kate was still

murmuring as she awakened from the sweetly sensual dream. "Please don't leave me."

Her breath coming fast, her heart pounding, she lunged up and frantically looked around, half expecting to see a bare-chested Travis. A sense of crushing disappointment swept through her when she swung her bare feet to the floor. Her hand went to her throbbing heart. She shook her head to clear it.

The dream had been so incredibly real that she could almost taste Travis's burning kisses on her lips and feel his warm caressing hand on her breasts. Shaken and wistful, she squeezed her knees together and her eyes tightly shut.

Then she exhaled heavily and leaned back against the sofa's tall headrest. When finally she began to calm, she assured herself that it had just been a dream and dreams meant nothing. Nothing at all.

But she was reluctant to go back to sleep for fear she might continue to dream of Travis McCloud. An even worse fear plagued her. How would she feel when next she encountered the sheriff? Would she be so embarrassed and red faced that he might guess she had dreamed about him? Would he read her guilty thoughts?

Kate shivered, remembering what he had said when he'd deposited her on the front porch and plucked at her damp nightgown.

You'd be surprised what I can make you do.

* * *

Naked, she rose up out of the water and brazenly walked toward him, making no attempt to cover herself. God, she was beautiful, with her high, rounded breasts, her flat belly, flaring hips and long shapely legs.

He stared at her unclothed body and knew he had to have her, that he could wait no longer. He was going to make love to her this very night as no one ever had.

She paused when she was still a few feet away. She lifted her arms and swept her sopping golden hair back off her face. She smiled seductively and walked to him.

When he reached for her, she warned, "I'll get you wet, Sheriff."

"And I'll return the favor. Now come here." He caught her close and pressed the naked length of her against him. He could feel his clothes soaking up the moisture from her bare, silky body. He ran his hands over her wet back, her hips, her rounded buttocks. He kissed her and she looped her arms around his neck.

He filled his hands with the twin cheeks of her bottom and strongly considered taking her right where they stood. When he lifted her, she wrapped her long legs around his waist. He clasped his wrists beneath her and kissed her.

Then he turned and carried her up to the house. In the moonlit drawing room, he lowered her to the sofa, and while she lolled there, leaning back, looking breathtakingly beautiful, the water glistening on her breasts and shoulders and long legs, he undressed. In seconds his gun belt and clothes lay on the floor. Naked, he knelt before her, pushed her legs apart, wrapped a hand around the back of her neck and drew her face down to his.

She pleased and surprised him when she said, "I want you to make love to me in every way possible." Her eyes sparkled with deviltry. "You're not leaving until you do."

"Ah, baby, I'm going to love you till you're begging me to stop."

"That will never happen," she said. "I'll never get enough of you."

"Promise," Travis murmured. Then he wrapped his hands around the backs of Kate's knees and drew her to the sofa's edge.

She gripped his ribs with her knees and clutched the strong column of his neck when he grabbed a handful of her soaked hair, urged her face down to his and kissed her.

By the time the long, lusty kiss ended, Travis had managed to maneuver her about so that she was lying on her back with one leg raised and draped along the sofa's high back, the other bent at the knee and cocked outward.

He was between.

He swept a hand over her flat belly and gazed at her. She smiled seductively, licked her lips, lifted her hands and beckoned him into her arms.

He shuddered.

She was wonderfully wanton, wild and wet and open to him. And he was driven half-insane by the raw hunger she evoked. Blinded by passion, he could wait no longer.

His heart hammering, he rose up onto his knees and moved into position. Gripping his painfully swollen cock, he was poised to plunge into her wet warmth when she rolled up onto her elbows to watch and urge him on.

"Give it to me, Travis," she invited eagerly. "Put it in me where it belongs."

"I will, baby," he whispered. "I will."

"I will, I will," Travis was muttering when he awakened abruptly from the highly erotic dream. "I will," he mumbled, lunging up and foolishly looking around, half expecting to see a naked Kate in his bed.

Perspiring, his heart beating wildly, Travis realized it had been a dream. Just a dream. A dream that meant nothing. Nothing at all.

He had no burning desire to make love to Kate VanNam. He had dreamed of her because he'd seen her shortly before going to sleep. Now he cursed the golden-haired beauty for foolishly taking a late night swim in the nude. She sure as hell should have known better. Her lack of judgment was responsible for the carnal dream and for the aching erection now lifting the sheet like a tent.

"Damn you, Kate VanNam."

Nineteen

"Cal, come here. You heard me! Come here. What on earth do you have in your mouth?" Kate called out as the big calico padded down the mansion's central corridor shortly after sunup. She frowned and snapped her fingers loudly. "Come here this minute!"

The cat made no effort to obey, but he headed directly for the open front door. Something—she couldn't tell what—was dangling from a string clamped firmly between his teeth. The object was swinging back and forth.

"Oh, no you don't!" Kate shouted, and dashed after him.

She caught up to the cat, sank down on her heels and grabbed him. She snatched the small leather pouch from his mouth and studied it carefully.

"Oh, my Lord," she lamented, "this is Chang Li's savings. He hid it here in a secret place, but of course you snooped around until you found it! You're a bad,

bad boy, Cal," she rebuked him. He just placed his front paws on her knees, lowered his head and rubbed it against Kate's chin, softly purring.

"That won't work, my friend," she warned, and rose to her feet.

Her brows knitted, Kate held the pouch in her hand and considered what she should do. She had no idea where Chang Li had hidden it, so she couldn't put it back in its place. She had no choice. She would have to tell him the truth and suggest he choose a new hiding place.

For now she'd put the little purse under a sofa cushion and ask Chang Li to stop by at day's end to either take it with him or hide it again somewhere in the mansion. That was the best she could do.

Kate walked into the drawing room and went directly to the sofa. She lifted a cushion and started to slip the pouch underneath, but hesitated. She was curious. Almost as curious as Cal.

She knew that Chang Li had been saving for a long time in hopes of accumulating enough to bring his family to America. She wondered how much he had managed to put away.

Kate looked around guiltily.

Cal meowed and she jumped as if she'd been caught in some heinous crime. She glanced down, saw the cat seated regally at her feet, his tail curled around him, staring up at her with narrowed eyes as though he knew her intention.

"You're a good one to talk," she accused, frowning at him. "You're who went snooping around, not me."

Kate sat down and ignored Cal when he leaped up onto the sofa to watch her. She carefully loosened the drawstrings, reached inside, withdrew the money and laid it atop a cushion. Gently shoving Cal away when he pounced on the money and sniffed at it, she carefully counted the bills. Then she recounted them, to make sure she had tallied correctly. Holding the hardworking Chang Li's entire fortune in her hand, Kate shook her head sadly.

Two hundred seventy-eight dollars.

That's all the poor man had been able to save after three or four years of slaving away in the heat and the cold of the rugged Sierra Nevadas. He saved every cent he possibly could. He lived in a canvas tent. He never ate fancy meals. He never drank or gambled. All he had to show for his hard work and self-denial was two hundred seventy-eight dollars.

Yet he never complained about his lot in life. Never whined no matter how hungry or tired or lonely he was. He was always smiling and cheerful. Never gave up hope.

Kate put the bills back into the leather pouch, tightened the drawstrings and stuck it under a sofa cushion.

She turned to the portrait of her aunt Arielle and said, "I know you would never have left me a worthless claim. There has to be gold in the Cavalry Blue."

Determined she'd be as optimistic as Chang Li, Kate left the house with the unrepentant Cal right on her heels. Dressed in a work shirt, britches and rubber boots, Kate hummed as she headed for the mine and another hard day's labor.

As she trudged through the thick forest and up the rocky hill to the side of the steep mountain where the mine's entrance was located, she looked to a bright future ahead. One of these days she and Chang Li would find the gold, and when they did, he could bring his family to California. And she could restore the mansion to its former splendor.

It was just a matter of time.

The courtship continued.

The handsome Winn DeLaney was vigilant in his single-minded pursuit of Kate. He made no effort to conceal his growing affection for her, and yet he was ever mindful of her reputation. He knew that she was a refined young lady, so he behaved unfailingly as a consummate gentleman.

DeLaney delighted in escorting Kate around Fortune. He told her he was the envy of every male in town, and that there was nothing he liked better than showing her off, knowing that everyone was jealous of him.

Kate believed it was true, because many evenings after they shared a leisurely dinner at one of the hotels, Winn would suggest that they take a stroll through town. When she agreed, he'd hold her hand while they sauntered aimlessly up and down the sidewalks. Winn would nod to passers-by, clearly wanting everyone to know that she was with him, that she was his sweetheart.

Kate was flattered. And she was almost as eager as he for everyone to know that he was courting her.

Especially Travis McCloud.

Anytime they caught sight of the sheriff, Kate made it a point to either cling to Winn's arm and gaze fondly up at him, or to laugh merrily as though she were having the time of her life.

And, she reminded herself, she was.

Winn DeLaney was handsome, sophisticated and charming, and he adored her. She was a lucky woman indeed to have such an entertaining beau. Furthermore, she was glad that Winn's good-night kisses continued to be restrained. That was as it should be. He would *never* have kissed her against her will. And when she gave him permission, he didn't dare kiss her passionately as the arrogant Travis McCloud had done!

Thank heavens.

"Thank you for a lovely evening," Winn said now, at the end of an evening, as they stood outside the mansion in the July moonlight.

"I had a wonderful time, Winn."

"I'm glad, my dear. By the way, have you heard? A traveling Shakespearian troop is coming to town

for a week-long engagement at the Bird Cage. Shall
we attend?"

"Oh, yes, absolutely. I wouldn't want to miss that."

Winn smiled, took both her hands in his. "I
wouldn't want you to miss anything you'd like to do,
Kate. If there's anything at all that you…"

"There is, Winn," she said, her eyes flashing. "In
a couple of weeks, on August 11, there's to be a big
street dance to celebrate the sixth anniversary of gold
being discovered here in Fortune."

He frowned slightly, slipped his hands up her arms
and let them settle on her shoulders. "My dear, surely
you don't mean it. Why, that will be no place for a lady."

Kate cocked her head to one side and smiled. "It's
not a saloon or gambling hall, Winn. It's the street.
And it'll be fun, I know it will. Doc Ledet says everyone will be there, including the handful of miners'
wives that live in Fortune. It will give me the opportunity to meet—"

Interrupting, he said, "Miners' wives won't be the
only females present, Kate. Saloon girls and bordello women will turn out, as well."

"So?" She lifted her hands, laid them lightly on
his chest. "They won't bother me and I won't bother
them. Please, Winn, say yes."

He finally smiled. "I can refuse you nothing." He
drew her closer. "Now, it's quite late, my sweet. Kiss
me good-night."

Kate nodded, tilted her face up and closed her

eyes. His lips brushed hers tenderly, but only for an instant. And once again she felt nothing.

"Sleep well, Kate," Winn whispered against her cheek, carefully keeping his passion in check.

"And you as well," she replied.

"It's straight to bed for me," he said, as he touched her hair. Then he was gone.

Twenty

Winn DeLaney whistled as he hurried back to town.

But as soon as he reached the Bonanza Hotel, he yawned sleepily and entered the lobby. Dwayne, the clerk on duty, looked up, saw Winn and reached for his room key.

Handing it across the counter, Dwayne commented, with a sly grin, "All tuckered out after another evening with that pretty Kate VanNam, Mr. DeLaney?"

Winn said nothing, just smiled, turned and climbed the stairs. He paused outside the door of his suite. He took a deep breath. He cautiously looked around and, seeing no one in the corridor, reached out and opened the door. A door that he had purposely left unlocked. He quickly stepped inside.

He immediately smiled with pleasure.

Winn DeLaney closed the door and leaned back against it, pleased with what he saw.

A straight-backed chair that had been turned around to face away from the door was six feet away. And there in the shadowy, lamplit room, a woman sat straddling it. She was smiling at him. She had clear olive skin, ruby-red lips, emerald-green eyes and dark, dark hair that was held off her face with a flashing golden dagger.

The dagger was her only adornment.

The woman was naked as she sat astride the chair, her strong thighs widely parted, her heavy breasts looking like succulent melons. She was a sight to arouse any man's passions. The habitually cool, calculating Winn DeLaney took one look at her and was instantly excited.

He anxiously came to her, thrust his hands into her lustrous dark hair, yanked her head back, bent and aggressively kissed her. His tongue searched and found fervent answer, a seeking, sucking response that quickly set his heart to hammering. Her lips beneath his were blazing hot, and all logical thought quickly burned away in the sexual heat.

While her generous mouth devoured his in a kiss he felt down to his toes, the woman's nimble fingers found the buttons of his shirt and swept it apart. When finally she ended the prolonged kiss, a totally conquered Winn DeLaney sank weakly to his knees before her as if to worship her.

The woman laughed throatily and sat up straighter

so that her naked breasts rested on the chair's top edge and were fully accessible to him. She arched her back and boldly invited, "See anything you'd like to taste, Mr. DeLaney?"

"Oh, Melly," he managed to gasp.

Again she laughed as she placed a hand in his golden hair and guided his face to a waiting nipple. Anxiously, he opened his mouth and began to suck greedily, noisily.

"I start to work at the Whiskey Hill Saloon tomorrow night," she casually told him, her red-nailed fingers toying with a lock of his gleaming hair while he suckled her. "I suppose I'll be expected to laugh and flirt with the miners I serve drinks to." She purposely needled him by adding, "You won't be jealous if I'm required to do more than flirt, will you, Winn?"

Winn's lips released the wet nipple and he abruptly raised his head. "Don't torture me like that, Melly. Promise me all you'll do is serve drinks, nothing more. Swear it. Tell me you'll behave. You know how jealous I am."

"What about your behavior? What have you been doing with that little Boston blonde before I got here?"

"Nothing. Not a thing." He cupped her face in his hands. "You're the only woman for me, you know that. I'm crazy about you, Melly."

"That may be, but I don't like the idea of you being with her, and I don't like the idea of having to serve drinks to a bunch of dirty miners in a smoky saloon."

"It'll only be for short while, my love."

"It had better be," she warned, and, moving his hands from her face, urged him back to his feet. "Stand up, Winn. Let's get you undressed."

He rose, and while he shrugged out of his jacket and shirt, she unbuttoned his trousers. In seconds his clothes lay on the floor and he was as naked as she. He stood before her and shuddered when she looped her arms around him and pressed kisses to his bare abdomen.

Knowing her well enough to realize that she was not yet ready to get into bed, that she preferred making love the first time somewhere else, Winn took her arms from him, stepped around and sank down onto the chair behind her.

She sighed and squirmed and clung to the twin newels of the chair as his hard, heated flesh surged against her naked buttocks and he crushed her up against the chair's back. Sliding his lips up and down the side of her throat, he slipped his hands under her heavy breasts and plucked at the peaking nipples with his fingertips. Winn listened and murmured in agreement as she told him exactly how she wanted him to make love to her.

"I want it right here in this chair, Winn DeLaney," she commanded. "I want to climax in this chair. It's up to you to figure out just how to go about it."

"That should pose no problem, my love," he said, brushing kisses across her bare shoulder.

He raised his head, straightened, reached up and plucked the decorative golden dagger from her dark hair. Melisande waited, tensed. She trembled when his hand, clutching the dagger, came up in front of her.

"Lick it," he said.

"Now, Winn," she half protested, but was eager to do anything he might suggest.

"You heard me, Melly," he said, knowing she would do as ordered. That's what he liked best about Melly. Nothing shocked her, nothing repelled her. In the realm of sex, she was willing to do anything he wished. "You know the dagger's not sharp," he said. "You won't get cut. I'd never hurt you. Now, lick the blade."

Melisande put out her tongue and licked the tip of the dagger.

From just above her ear, he said, "Put it in your mouth. Suck on it. Pretend it's me."

Her heart racing, her face flushed, Melisande lifted a hand, placed it over his and carefully guided the dagger's dull tip into her mouth. As she did so he whispered, "Ah, yes, gold, precious gold. Soon, darling, we'll have the gold." He carefully took the dagger out of her mouth. He murmured, "Isn't the thought of all that gold enough to bring you immediate sexual fulfillment?"

"You really believe we'll get the gold?" she asked, panting now.

"I know we will," he said, and very carefully drew the tip of the dagger around each of her diamond-hard nipples before lowering it and placing its flat edge between her parted thighs. While he cautiously pressed the gleaming blade against her wet, throbbing flesh, he spoke of all the lovely nights to come when they would be so rich they would make love in a bed fashioned from gold.

Melisande climaxed as Winn regaled her with tales of the wealth that would soon be theirs. When she collapsed back against him, Winn dropped the golden dagger to the floor, lifted Melisande up, bent her forward over the chair and entered her from behind. Once he was inside her, he brought her back down onto his thighs.

And he made urgent love to her.

Melisande's bare bottom slapped up and down atop his thighs while the chair banged up and down against the floor.

"Gold," she murmured as he thrust deeply into her. "Bright, shiny gold."

"Gold," he groaned. "Valuable, spendable gold."

"*Our* gold," she gasped, her second climax rapidly coming on. "More gold than we can spend in a lifetime."

"And all of it ours. Just yours and mine," he moaned, his own release starting.

"Gold!" they cried out together in orgasmic ecstasy, and when both collapsed forward against the chair back, Winn swept Melly's dark hair up and kissed the blue trinity tattoo on the side of her neck, which was glistening with sexual perspiration.

Twenty-One

"Look, Trav, over across the street," said Doc Ledet, gesturing out the front window as he walked into the jail. "There they are again. That sweet Kate VanNam and that well-heeled San Francisco fellow." He smiled, admiring the pair. "They're off to the Bird Cage to see that Shakespearian troupe perform this evening. Kate told me about it last week. My, my, aren't they just the handsomest couple you've ever laid eyes on?"

Travis never turned his head, never glanced out. "Doc, I'm in a bit of hurry here," he said, lifting his battered, bloody right hand.

"Oh, sorry, sorry," murmured the white-haired physician, and set his black bag down atop Travis's desk. "Have a seat and I'll fix you up good as new."

"Thanks." Travis sat down, clasped his wrist and gently placed his throbbing right hand on the desk.

Opening his black bag, the doctor said, "It looks
to me like Winn DeLaney is pretty well smitten with
that little golden-haired girl." He waited for Travis to
comment. The sheriff said nothing. "Wouldn't you
say so, Trav?"

Travis rolled his eyes.

"Sheriff?"

"Beats me, Doc."

"Well, it's just my opinion, of course, but I really
believe DeLaney is more than a little sweet on Kate.
No sir, it wouldn't surprise me if he soon proposed
marriage. And she could do a whole lot worse, if you
ask me, so if they—"

"Doc, I hate to interrupt these newsy bulletins, but
I haven't had any supper and it's coming up on eight
o'clock."

The doctor nodded. Then, squinting, he leaned
close, studied Travis's injured hand, shook his white
head and reached into his bag for a bottle of rubbing
alcohol and a roll of bandages.

"The hand is already badly swollen," the doctor
said, as he cleaned Travis's bruised, bloody knuckles
with the alcohol. His white eyebrows rising, he
asked, "Is it throbbing yet, son?"

"A little," Travis replied, and shrugged his wide
shoulders.

The physician released a long sigh. "You know,
Trav, you ought to try and avoid getting into so dan-
ged many fistfights. You're not a kid anymore. Be-

sides, you can't expect to lick the whole town and if you—"

Again interrupting the talkative physician, Travis said, "Doc, what do you suppose a man like DeLaney is doing in Fortune?"

"What do you mean?" The doctor was puzzled by such a foolish question. "I understand Mr. DeLaney is a very successful entrepreneur. I would imagine he travels extensively."

"Exactly. What's a 'successful entrepreneur' like DeLaney doing in a little mountain mining town?"

"Winn DeLaney says he buys and sells gold mine claims," said the doctor with great authority. "Purchases and sells claims all the way up and down the western side of the Sierra Nevada foothills. From the far southern fields on up here through the northern diggings. There," he said, "that should do it." He tossed the soiled gauze away and began wrapping a clean white bandage around Travis's hand.

"Has he bought any claims since he got here?" Travis asked.

"Well, I'm not sure. He might have and—"

"Doc, you pride yourself on knowing everything that goes on in this town. If he had bought or sold any claims in or around Fortune, you'd have heard about it."

The doctor stopped wrapping Travis's hand. He screwed up his face in thought. "You know, you're right. DeLaney hasn't really bought or sold much of anything. What the devil *is* he doing here?"

With his good hand, Travis opened the bound leather crime ledger resting on his desk. He said, "Doc, in this ledger is the record of an assayist's murder that took place in San Francisco several years ago."

"What's this got to do with DeLaney?"

Travis shrugged. "Nothing. But DeLaney was in San Francisco at the time of the murder."

The two discussed Winn DeLaney, Kate VanNam and Kate's great-aunt Arielle Colfax. They talked about the fact that Arielle's husband, Benjamin Colfax, had been with John C. Freemont when he'd mapped out the area in 1844.

"You think DeLaney believes there's gold in the Cavalry Blue, Travis?" Doc Ledet asked. "You figure that's what he's after?"

"Don't know," said Travis, his eyes narrowing. "I do know that since he's been in Fortune, DeLaney's done nothing other than diligently court Kate VanNam."

"That's true. But he couldn't have come here just to court Kate. After all, what were the chances of him finding a pretty young lady like her in a rough mining town like Fortune?"

"My point exactly."

"You think Delaney somehow knew that Kate was…"

"Finish up, will you, Doc?" Travis prodded. "I may need this fighting hand again before the night is over."

* * *

"Yoo-hoo! Miss VanNam, you in there? Is any-body home?"

Kate was in the back of the house on a late Sun-day afternoon when she heard someone calling her name. It was clearly a woman's voice, so Kate dropped what she was doing and hurried toward the front door. Cal, the cat, beat her there.

Kate paused before the closed door, smoothed her uncombed hair back off her face, looked down and frowned at her bare feet. She was afraid that if she took the time to put on shoes and stockings, her unex-pected visitor would leave, so she yanked the door open.

A tall, slender woman with chestnut hair, green eyes and a friendly smile stood on the porch with a covered plate in her left hand.

The woman stuck out her right one and said, "Kate VanNam? I'm Alice. Alice Hester."

"I'm so pleased to meet you, Alice," Kate said, and warmly shook the offered hand.

"Hope I haven't come at a bad time," said the woman, her wide-set green eyes sparkling. "Doc Le-det said it would be okay if I visited you this afternoon."

"Oh, Alice, yes, by all means, come in, come in," Kate said, delighted. "You're welcome here anytime."

"Well, thank you."

Staring at the young woman, whose face was too

thin, but whose flashing green eyes made her almost pretty, Kate told her, "You're the very first woman I've met since arriving in Fortune."

"I know, and I apologize for not coming up sooner," Alice said, stepping into the corridor and handing the covered plate to Kate. "It's a pie, Kate. An apple pie. I hope you like apple."

"Apple is my all-time favorite, Alice. I can't afford the pies at Hester's Bakery so I...so..." It suddenly dawned on her who this was. "Hester! Alice Hester! You must be the Mrs. Hester of Hester's Bakery!"

"That I am, Kate," she said, her eyes twinkling. "The Mrs. Hester that charges a dollar-fifty for a pie. Still glad to meet me?"

"You know I am," Kate assured her, directing her into the drawing room. "You must excuse the looks of the place. It needs a bit of fixing up. Well, more than a bit. But please, won't you have a seat here on the sofa while I go cut us each a slice of the pie?"

"None for me," said Alice, making a face. "You bake pies all day every day and you lose your taste for pastry of any kind."

Kate smiled, nodded. "I'll be right back. Do sit down." She caught the curious Cal starting to leap up onto the sofa to more closely examine their guest. "No," she warned, and snapped her fingers at the cat. He hissed, looked at her coldly, but turned and padded out of the room while both young women laughed.

Kate hurried out to the kitchen. When she returned, she apologized for the lack of furniture and for the ruined carpets.

"Why, this place is a palace," Alice said. "Wait until you see where I live."

"I fully intend to have the mansion restored once I can afford it," Kate explained. "I know it will be very expensive, since I'll have to hire craftsmen out of San Francisco."

"Maybe not," Alice offered thoughtfully. "There's this skinny, toothless old sourdough in Fortune that is an amazing carpenter and talented jack-of-all-trades. Built all the shelves in my bakery. Nothing he can't do in the way of building and remodeling."

"Really? What's his name?"

"Blankenship. H. Q. Blankenship."

"The name's familiar," Kate said, trying to recall where she'd heard it. She snapped her fingers again. "I know! He helped me get Chang Li to the doctor's office when Chang Li was badly beaten. He was the only man who offered."

"That's old H.Q.," Alice declared.

"He's a bit strange," said Kate.

Alice chuckled. "A couple of years ago the state board of health tried to have H.Q. sent to the lunatic asylum down in Stockton. The asylum was founded to treat those driven mad by the goldfields. The board claimed H.Q.'s madness had to do with 'his speculative and gambling spirit.'"

Kate was astonished. "That being the case, everyone in Fortune needs to be in the asylum. Including me!"

Both women laughed. When they quieted, Kate said, "They never really locked him up, did they?"

"No. Sheriff McCloud went before the board and vouched for H.Q. Told them the old sourdough was perfectly sane and a harm to no one. He said they could hold him responsible should H.Q. prove him wrong. H.Q. was so grateful, he's been on his best behavior ever since. And, naturally, he thinks the sheriff hung the moon."

"Naturally," Kate said, adding, "I'll definitely call on Mr. Blankenship when I start my restoration."

She took a seat beside Alice. For a long moment the two young women simply stared at each other in wonder, each clearly starved for the companionship of another woman. Then, realizing they were gaping, they laughed, threw their arms around one another and embraced as of they had known each other for years.

In that instant they became friends.

Alice Hester stayed at the mansion until almost sunset, and Kate was glad she had turned down Winn's invitation to go for an afternoon buggy ride. She hadn't realized just how much she had missed having a female friend, especially someone as likable and as cheerful as Alice Hester, who, she soon learned, had plenty to complain about, but didn't.

The two talked and talked, eagerly getting to know

each other. Kate told her new friend how she'd traveled all the way from Boston to claim the inheritance left her by her great-aunt Arielle Colfax.

Then, eager to know more about Alice, Kate prompted her to talk about herself. She learned that her new friend had been in Fortune for the past three and a half years. She had arrived from her Missouri home with her bridegroom, Elmer Hester. They'd been in Fortune for less than six months when Elmer was killed in a mining accident. Left alone with no money to get back home, she'd opened a bakery.

Alice laughed now when she said proudly, "I make more money than most of the miners!"

"Good for you!" Kate declared.

"And," Alice confided, "I've a new fellow in my life. For the past six months he's been my beau. He's a good man. A little shy and quiet, but he treats me like a queen and I'm quite fond of him."

"Why, that's wonderful," said Kate. "Is he a miner?"

Alice shook her head. "No. He's a brave lawman."

Kate felt her heart mysteriously squeeze in her chest. This lively, enterprising widow was Travis McCloud's sweetheart? Kate swallowed hard and tried to sound casual when she said, "Oh? So your beau is the town sheriff?"

"Yes," Alice said with a shy smile.

"Ah…that's…nice," Kate managed to reply.

"Well, deputy sheriff," Alice corrected.

"Oh." Kate felt relief flood her. "I thought you meant…"

"Travis? That big, handsome devil? Heavens, no. A man like Travis would never look twice at a woman like me. My beau is Jiggs Gillespie. You know him?"

"I've never actually met him, but when I came up-river on the steamer, Deputy Gillespie was on board escorting a prisoner to jail."

"That's my Jiggs," Alice said proudly, then talked at length about the quiet good times the two of them had together.

When she concluded, Kate couldn't keep from asking, "Is there a special woman in Sheriff Mc-Cloud's life? Not that I care. I'm just curious."

"I hear whispers that Valentina Knight, the Creole beauty who owns the Golden Nugget, frequently entertains the sheriff." Alice raised her eyebrows and lowered her voice. "But you want to hear the most exciting gossip about Travis?"

"Yes."

"When he was very young, he fought a duel over a woman. Killed a man for the love of a beautiful lady. Isn't that the most romantic thing you've ever heard?"

"It is," Kate murmured, dying to know more. Instantly she wondered who the woman was and what happened to her. Why had there been a duel? But she kept her own counsel.

"…and hope you and your handsome beau will attend."

"Sorry? What? What did you say?"

"I said, will you be coming to the street dance the first Saturday in August?"

"I wouldn't miss it," Kate replied. "Everybody will show up for the dance, won't they?"

"You bet." Alice laughed. "The miners are amazing. They dig all day and dance all night. So be prepared to dance with every male in Fortune."

Twenty-Two

All week long the male population of Fortune had looked forward eagerly to Saturday night's big street dance. Doc Ledet was one of the celebration's organizers, and he took his assignment seriously.

The first thing he had done was to hire a quartet of strong-backed men to build a raised wooden platform to serve as the dance pavilion. It was the same quartet that always built the gallows when the Committee of Vigilance requested it. The doctor had been in Fortune long enough to know that a sudden rainstorm could make for a very muddy street. He well remembered the town's fourth anniversary two years ago. Just as the dance began, so had the rain. In minutes the women's best dresses were badly soiled and their shoes ruined. He'd never let that happen again.

Next he managed to engage a five-piece orchestra from San Francisco to play for the big event. They would stay until 2:00 a.m., and longer if need be. Then he'd enlisted the help of the saloon girls to festively decorate the town.

By early afternoon on that blistering hot Saturday in August, colorful bunting graced the pavilion's bottom perimeter and hanging oil lamps, carefully covered with green tissue paper, swung from every porch pillar up and down the street. Miners' lanterns, swathed in the green tissue, sat evenly spaced around the edge of the dance floor.

Well before sunset on the big day, intense grooming was taking place in hotel rooms, boardinghouses, canvas tents and open-air camps all over town. Scruffy miners who hadn't bathed or shaved for weeks were scrubbing their dirty bodies with stiff-bristled brushes, and either shaving away all facial hair or neatly trimming their beards.

Travis McCloud, a man who was always immaculately groomed, sat in his nightly tub of soapy water as the hour of the dance approached. Before his bath Travis had carefully shaved. Then shaved once more. He told himself, as he drew the straight-edged razor down his left jaw, that he was shaving the second time because he wanted his face to be as smooth as a baby's butt when he danced with all the saloon girls. He recalled last year's commemoration, when he'd been obliged to dance with every female in town if he wanted to keep the peace.

This closer-than-usual shave had nothing to do with the prospect of pressing his face against the soft cheek of Kate VanNam, because he had no intention of dancing with her.

With a thin black cheroot clamped between his teeth, Travis vigorously ran a soapy washcloth over his broad chest, his muscled arms, his long legs. When he had scrubbed every inch of his lean body, he snubbed his cigar out in a dish by the tub, rose to his feet and stepped out of the water.

He grabbed up a towel and glanced at the clock on the bureau. Seven o'clock. Too early to get dressed. Travis toweled himself dry, then padded across the room to his big double bed. He tossed back the covers and stretched out on the clean white sheets, intending to doze for half an hour. He'd need all his strength to keep the miners in line tonight.

But as soon as he folded his hands beneath his dark head and closed his eyes, he saw again the beautiful golden-haired Kate VanNam shedding her nightgown and plunging into the moon-silvered lake by her house. The vision haunted him. He felt his groin stir, and in seconds he was sporting a full-blown erection.

Swearing, Travis opened his eyes and laid a restrictive hand over the rigid flesh bobbing involuntarily on his belly. There had been just one other woman in his entire life who was capable of arousing him just by thinking about her.

Travis rolled over and anxiously pressed the unwanted, unwelcome erection into the mattress in a vain attempt to rid himself of it. It didn't work. He flopped back over and angrily gave the offensive flesh a smart thump with his thumb and middle finger.

He exhaled heavily, swung his long legs to the floor, snatched up his clean white underwear and stepped into it as if a dangerous she-devil was trying to get her hands on him.

Travis poured himself a stiff drink of bourbon and tossed it back in one long swallow.

Just before eight o'clock, he dressed in a pair of neatly pressed black trousers, a freshly laundered white shirt with his shiny silver sheriff's star resting on his chest and a pair of well polished black cowboy boots, before leaving his quarters.

He would never have admitted it to anyone, but he was almost as excited about the dance as the lonely miners.

From the minute she'd heard about the festivities, Kate had looked forward to the celebration. Nothing dampened her excitement, not even her friend Alice Hester's dire warning that she would have to dance with every miner in Fortune. Nor had Winn's admonition and plea that she change her mind and skip the party caused her to have second thoughts.

Kate hummed happily on that late Saturday afternoon as she sat in her zinc tub. Cal lay stretched out on the couch, purring. Kate suspected the reason for the cat's serenity. Earlier in the afternoon she had spotted, down by the lake, a yellow, long-haired tabby. Cal had immediately shot out of the house and raced down there. The tabby had hissed at him and sprinted away, but, not giving up easily, he had followed. Both felines had disappeared into the forest, and Cal had come home an hour later looking pleased with himself and all tuckered out.

"You have it made, don't you, Cal?" Kate asked now as she soaped a slender arm. "All you do is eat and sleep and…"

She giggled then, and Cal raised his head. He glared at her as if to say, *Silence, please. I'm trying to get a little rest.*

Kate continued to laugh as she lifted a slim leg into the air and gave it a good scrubbing with her washcloth. When her laughter subsided, she began to hum once more and to swirl the soapy cloth around each breast. While she was at it, an unbidden image of Travis McCloud arose out of the blue: the sheriff with his shirt off and perspiration gleaming on his broad chest and bare, beautiful back. The vision that appeared far too often of late.

Kate winced as the mere thought of him caused her nipples to tighten and tingle and her belly to constrict. She silently berated him for doing this to her. The dark, seductive sheriff was capable of stirring her senses when she merely thought about him. Kate took a shallow breath and looked at herself in the tall mirror that leaned against the wall. She blushed when she saw her nipples jutting out in twin peaks of sheer sensitivity, looking for all the world as if they were waiting for a man's gentle touch.

She dropped the soggy washcloth in the tub, slowly raised her hand and cautiously plucked at a pebble-hard nipple with her fingertips. Closing her eyes, she imagined the sheriff's tanned fingers taking the place of hers. She toyed with and teased the aching tips and wondered how it would feel to rub them against the sheriff's naked chest.

Immediately ashamed of her forbidden thoughts, Kate dropped her hand away and opened her eyes.

She grabbed up a towel, shot to her feet and gave her body a brisk, quick rub, anxious to get her undergarments on. She snatched up her pantelets and camisole as if Satan himself were reaching for her. When her underwear was in place and modestly covering her, Kate began brushing her hair before the mirror.

After several long strokes through the freshly shampooed locks, she stopped the brush in midstroke and made a face in the mirror. Why, she wondered, had it been McCloud's dark hand she had envisioned intimately touching her and not Winn's?

Kate suddenly trembled.

There was something about the sheriff. It was more than just his masculine good looks that aroused her. He was a little dangerous. He harbored a secret. No one really knew him. No one frightened him. No one could get close to him.

Cal abruptly leaped down off the sofa, the movement pulling Kate from her reveries. Winn was coming to collect her at any moment.

She drew her blue silk dress over her head, reached behind her and deftly fastened the hooks running down the back. She then smoothed the billowing skirts and studied herself in the mirror. Earlier in the week she had purchased a strand of expensive ivory Irish lace. She'd carefully sewn it into the low-cut bodice so that the dress would look more chaste and proper.

She was pleased with her handiwork. The fragile lace concealed the swell of her breasts. Still, she wished she had a new dress to wear, something no one had ever seen. The blue silk was the best she had, but she had worn it every time Winn took her out to dinner or to the Bird Cage. He was surely tired of seeing her in it.

As Kate stared at herself in the mirror, Cal sauntered over to stand beside her. "So? What do you think? How do I look?" she asked him.

The cat ducked his head and rubbed up against her full skirts. She laughed, sank down and petted his head while he meowed softly. "Now listen to me, Cal," she said, stroking him affectionately. "Mr. DeLaney will be here any minute and I'll be leaving.

But I expect you to be right here in this room when I return tonight. Can I count on you?"

The cat began to anxiously wiggle from her grasp, backing away, making a rattling sound. Kate sighed and rose to her feet. The cat behaved strangely every time Winn came to the mansion.

"What is that you don't like about Winn De-Laney?" she asked, hands on her hips.

The cat's eyes narrowed into slits and he made strange growling noises.

"Yes. Well, I'm sorry you feel that way. He's a fine man and I'm quite fond of him."

Twenty-Three

"Just look at them, Winn," Kate whispered from behind her hand when a laughing, whooping group of saloon girls spilled out into the street shortly after eight o'clock on that warm Saturday night.

"I warned you," he replied.

Kate tried not to stare, but that was impossible. The women were garishly painted, their lips and cheeks rouged scarlet, their faces heavily dusted with rice powder. They wore gaudy dresses of every bright hue known to man, the necklines of which were cut so low that their full bosoms were barely covered.

One flamboyant woman in particular caught Kate's eye. She was an exotic looking dark-haired, olive-skinned beauty in a shimmering, yellow satin gown. Her shoulders were bare, her waist was well cinched, and her heavy black hair was held off her face on one side with a unique golden dagger.

"Look at that one, Winn," Kate whispered, directing his attention to the woman in yellow. "She has a dagger in her hair. A golden dagger!"

Just then the five-piece orchestra struck up "Buffalo Gals Won't You Come Out Tonight" and eager dancers took to the floor amid much laughter and shouting.

"Shall we, my dear?" Winn asked, after covertly casting another quick glance at the dark-haired woman in yellow.

"Let's wait for the next one," Kate said, studying the crowd. "I'm looking for my friend, Alice Hester. She promised she'd be here at eight sharp."

"As you wish." He was congenial, slipping an arm around her waist and smiling down at her.

Kate's eyes shone with excitement as she watched the dancers spin rapidly about the floor. Most of the big, rough miners were terrible dancers, but that didn't seem to bother their partners. The women in flashy clothing laughed and flirted and didn't object to being held in a crushing bear hug.

"Why aren't you two dancing?" Doc Ledet asked as he stepped up beside them.

"I've asked her," said Winn with shrug of his shoulders, "and she turned me down."

"I'm having too much fun watching the others," Kate said, clapping her hands in time to the music. "Looks like the entire town has turned out. The miners' wives, what few there are, and all the women from the saloons. And obviously every miner in Fortune and some from the other camps."

"Yes, we've got a fine crowd indeed," said the doctor.

"You know who I haven't seen yet," Kate commented. "That beautiful dark-haired woman I ran into at your office that day." She held her breath, waiting to see what he'd say.

"Valentina? Valentina Knight?" asked the doctor.

"Yes. Will Miss Knight be at the dance?"

"Not this year. I understand she has business in San Francisco and won't be back until sometime next week." The physician chuckled then and added, "I've an idea Valentina missed the celebration on purpose."

"And why would she do that?"

"Well, at last year's shindig she was forced to dance with every miner present. They fought over her, Valentina being so beautiful and all." The doctor smiled wryly, remembering. "No doubt about it, a woman has to be a real good sport to attend a dance in a mining town."

"I tried to warn her, Doctor," Winn stated. He looked at Kate. "You're the prettiest woman here and once the liquor starts flowing I won't be able to protect you from these big lonely brutes. You'll have to dance with them. You'll have no choice."

"I don't mind so much," Kate said, not really believing that she'd be expected to dance with many of the men.

She knew of only one man with whom she had no intention of dancing.

Sheriff Travis McCloud.

Not that he would ask her. He wouldn't. But if he did, he would get a resounding no. She didn't like the sheriff. Didn't like the way he made her feel. Nervous. On edge. Unsure of herself. She was half frightened of him.

And of herself.

But she wouldn't worry about McCloud tonight. The town sheriff would surely have no time for dancing with anyone.

"There's Alice," Kate said to Winn, raising a hand to wave.

Alice nodded and hurried their way. Right behind her was the skinny deputy sheriff, Jiggs Gillespie, smiling shyly. Introductions were made. Pleasantries were exchanged. The two women hugged and whispered, and soon everyone, Doc Ledet included, had taken to the dance floor.

An hour passed.

Kate was exhausted. Winn had been right. Not only did the miners all insist on dancing with her, but they argued over who got to be her partner next. They pulled her this way, then that. Unable to successfully get out of one man's arms before being grabbed and clasped by another, Kate was dizzy and hot from spinning about on the floor. And now she was slightly puzzled, as well.

When she'd first been ushered up onto the floor by a big, burly fellow in denim overalls, Winn had been standing just below the dance platform. Right where she'd left him, with his arms crossed and a smile on his face. He seemed content to wait for her.

But when the tune ended, a jolly bearded man grabbed her and wouldn't let her return to her escort. By the fourth dance Kate had lost sight of Winn. He was no longer where she had left him. And he wasn't on the dance floor.

Winn had dutifully watched while Kate spun about the dance floor to one, two, three lively tunes. When the fourth began, he felt confident she'd be kept busy for the next half hour and never notice his absence. He began to slowly back away from the crowd.

Finally he turned and hurried to the wooden sidewalk, where he slipped into a darkened alley.

He found her waiting there, leaning back against the side of a building, eyes sparkling, perfume wafting over him.

"You little fool," he scolded when she threw her arms around his neck. "We're taking one hell of a chance."

She kissed him hotly, hungrily. Then she laughed

and said, "A little danger is always great fun. You've said so yourself."

"Very well, but we'll have to hurry."

She laughed throatily. "I'm ready, darling."

Winn lowered a hand. And he laughed with her. The skirts of her yellow satin dress were shoved up over her belly and tucked into a wide sash at her waist. She was naked beneath the raised dress. In seconds she had deftly unbuttoned his trousers and freed him. She raised a knee, wrapped her leg around his hip.

When he touched her, he found she was dripping wet and ready. He gripped his hard flesh and roughly impaled her on it.

"Ahh." She moaned with pleasure and wrapped her other leg around him while he lifted her, shoving her up against the wooden building and pinning her there with his body.

While the music, laughter and loud talk drifted on the night air, Winn and Melly made lusty love there in the alley not seventy-five feet from the dance floor. His hands gripping her soft buttocks, his lips sucking at the curve of her neck and shoulder, Winn thrilled to the wild, impromptu coupling. He hadn't planned on it, and had even cautioned Melly that she was to come nowhere near him during the celebration dance. It was far too dangerous. They didn't dare risk everything they had worked so hard for to indulge in a few stolen moments of passion.

But then Kate had innocently directed his attention to Melly. One glimpse of his lover in that low-
cut yellow gown had weakened his resolve. She must
have sensed it because she had made it a point to drift
away from the crowd. When he had gotten the opportunity to look around, he had seen her alone on
the sidewalk, leaning against a porch pillar, the oil
lamp hanging above her head casting a glow over her.
Feeling his eyes on her, she had extended the tip of
her tongue, licked her lips, raised her dress to her
knee and indicated the alley behind her.

And he had been unable to resist.

Now, as he drove furiously into her moist heat,
Winn raised his head and murmured, "Have you any
idea what I'm risking for you?"

"Tell me," she said, tipping her head back, pump-
ing her pelvis, sliding up and down to meet each
plunging thrust of his rigid flesh.

"If my innocent little sweetheart knew that I was
inside you right this minute, we'd never get close to
that fortune."

Melly laughed, then threatened, "And if I knew
you were inside her at any time or place, you wouldn't
have to worry about the fortune. You'd be dead."

"Melly, darling, if she's to be my wife I'll have
to—"

"Shut up and give it to me good. Nail me to the
wall. Show me I'm your only love."

Winn showed her.

Twenty-Four

Once both were satiated, Winn immediately set his gasping lover back on her feet, and began hurriedly adjusting his clothing.

Already he was sorry he had taken such a foolish chance. Anxious to return to the dance before Kate had time to miss him, he felt his anger flare when Melisande deviled him by saying she would walk with him.

Winn grabbed her by the hair, forced her head back and said through clenched teeth, "Damn you, woman, you'll do no such thing! And you'll wait at least a half hour to return to the dance. Alone. Once you're there, you're to stay away from me. Don't try to dance with me, don't even look at me." He gave her hair a hard yank. "You hear me?"

"I hear you!" Her eyes flashing, breasts heaving, she snarled, "But don't expect me to stay in this primitive gold camp forever while you dilly-dally with that uppity little Boston blonde."

"You'll have to be patient for a while. The girl's not the easy mark I had hoped. Often as not, she turns down my invitations."

"Surely you can charm—"

Interrupting, he said, "Even when she does agree to go out to dinner or the opera house, I feel like there are several pairs of eyes on us, watching my every move."

"You're imagining things, Winn."

"No, no I'm not. There's the protective little Chinaman that works with her. And the nosey Dr. Ledet. And especially the town sheriff. Marshal McCloud has the annoying habit of turning up everywhere we go. I strongly suspect his interest in Kate is more than a simple concern for her safety."

"You think the sheriff wants her for himself?"

"I wouldn't be a bit surprised."

Melisande worriedly shook her head. "You can't let that happen. If McCloud gets his hands on her, we're sunk."

"So you're saying that big, sullen lawman could sweep her off her feet and I can't?"

"If you can, do it," she said. "Stop wasting time. Charm her, seduce her, make her marry you. And the sooner the better."

"I'll do what I can," Winn said, and kissed her.

* * *

Kate had been anxiously looking for him all evening.

She had not seen him.

He was not here and the dance had been under way for more than an hour. Kate felt a great sense of relief. Obviously the sheriff was not planning to attend the street dance. Now she could relax and enjoy herself.

"No, please, I really must catch my breath," she begged as a grinning, gap-toothed miner stepped up to claim the next dance.

"You're not next, I am," said a big man with curly salt-and-pepper hair, taking her arm.

"The devil you are," said the gap-toothed fellow as he attempted to pull the struggling Kate into his arms.

An argument ensued.

Kate backed away as Deputy Jiggs Gillespie—on the floor dancing with Alice Hester—moved in quickly to settle the dispute.

"The young lady is dancing with neither of you." The deputy fearlessly stepped between the two big men. "And you'll both spend the night in jail if you cause me any trouble."

Dancers stopped and stared.

Alice Hester beamed with pride.

Kate seized the opportunity to exit the dance floor. She hurried off the platform and left. Feeling warm, and tired from spinning dizzily about and having her toes stepped on, she fanned herself as she walked away from the crowd, heading for the refreshment table that had been set up on the sidewalk in front of the Eldorado Hotel. There she eagerly accepted a cup of fruit punch from a painted, smiling woman behind the table. Then she turned and wandered on down the deserted sidewalk.

She stopped to drink her punch, not noticing that she was just outside the Golden Nugget saloon. With her back to the saloon's slatted bat-wing doors, she stood and watched the crowd, searching for the one man she hoped she wouldn't see.

She didn't.

But when a chill suddenly skipped up her spine despite the warmth of the August night, Kate sensed the cause. She could feel his presence, and she knew without a doubt that he was close to her. Very close.

She tensed, waiting.

Travis had been standing at the bar when he'd looked out and seen her. He had tossed down his whiskey and walked out of the empty saloon.

Now he was directly behind her. He didn't speak. Didn't say a word. Just stood there waiting for her to turn and see him.

"I know you're there," she finally said.

"I know you know," he replied in his low, rich baritone.

Kate squared her slender shoulders. She would not

be intimidated by Sheriff McCloud, and whirled about to face him. She felt her heart stop beating, then race madly.

He was strikingly handsome and awesomely male. He wore a well-cut frock coat as black as his neatly brushed hair, and a shirt as white as freshly fallen snow. His dark eyes and white teeth flashed in his smooth tanned face. Everything about him spelled excitement and danger. Kate felt herself swaying toward him and quickly caught herself.

Travis grinned cynically, and in his eyes was an impertinent gleam that shrewdly masked the fact that she absolutely took his breath away. She was unbelievably beautiful and fabulously female. Her golden hair framed her lovely face and fell in soft waves atop her bare shoulders. She wore a gown of pale blue with wisps of lace lining the low-cut bodice. Beneath that lace the tempting swell of her breasts rose and fell with her breaths, making him long to lean down and press heated kisses to the soft pale flesh until he felt her heart beating rapidly beneath his lips.

Kate finally broke the strained silence. "If you'll excuse me, I'd better get back to the dance."

"What's your hurry?"

"My escort will miss me and be worried."

"Oh? Where is your gallant protector?"

"At the dance, of course." She was instantly defensive.

Travis looked over her head and squinted toward
the crowded dance floor. "I don't see him." He lowered his gaze to meet hers. "You sure about that?

"I'm not a prisoner to be questioned by you, Marshal," she told him haughtily. She shoved her empty
punch glass at him. "Good evening to you, McCloud."

"I'll walk you back to the dance," he said, slipping
the handle of the cup around his little finger.

"Not necessary, Sheriff."

He took her arm and told her, "You know, it might
be wise to make your beau a little jealous."

"Winn DeLaney jealous of you?" she said with a
derisive smile. "That's comical, Marshal."

"You're not laughing, Miss VanNam."

Kate's temper flared. She pulled her arm free and
warned, "Leave me alone, McCloud. And I mean
it!" She lifted her skirts and hurried away from him.

Tapping the cup against his trousered thigh, Travis
stood and watched as she reached the crowd and began anxiously looking for her escort. With one shoulder resting against a porch pillar, Travis turned his
head and saw Winn DeLaney emerge from an alley
and hurry back to the dance.

"Kate," Winn said, stepping up beside her, "there
you are."

"Yes, here I am, but where were you?"

"I'm sorry, my dear," he exclaimed. "You were so
busy dancing I didn't think you'd miss me."

"But where were you?"

Winn took her arm and ushered her onto the dance floor as the orchestra began a rousing rendition of "Oh, Susanna."

"I was thirsty so I stepped across the street to have a quick beer," he explained. "Say you forgive me."

"I forgive you."

"Thank you, Kate. Shall I get you a cup of punch? There's a table set up—"

"I'm not thirsty."

"No?" Winn flashed his most winning smile, leaned close and kissed the tip of Kate's turned up nose. "Then dance with me," he said, and took her in his arms.

They spun about the floor to the quick tempo of the tune, Kate having to hang on tightly, Winn keeping an arm wrapped securely around her waist. The floor was crowded with dancers.

Kate never noticed him.

But Winn did.

The town sheriff.

Standing just below the dance floor with his arms crossed, watching. Watching the dancers. Watching them. Watching Kate.

With his cheek pressed to Kate's, Winn wondered if she was looking at McCloud over his shoulder. He sensed an attraction between McCloud and Kate, despite her open animosity toward the sheriff and McCloud's seeming disinterest in her. On more than one occasion he'd been aware that Kate and the sheriff were overly conscious of each other.

Laughing merrily now, Kate clung to Winn's neck as he turned her rapidly about. Then she, too, caught sight of Travis McCloud. Her laughter stopped. She made a misstep.

"What is it?" Winn said against her ear.

"Nothing." Kate tried to sound casual. "Just clumsy. Don't let me fall."

"No need to worry, I've got you," he said. "I won't let you go."

The song ended.

Everyone applauded and called for more.

The fiddler in the five-piece orchestra began to play the first stirring strains of the hauntingly sweet ballad "Believe Me If All Those Endearing Young Charms."

"That's more like it," Winn said, and reached out to draw Kate back into his arms.

Before he could manage, a laughing, rotund woman who was more than a little tipsy grabbed his arm and insisted he dance with her. Winn gave Kate a helpless look. She smiled and turned to leave the floor, but bumped squarely into Sheriff McCloud. Travis didn't ask permission. He took her in his arms before she could object. Kate struggled only briefly, then acquiesced so he wouldn't cause a scene. She would, she decided, keep a stiff upper lip and endure.

That was her intent. Once she was in Travis's

arms, however, that plan quickly changed. He was an incredibly graceful dancer and so easy to follow that she could sense his movements before they were made. He respectfully held her at arm's length, yet she could feel the incredible heat and muscled power of his tall, lean body as if she were pressed flush against him.

He looked directly into her eyes as they swayed together to the beautiful love song. Much as she wanted this dance to be an unpleasant experience, it was not. Although she disliked him, she found it undeniably thrilling to be in his arms.

She was fascinated with Travis McCloud. Afraid of him, yet drawn to him. As they turned and sensuously glided across the floor, the crowd miraculously disappeared. There was only the two of them, dancing, moving together as one lithe body. They gazed into each other's eyes, wordlessly communicating a message as old as time itself.

With her hand lightly clasped in Travis's and folded against his chest, Kate looked into his dark eyes and felt them burning right through her clothes. Clothes that had suddenly become uncomfortably tight.

Kate was confused.

She was intensely uneasy, yet she was totally relaxed. She desperately wanted Travis to release her, yet at the same time she wanted him to hold her closer. So close she could feel his hard, ungiving body pressed against hers. She was sure he felt the same even if he would never have admitted it.

Kate could tell he wanted to kiss her the way he had that night at the mansion. She also knew that Travis wished he didn't want to kiss her. There was a mixture of physical yearning and puzzling melancholy in his beautiful eyes.

Instantly it was gone, replaced by the cool, cynical gleam she'd come to expect.

Travis grinned devilishly and said right out loud, "Taken any naked moonlight swims lately, Miss VanNam?"

Twenty-Five

"Shh!" Kate scolded, and anxiously looked around to see if anyone had heard. She struggled vainly to free herself from Travis's encircling arm, and muttered under her breath, "You are despicable and I will not spend one more minute dancing with you. Let go of me you…you…"

"Bastard? That the word you're searching for?"

"Yes! That's exactly what you are and I refuse to—"

"Better be careful, Kate. Your knight in shining armor is looking this way."

Kate glanced at Winn. He appeared concerned. She waved a hand as if to say nothing was wrong. And forcing a smile, she said to Travis, "Why do you insist on harassing me, Sheriff? What have I ever done to you?"

"It's not what you've done, it's what you could

do," Travis said, his grin slipping slightly, "if I let you." That enigmatic look was in his eyes again.

Sensing she momentarily had the upper hand, Kate wasted no time pressing her advantage. Rising up onto tiptoe, she suggestively whispered in his ear, "Know what I think, Marshal? I think you'd like to take a naked moonlight swim with me." She pulled back to judge his response.

But Travis was grinning impishly once more. "Only if you twist my arm."

"And you're afraid," she added, taunting him, "that I might be taking those moonlight swims with Winn DeLaney." Travis made no reply. "Aren't you, Sheriff?" she needled. "Think about it when you can't sleep."

"I sleep like a baby," he assured her.

"You won't tonight." Again she rose up on tiptoe and whispered, "You'll lie there in the heat, miserable and perspiring. And while you're burning up, I'll be slicing through the cool, clear waters of the lake. Gloriously naked. And you'll wonder if I'm swimming alone or if…" She lowered her lashes and let her words trail away.

She could tell she'd gotten to him when he said, "Don't be a fool, Miss VanNam. You know nothing about Winn DeLaney."

"I know enough," she replied with a meaningful smile, intent on leaving the wrong impression.

The music ended.

Kate slipped out of Travis's arms. Winn stepped up beside her and possessively took her hand. He turned to Travis. "Am I not the luckiest man alive, Marshal?"

"So it would seem."

It was late. The dance had lasted until well past one in the morning. Now it was after 2:00 a.m.

Kate and Winn stood on the front veranda of the mansion saying their good-nights.

"I really must go in now," Kate said for the second time.

"No, wait. I'm curious, my dear. What were you and the sheriff talking about while you danced?"

"Oh, I don't remember. Inconsequential things like the weather, the turnout for the dance. Nothing, really."

"Nothing? You looked angry, Kate. Did McCloud say or do something that…"

"No. Certainly not," Kate said.

"You'd tell me, wouldn't you?" When she nodded, he continued, "I'm not sure McCloud is a man who can be trusted, Kate."

"Whether he can or can't is of no importance to me," she declared.

"You sure about that?"

"What's this all about, Winn?" Kate asked, her brow furrowed. "I danced with the town sheriff. So what? I danced with at least a dozen miners as well."

Winn smiled. "So you did. Enough about Mc-Cloud. Let's forget about him."

"He's forgotten," said Kate, wishing it were true.

"Let me come inside," Winn murmured persuasively.

"No, Winn. I'm very tired and it's late."

"Just for a few minutes," he coaxed. "You know I won't take advantage of you. Don't you trust me, Kate?" He clasped her waist lightly in his hands.

"Yes, I do," she said, her own hands resting on his chest. "But I'm so sleepy I can barely hold my eyes open."

Winn smiled, brushed a kiss to her lips and said, "I'd love to hold you while you sleep."

Kate laughed it off. "Good night, Winn."

She turned, went inside and closed the door behind her. Cal roused from a nap when she walked into the darkened drawing room. He followed Kate to the front window. She peeked out, saw Winn exiting the front yard, and sighed with relief.

She looked down at Cal, smiled and said, "You may stop that infernal rumbling, he's gone."

As if he understood, the cat rubbed against her skirts, meowed contentedly, then stretched out beneath the window to go back to sleep. Yawning, Kate didn't bother lighting the lamp. She undressed in the darkness, drew on her nightgown and got into bed.

She turned onto her side, folded an arm beneath her cheek and thought about Sheriff McCloud. Her eyelids closing, Kate smiled foolishly, sighed deeply and drifted toward slumber, recalling how handsome Travis had looked when she'd turned to face him on the sidewalk in front of the Golden Nugget. And how it had felt to be in his arms when they'd danced.

Her last waking thought was to wonder if he was now sound asleep, or if he was as wide awake and miserable as she had predicted.

It was hot—miserably hot—and there wasn't a hint of a breeze to stir the warm air in his Spartan quarters behind the city jail.

Travis tossed restlessly in his bed, unable to fall asleep despite the lateness of the hour. The damnable heat was making it too hot to sleep. His restlessness had nothing to do with the fact that every time he closed his eyes he saw Kate VanNam as she'd looked when she had turned to face him on the sidewalk outside the Golden Nugget.

No, his sleeplessness had nothing to do with her.

"You won't be able to sleep tonight," she had taunted. "You'll lie there in the heat, perspiring and miserable. And while you're burning up, I'll be slicing through the cool waters of the lake naked."

"Damn you, lady!" Travis muttered aloud. "Think you can devil me? Lots of good old-fashioned luck to you!"

He convinced himself, as he lay there in the darkness, that the only reason he paid Miss Kate VanNam any attention was to try and keep her off balance so that she wouldn't fall under Winn DeLaney's spell.

Travis considered himself a good judge of character, and he found DeLaney suspect. Something was not right. Why was DeLaney in Fortune? What was the man up to?

Travis mused on it, and not for the first time. He'd done his homework. Correspondence with San Francisco authorities verified what he strongly suspected. There was indeed a connection between the Cavalry Blue Mine Kate had inherited and Winn DeLaney's arrival in Fortune.

Kate's late aunt Arielle had accompanied her husband, Benjamin Colfax, a noted geologist, out here on Freemont's earlier explorations. And the widowed Arielle Colfax had been living in San Francisco at the time of her death. From his own crime ledger, Travis had learned that around that same time, the assayist George McLoughlin had been murdered in San Francisco and his records stolen.

Winn DeLaney was from San Francisco. And DeLaney had shown up in Fortune less than six months after Arielle Colfax's death, seemingly coincidental with Kate's arrival. He'd immediately begun courting her.

Travis frowned. Pieces of the puzzle were missing. He'd have to investigate further. He couldn't help worrying about Kate, even though she annoyed the hell out of him. She was so stubborn and combative he couldn't just come right out and warn her about her choice of companions. She would think he was jealous.

And maybe he was. No getting around it, he felt the blood zing through his veins anytime he caught sight of her gleaming golden hair. The sound of her soft, cultured voice never failed to warm the heart he had sworn would remain forever cold.

Travis felt his bare chest tighten. Holding her in his arms at tonight's dance had been sweet agony. He had wanted her, desired her, yearned to make love to her. And she had tormented him, hinting that she allowed DeLaney to swim naked with her in the lake.

Travis cursed them both.

He sat up and swung his legs to the floor. He lit a cigar and drew the smoke down into his lungs. He rose, pulled on his discarded white underwear and stepped outside, hoping to catch a breeze.

There was none.

It was just as hot outside as it was in. Travis exhaled with irritation and sank down onto the stoop, his cigar clamped firmly between his teeth, his forearms resting on his raised knees. He sat there in the late night silence and vowed he would try to save Kate VanNam from herself where DeLaney was concerned.

But he'd be damned if he would allow the willful young beauty to get her soft hands on his heart.

Twenty-Six

On Sunday afternoon the town was quieter than usual, the streets nearly deserted. A majority of the revelers from the previous night's street dance hadn't yet ventured out of their rooming houses or tents or campsites. Many lay prostate on their cots, suffering with headaches and upset stomachs from drinking too much rotgut whiskey. They cursed anybody who made so much as a peep.

A trio of rowdies who'd tried to shoot up the town were now sleeping it off in the city jail. Their loud, annoying snores had driven Travis and his deputy outdoors.

With their chairs tipped back and their booted feet resting on the hitching rail in front of the jail, Travis and Jiggs relaxed. They were enjoying the rare tranquillity.

"So…" After nearly half an hour, Jiggs finally

broke the silence. "Valentina gets back this afternoon, does she?"

Travis nodded. "Around five." His hands laced on his stomach, he twiddled his thumbs restlessly.

"You going down to the river to—"

"No. I'm to join her later this afternoon. We'll meet up at her suite above the Nugget around six o'clock. She wanted it that way." He smiled and added, "Valentina's a vain woman. She'll want a chance to bathe and change before I get there."

"I see."

Another ten minutes passed in silence.

"I'm bored, Jiggs," Travis finally announced. "Think I'll take a walk. Kill some time before I head up to Val's."

"Sure," said Jiggs. "Go on. I'll hold the fort here."

Travis took his feet off the rail, tipped his chair legs back down and stood up. He raised his long arms above his head, stretched and said, "You having supper with Alice Hester again tonight?"

Jiggs's narrow face lit up like a summer sunrise. Bobbing his head, he said, "Chicken and dumplings and cherry pie."

Travis grinned. "Same time as always? Eight o'clock?"'

He shrugged narrow shoulders. "Or thereabouts."

"Eight is fine, Jiggs. Val will get ready to sing around eight, so I'll be back here to spell you."

"Good enough," said the deputy.

Travis considered going inside to get his hat, but decided against it. He stepped down off the sidewalk and crossed the street. He had no particular destination in mind, but within minutes he had sauntered into the dense forest. The cooling shade was a welcome change from the harsh August sunshine.

Travis knew every inch of this pine forest and every landmark for miles around the town. Ducking tree limbs and weaving in and out, he soon began the climb to a favorite spot, a place he'd discovered on his first week in Fortune. At timberline, high above the town a smooth, flat shelf of rock jutted out from the side of the mountain.

Travis had gone there often during his first year in California. Young, homesick and lonely, he had found solace on the lofty windswept overhang. He hadn't been there in a long time. Not in two or three years. He didn't know why he was going there now.

Halfway up, Travis was perspiring. He stopped, unbuttoned his shirt, yanked it out of his trousers and whipped it off. He dropped it where he stood. He'd pick it up on the way back down.

He trudged rapidly on up the sharp incline, his legs growing weak, his breath short. At last he stepped out of the forest and onto the rocky overhang.

And then he saw her.

Kate VanNam was lying on the sun-heated promontory, drying her golden hair. She was barefoot. She wore a beribboned camisole and cotton pantelets. Her petticoat and dress lay folded neatly beside her.

Travis didn't dare move or take a step toward her. He stood as still as a statue and stared.

When Kate turned her head and saw him, she felt her stomach clench. He was bare chested and bare headed, his raven hair gleaming in the sunlight, his muscular torso and shoulders glistening with a sheen of perspiration. His gun belt rode low around his hips. So did his tight trousers. His belt buckle rested well below his navel.

Kate shaded her eyes with her hand and stared. She did not scold him or order him to leave. Nor did she anxiously reach for her dress and cover herself.

For a long, tense moment they simply stared at each other. Then Travis, holding her gaze, slowly unbuckled his gun belt and laid it down on the rock. Kate said nothing. She didn't move.

Travis edged closer.

When he stood looking down at her, Kate lifted a hand. She gently grasped the fabric of his neatly creased trousers and tugged playfully at the pant leg. She saw him swallow anxiously and she felt a sudden surge of female power. Sliding her fingers around the back of his leg, she felt the muscles bunch and flex.

Travis tensed at her touch, and his low-riding trousers fell away from his drum-tight belly. His heart was racing as he sank to his knees beside her. Kate slowly sat up. A strap of her camisole fell from her shoulder and down her arm. Travis hooked his little finger beneath the fallen strap and drew it back up into place.

Kate looked into his beautiful midnight black eyes and her lips parted. She nervously smiled. Travis clasped a handful of her damp golden hair, lifted it to his face and inhaled deeply of its perfumed scent. Kate waited, not daring to move. He released the silky hair, letting it spill slowly through his fingers.

Then, without a word, he drew her up onto her knees to face him, gathered her into his arms, bent his dark head, hesitated for a couple of heartbeats, then kissed her.

Just as it had been that night at the mansion, his kiss was at once utterly brazen and blazing hot. With one long arm wrapped securely around her, Travis clasped Kate's chin with his thumb and forefinger and feasted on her tempting lips like a man too long starved for the taste of her.

Kate thrilled to the bold invasion of his kiss. His lips and tongue plundered her open mouth, and she melted against him, having neither the strength nor the inclination to stop him. She wanted him to keep on kissing her forever.

The instant Kate felt his heartbeat against her breasts she knew she was his to do with as he pleased. No one had ever kissed her the way Travis was kissing her, and she gloried in the intimate pleasure.

When his hand left her chin and settled warmly on her bare shoulder, Kate shivered expectantly. Would he lower the camisole strap back down off her shoulder?

As if he had read her thoughts, he teasingly plucked at the lacy strap, but did not brush it away. Instead he wrapped both arms around her and crushed her against his bare chest. While his masterful mouth molded her lips to his and his tongue did wonderful things to the sensitive insides of her mouth, Kate anxiously pressed her breasts against his naked torso.

Through the thin batiste of her camisole she could feel the crisp black hair and the muscled flesh of his hot, hard chest. Her breasts were flattened against him and her nipples tightened and ached. She moaned softly, anxiously clasping his biceps as she arched her back in an attempt to get even closer. His raw masculinity was like a powerful magnet pulling her into a fire that was rapidly burning away all her inhibitions.

His lips never leaving hers, Travis took hold of Kate's slender arms and lifted them up around his neck. She clasped her wrists behind his head and clung to him. She felt his hands slide caressingly down to her waist, then her hips. While his tongue stroked hers and she eagerly slanted her lips to his, Travis skillfully insinuated a knee between her legs, nudging her knees apart. With his palms cupping her bottom, he drew her down onto his hard thigh.

Again she moaned and anxiously rode him, rubbing herself against his steely thigh just as he'd intended. His hands caressed her all over as, with his heart thudding in his chest, Travis kept kissing her, exciting her, arousing her.

While the hot August sun beat down on their heads, the pair kissed and touched and sighed until they were burning up with a sexual heat far hotter than any blinding summer sun.

They kissed until they were breathless and wanting each other so badly they shuddered with barely leashed desire. One more minute and it would have been too late.

But just in time, Travis came to his senses. He realized what was about to happen and anxiously tore his heated lips from Kate's. Much as he wanted her, he couldn't, wouldn't allow this sudden summer madness to go any further. He was afraid of this angelic-looking blond beauty. He knew that if he made love to her, he'd pay for it, and that the price was too high. His heart for her body was too great a cost.

No thanks.

Kate's eyes flew open in surprise and confusion. Travis gritted his teeth and sat her back.

"Sorry, Kate," he said, a tortured expression in his dark, expressive eyes. "My fault. That shouldn't have happened. It will never happen again."

Too stunned and shaken to respond, she stayed there on her knees as he rose to his feet. Mystified, she watched as he turned and walked away. He stopped, yanked up his gun belt, slung it over his shoulder and disappeared.

With her lips swollen from his kisses, her nipples stinging from being pressed against his chest, her groin aching from the contact with his hard thigh, Kate weakly sank back onto her heels.

She stared after him, longing to have him come back and keep on kissing her. She didn't understand why he'd left so abruptly. She hugged her arms to her chest and trembled, hurt and humiliated.

And finally she became angry.

Angry with him.

Angry with herself.

With him because he had obviously taken perverse pleasure in showing her just how easily he could seduce her, if he so desired.

She chastised herself for falling right into his arms and proving him right.

Tears springing to her eyes, Kate cursed his name and vowed she'd never speak to him again, much less kiss him.

Twenty-Seven

His blood up, Travis stopped, picked up his shirt, put it back on and headed directly to the Golden Nugget and the arms of the beautiful Valentina Knight.

He caught her in her bath. Her French maid was there, kneeling beside the tub, scrubbing her mistress's back with a long-handled brush.

"Darling!" Valentina happily greeted Travis and snapped her fingers at the maid. The woman nodded, rose and promptly disappeared. "I'll just be a minute, my love," Valentina said, and then squealed with girlish delight when Travis stalked over to the tub and snatched her up out of the sudsy water.

Dripping all over the fine Aubusson carpet, Valentina joyfully threw her arms around his neck and leaped up onto him, wrapping her legs around his waist. While she clung to him and scattered kisses all over his face, Travis unbuckled his gun belt and dropped it to the floor.

As agile as an acrobat, Valentina climbed all over Travis, quickly saturating his clothing. Then she delighted in stripping those wet clothes from his body. Swinging on him, laughing merrily, she unbuttoned his shirt and pushed it off his shoulders and down his arms.

She was sprinkling kisses along his bare shoulder when Travis sank to his knees and sat back on his heels with her astride his spread thighs. Valentina didn't hesitate. She knew just what to do. Kissing his well-cut chin and firm jawline, she deftly reached between them, unbuttoned his trousers and freed him.

"Well, what have we here?" she teased, and rubbed her wet body against his awesome erection. "Is this for me?"

"Just for you," Travis said, wishing he meant it, knowing that he did not.

Still, she was incredibly beautiful and a skilled and innovative lover, and when she clasped him in her soft hands and guided him up inside her, Travis momentarily lost himself in her. Physical ecstasy was theirs for a few fleeting minutes. The slippery Valentina glided up and down the throbbing length of her lover with a mastery honed earlier. She knew how to please, how to take a man almost over the top, then pull back just in time.

She didn't do that this afternoon.

Travis wanted, needed to climax quickly. She sensed it. Sadly, she sensed as well that this sudden burst of burning lust had not been generated by or for her. An astute woman, Valentina suspected she was in danger of losing her lover, but for the moment she put that thought out of her mind. For this pleasurable minute, he was hers, and she gave him her all, determined to please him. Within minutes the two of them were shuddering in shared release.

Later, when both were fully undressed and lying stretched out in Valentina's big soft bed, they made easy small talk. Valentina told Travis about her brief stay in San Francisco, said she'd gone to her dressmaker's and had some exquisite gowns fitted. She'd done some shopping, went to the theater and dined at her favorite restaurants.

"But I missed you," she said. "Now, tell me about last night's street dance." She turned onto her stomach beside Travis and folded her arms over his chest.

"It was pretty much like last year's wild celebration," Travis said. "All the miners got drunk and danced with all the women."

"Did you?"

"Get drunk?"

"No, silly. Dance with all the women."

"I danced a time or two."

"Did you dance with Kate VanNam?"

"Yes, once," he said.

"Was she there with Winn Delaney?"

Travis nodded.

Valentine made a face and said, "There's something going on there that puzzles me, Travis."

"What's the mystery?" he said. "DeLaney is ardently courting Miss VanNam. I would assume he has marriage in mind."

"Perhaps. But when he's not with Kate VanNam, DeLaney—so I hear—is in bed with the new girl who works at the Whiskey Hill Saloon."

Travis said nothing, but his lean body automatically stiffened. Valentina felt it. She continued, "You may have seen the woman. She's not exactly pretty, but she's exotic looking. She's dark complected with green eyes. She wears a decorative golden dagger in her black hair." Valentina paused, looked thoughtful, then added, "And, the strangest thing, she has a blue trinity tattoo on the side of her neck. Now why would a woman do that to herself?"

Travis eased Valentina's arms off his chest and sat up. "She wouldn't," he said as reached for his clothes. "A blue trinity tattoo is the mark given to Australian prisoners. Apparently the lady in question is a felon." He stood up and stepped into his trousers.

"What are you doing? So she's been in prison, who cares?" Valentina said, and scrambled up out of the bed. She laid her hands on his chest. "Don't go, darling. We have another hour before I'm due downstairs."

Travis thrust his arms into his shirtsleeves. "I promised Jiggs I'd hurry back to the jail so he can have dinner with Alice Hester."

Feeling as if her world was spinning out of control, Valentina pressed herself against Travis and said, "To hell with Alice Hester! I don't care if that plain-faced widow ever has dinner with Jiggs. Let her bake some more of her overpriced pies!"

"Now, Val, it's not like you to be unkind." He gently tore her arms from around him. "I have to go."

"So go!" she said angrily, "Get out of here."

Travis smiled, touched her cheek affectionately, turned and left. For a long moment Valentina stood there and stared at the door he'd closed behind him. She felt tears come to her eyes. She had the sinking feeling that the handsome sheriff might never come through that door again.

And she knew why.

Her keen intuition told her that what she'd suspected for weeks was true. The man she loved was falling for the Boston blonde.

"You back already?" Jiggs said when Travis walked into the jail at five minutes of seven that evening.

"Val ran me off," Travis said. "She has to get dressed for tonight's performance."

"So I can go on over to Alice's?"

"Sure, Jiggs." Travis dropped down into a chair behind his desk. "One thing, before you leave… I hope you'll continue keeping a close eye on Kate VanNam. Just in the daylight hours. I'll handle the nights."

"Something happened that…?"

"No, no." Travis cut him off. "It's just that she's such a pretty, naive young thing and I don't completely trust DeLaney."

"Me neither," said Jiggs, rubbing his chin thoughtfully. "There's something about that fellow I can't quite put my finger on."

"Well don't worry about it," Travis said. "Go on. Enjoy your evening."

Travis was still seated at his desk when, at shortly after eight, he glanced up and caught sight of Winn DeLaney and Kate. They were across the street, strolling down the sidewalk. When they went into the Bonanza Hotel, Travis pushed his chair back and got to his feet. DeLaney had a suite at the Bonanza. Did he mean to take Kate up there?

Travis wasted no time.

He looked in on his three prisoners. All were sound asleep in their cells. Travis left the jail, crossed the street and went into the Bonanza. He nodded to Dwayne, the room clerk, and crossed the lobby to the dining room. He stood in the arched doorway and looked inside. Kate was seated across from DeLaney at a linen-draped table for two.

Travis turned away, chose an overstuffed chair in the lobby and sat down to wait. An hour passed before the couple came out of the dining room. Travis stayed where he was. But if DeLaney had made one move to take Kate upstairs, Travis would have intervened immediately.

"Why, if it isn't the town sheriff," DeLaney said, looking up to see Travis. "What terrible mischief is going on in the Bonanza this evening to bring out the law?"

Travis rose to his feet and acknowledged the pair. "Delaney. Miss VanNam."

Kate said nothing, just nodded silently, but Travis caught a look in her eyes that he'd never seen before. He wondered if that same expression was mirrored in his own.

"My sweetheart is quite tired this evening for some unexplained reason." DeLaney broke into Travis's thoughts. "Kate insists I take her straight home, despite the early hour. Why don't you come along with us, Marshal?"

"No, thanks."

"It would save you the trouble of following us," DeLaney stated sarcastically, and slipped an arm around Kate's waist. "That's what you'll do, isn't it?" He laughed then and ushered Kate out the door.

Travis sat back down.

He debated doing just what Delaney accused, but decided against it. Instead Travis returned to the jail, where he took out a deck of cards and played Klondike.

But his mind wasn't on the game.

It was on the beautiful blond-haired Kate. He kept seeing her lying on that sun-heated rock in her underwear. He kept feeling her lips moving sweetly beneath his own, and he kept hearing her softly sigh as he caressed her.

Travis was helplessly drawn to Kate even if she aroused conflicting emotions in him. He was not, however, confused about Winn DeLaney, and after what Valentina had told him about the woman who was DeLaney's mistress, Travis was doubly worried.

He looked up from his card game when he heard a loud knock on the frame of the open door.

Winn DeLaney walked in. "Evening again, McCloud."

"Something on your mind, DeLaney?" Travis said.

"You're following me, Sheriff, and I believe I know why. You want Kate for yourself and—"

Interrupting, Travis said, "DeLaney, I don't know what you're doing in Fortune, but I can't help but wonder. Did you somehow know that the heiress to the old Cavalry Blue claim was here?"

Travis saw the other man nervously swallow. "That's nonsense," DeLaney said defensively.

"Is it? Or did somebody tell you that the mine might actually hold a fortune in gold?"

"Don't be absurd! Everyone in this flea-bitten town knows there is no gold in that worthless claim of Kate's."

Travis pushed back his chair, rose and circled the desk. Towering over DeLaney, he said calmly, "Trifle with Kate or that mine and I'll kill you."

Twenty-Eight

Seployeptember came, and with it the rains.

Sudden and violent thunderstorms rumbled over the mountains. Their furious squalls were often followed by hours, then days, of steady rain that dampened Kate's already flagging spirits. The roof of the mansion leaked badly and she had no money to have it repaired. She stepped over puddles no matter how many times she mopped up the water. She had to shove the sofa against the wall to stay half-dry in bed at night.

And the nights were turning chilly.

Almost as chilly as the town sheriff.

Since the hot August afternoon on the rocky promontory, Travis McCloud had, without a doubt, gone out of his way to avoid her. Which was fine with her, if somewhat puzzling. She couldn't understand why he had kissed her and held her as if she were his treasured sweetheart, then abruptly pushed her away and left as if he loathed the sight of her.

But she was, in fact, relieved that McCloud had lost interest in tormenting her. The enigmatic sheriff was not the kind of man any woman in her right mind would choose to love. A broken heart would be the outcome.

Kate had enough real worries without giving Travis McCloud a great deal of thought. She was growing more and more doubtful that she was ever going to strike it rich, and she was nearly ready to concede that indeed there was no gold in the Cavalry Blue.

None.

All summer she and Chang Li had worked long hours, searching in vain for treasure. If there were any, they would have found it by now.

The meager amounts of placer had long since been taken from the streambed. The tiny gold-specked pebbles had provided precious few dollars, most of which Kate had already spent. She worried about what she would do once it was all gone.

Kate lay in her bed nights pondering her fate. She did not have the money to get back to Boston. How could she possibly support herself here?

They *had* to find the gold.

And soon.

Throughout that rainy September and on into a cold October, Kate and the loyal Chang Li continued to spend their days down in the abandoned mine shaft, hacking away at stubborn rock.

"What's the use," she said one bleak afternoon. She tossed her shovel aside and sank down onto the mine's rocky floor. "There's no gold here."

"Not to give up, Missy," Chang Li scolded. "We find treasure, you see." He smiled then, extended his hand and helped her to her feet. "You just tired. Work too hard for young slender woman. Look pale. Go home, rest."

"Good idea. Let's quit and—"

"I stay and work. Not tired."

Kate shook her head. "Of course you are."

"No, not weary, feel fine. You go."

Kate sighed and nodded. She knew Chang Li. It was no use arguing with him. The little man never faltered in his optimism. He started and ended each and every day with the belief that this could be the day good fortune would smile on them.

When Kate left him he was humming and hacking at the rock with the same enthusiasm he had on that very first day he had come to work with her.

How she envied him.

Kate stepped out of the mine and blinked in surprise. The rain had stopped. The sun had come out. The air was crisp and clear. The sky was an unclouded cobalt-blue. And in the northeast, just above the highest mountain peaks, a beautiful rainbow arched down from out of the heavens.

Kate hoped it was an omen.

She immediately felt better.

She took a page from Chang Li's book and walked home humming. Cal met her at the front gate and seemed to sense her lightened mood. He meowed and jumped up on her trousered leg with his front paws. She laughed, sank down on her heels and affectionately stroked his head. His eyes closed in pleasure.

Cal followed Kate into the house, zipped past her and raced down the hallway to the kitchen. Kate laughed again. He was hungry. As usual.

Kate fed the cat, then ambled into the drawing room, stripping off her work clothes as she went. She spent the rest of the afternoon lying on the sofa, reading a book Doc Ledet had loaned her from his extensive library.

"I believe you'll enjoy Sir Walter Scott's *The Lady in the Lake*," he'd said when he'd handed her the leather-bound novel. "It was a favorite of my dear wife, Mary."

Kate *was* enjoying the romantic tale. And she was enjoying being sinfully lazy for one lovely autumn afternoon. Chang Li was right. She was tired.

Well before dusk had settled in, the book she was reading had slipped from her hand and fallen to the floor.

She was asleep.

She was so physically exhausted that she slept soundly and didn't turn over all night.

* * *

Just before dawn Kate was violently shaken awake when her bed began to fiercely jump, the legs of the sofa slamming up and down on the wooden floor. Startled, unsure what was happening, she bolted up, looked around and ran out onto the porch, fearful that the walls would fall in around her. Cal was right behind her. Kate fought to keep her balance on the rolling, pitching porch.

Earthquake!

That's what it was. She'd heard about the California earthquakes and the destruction they could cause, with great fissures opening up and swallowing everything. Terrified, wondering if this was how she was to die, Kate offered up a quick prayer.

The tremor was over in less than a minute, but that minute seemed like an hour. Trembling, her heart racing with fear, Kate sank down on the porch steps. Cal climbed onto her lap and she hugged him close, taking comfort from his nearness, anxiously rubbing her cheek atop his head.

The calico tom would tolerate being held for only a short time. Soon he began struggling to free himself, and Kate released him. Both went back inside. Kate lit a lamp and walked through the mansion, checking for damage. There were a few broken dishes, an overturned chair, but otherwise the mansion was solidly built and had withstood the quake. Kate was relieved. The earthquake had scared her, but it had changed nothing.

Or so she thought.

* * *

Cal accompanying Kate to the mine each morning had become a habit. He walked at her side as though he were a dog.

Once they reached the Cavalry Blue, Cal would usually stay only long enough to go inside the mine, look around and check everything out. Then he'd get bored and disappear for the rest of the day. In the evening he would return just as Kate and Chang Li were quitting. The big calico seemed to have a built-in clock.

This morning Cal rushed on inside the mine ahead of Kate. He zipped right past Chang Li and vanished down into the darkness. Kate and Chang Li worked and talked about the early morning earthquake. The curious Cal was off somewhere in the mine exploring.

An hour had passed when Kate looked up to see Cal coming out of the dark reaches of the mine. When he stepped into the flickering light of the carbide lantern, Kate noticed that he was covered with dust and that tiny specks of rock clung to his fur. He was rumbling with annoyance and trying to shake himself clean.

"Look at him," Kate said to Chang Li. "Always into mischief." To Cal she said, "Come here, you bad cat. I'll brush you off."

She laid down her pick and sank to her knees. When the cat came to her, she grabbed his face in her hands and said, "Serves you right, always nosing into everything."

She began brushing the dust and particles from

him. Suddenly she stopped. Her brow knitted. Atop Cal's back, in the rich thick coat, a tiny speck of rock gleamed. Her lips falling open in astonishment, Kate plucked the fleck from the cat's back, and her blue eyes grew large and round.

Holding the tiny pebble between thumb and fore-finger, she said, "Chang Li, put down your pick."

"Why? Not tired, just get here."

"Put down your pick and come here, please."

Puzzled, Chang Li laid his pick against the wall, turned and came over. Kate held up the tiny speck for him to see. He looked at it. He looked at her.

"Gold!" they said in unison, their voices barely above a whisper.

"Chang Li make sure." The Chinaman put the small shiny pebble between his strong eyeteeth and bit down. He took it from his mouth and said, "Gold, missy. Real thing. Where you get?"

"From Cal's fur," she explained. "You know how he likes to investigate." She pointed and said, "He came out of there, covered in dust and…"

The sentence was never finished. Kate grabbed her carbide lantern and rose to her feet. Chang Li was right behind her. They went deeper into the mine to the rock wall where they had worked many times be-fore. They stopped abruptly when they spotted the narrow, newly opened fissure.

"The earthquake," Kate said, pointing to a crev-ice in the wall that revealed a natural vault cavern.

"Yes, tremor shift rock," stated Chang Li.

Kate shone her lantern through the opening.

She immediately spotted a wide vein of something shiny winking at her. With her bottom lip caught between her teeth, she slipped through the newly opened fissure and dropped her lantern in awe.

"Chang Li! Hurry! Come quickly!"

The little Chinaman eased through the crevice. His eyes widened in wonder. "Missy Kate, you rich, rich, rich!"

"We've hit the mother lode!" Kate shouted excitedly.

Smiling, clapping his hands, Chang Li declared, "Missy find treasure to equal the Incas of Peru!"

Twenty-Nine

"We've struck pay dirt! We've struck pay dirt!" Kate shouted gleefully.

"You millionaire big now, missy!" Chang Li joined in the fun.

"All thanks to this morning's earthquake!" Kate shrieked with delight.

"No tremor, no find treasure," Chang Li declared, his grin so broad his twinkling eyes disappeared into the laugh lines.

The happy pair whooped and hollered and danced dizzily around, giving thanks for the early morning earthquake. Both were aware that if not for the quake dislodging the wall of stone, they would never have stumbled across this colossal vein of gold-bearing quartz.

Clapping her hands, Kate laughed and said, "The

quake that shook me out of my bed has jarred the gold right into our hands!"

After several minutes of celebration, the pair finally calmed a little. They sobered, held the carbide lantern high and began to more closely study the wide vein of glittering yellow gold that streaked from the rocky ceiling above, all the way down to the cavern floor.

"We must have a sample assayed right away," Kate said.

"Yes, I do that this morning." Chang Li shot to his feet to go back after his pick.

"Wait." Kate stopped him. "We can't use an assay-ist here in Fortune."

Chang Li immediately understood. "I go over the mountain to assay office in Last Chance."

"No one knows you there?"

"Never been there before. Use older brother's name. They no trace."

"Good. How long will it take to get there and back?"

"Leave today, be back tomorrow."

Kate nodded. "I'll be on pins and needles until you return."

The two made a pact that very morning that they would tell no one of their discovery. Both knew that if word got out, they'd be in danger of claim jumpers and murderers swarming into the mine to steal the gold.

That evening after dark, Chang Li, riding a burro from the Wilson Livery Stable, slipped away from Fortune carrying a generous sample of the ore.

* * *

The next morning Kate, with Cal by her side, went to the mine, wondering if it was too good to be true. Had she dreamed it all?

She had not. Once inside the Cavalry Blue, she returned to the lower level where they had spotted the color. She raised her lantern and saw again the wide vein of yellow gold gleaming brightly.

Beaming, she said to the cat, who was seated at her feet, "Do you know what this means, Cal?"

He pricked his ears and his tail slowly swished back and forth on the stone floor as he looked up at her.

"You will dine on carefully prepared and cooked boned chicken. How does that sound?"

Cal meowed and his tail swished a little faster.

Kate laughed and said, "You deserve the very best, since it was you who discovered the gold."

Chang Li returned that afternoon and confirmed to Kate what both had hoped: the assay had proved incredibly favorable. He had been careful not to be followed back.

Now all they had to do was coax the gold out of the rock.

And keep their secret for as long as possible.

Neither dared tell anyone.

Kate had a dinner engagement with Winn that very evening. Although she was dying to tell him of her good fortune, she wisely refrained. But she couldn't hide her underlying excitement. Winn quickly picked up on it. He found Kate so extraordinarily happy and buoyant, he was sure that something good had happened. Her blue eyes were sparkling as never before and she couldn't stop smiling.

Winn strongly suspected that Kate had finally hit pay dirt in the Cavalry Blue. What else could make her so happy? The prospect made his heart beat faster. If it were so, if she had found the gold, riches would soon be his. Wondering why she was reluctant to share her good news, he gently probed. But she revealed nothing. And he was forced to hide his frustration.

When Winn told his mistress he believed Kate had found the gold, Melisande urged him to immediately propose to Kate. He agreed.

A couple of days later, after a sumptuous dinner at the Bonanza Hotel, Winn insisted on taking Kate for a carriage ride down to the river. She tried to beg off, saying it was much too cold, but Winn wouldn't listen.

He handed her up into the rented, one-horse gig, spread a warm lap robe over her knees and climbed up beside her. In minutes he'd parked the buggy near the river's edge, then turned and took her in his arms.

He kissed her and said, "Kate, you must know how I feel about you and…"

"Winn, please don't."

"Darling, I love you. I want you to be my wife.

I'm asking you to marry me, Kate. I want to take care of you."

"I'm very flattered, Winn, but no."

"Dearest, you can't mean that," he said. "I've been patiently courting you all summer, and I was under the impression that you've come to care for me just as I care for you."

"I've enjoyed your company very much," Kate told him. "But I'm not in love with you, Winn. I have no wish to marry you."

Astonished, he said, "Darling, is there someone else?"

"No, no. It's not that. I don't want to marry anyone."

"Kate, you don't know what you're saying. You told me yourself you have no family. You're all alone in the world. Let me take care of you, give you children. We'll be married right away and—"

"Winn, you're not listening," Kate interrupted. "I said no and I meant it. I am not going to marry you."

Seething and shocked that she would have the gall to flatly turn him down, Winn could barely hide his anger. He was desperate to make her his wife.

"Ah, Kate, Kate," he said softly. "I've been so careful not to take advantage of you that perhaps I've never really shown you how I feel about you. Let me show you now."

He reached for her, but Kate put up her hands and stopped him. "Take me home, Winn."

"Ah, darling girl, do you want to break my heart?"

"Certainly not. I'm fond of you and I consider you a friend. Can't we keep it that way?"

Winn knew it would do no good to press her. He smiled indulgently. "You'll continue to see me, I hope."

Kate replied, "It's late. Please take me home."

Winn was pacing the floor and muttering to himself when his mistress slipped up the hotel's back stairs well after midnight and into his top floor suite. She took one look at her lover and knew he had failed.

"She turned you down!" Her hands went to her hips.

"Yes! That ungrateful little bitch told me she didn't want to marry me. Can you believe it?"

"But she has to marry you! There's no other way," said an upset Melisande. "Damn you, Winn DeLaney, make her want to marry you. Use your charm, seduce her, sweep her off her feet."

Winn ran his hands through his disheveled blond hair. "And just how do you suggest I go about that?"

Melisande came to him, took the golden dagger from her dark hair and placed the point beneath his chin. She slid the dagger along his jawline, laughed throatily and said, "It's high time you stopped being a gentleman with Miss VanNam." She put out the tip of her tongue and licked her bottom lip. "Remember what you did to me last night?"

Winn finally grinned. "How could I forget?"

"Do that to her."

"God almighty, you can't be serious, Melly. She's a genteel young lady. She'd be horrified if I—"

"Do it," said Melisande, "and while she's still shuddering with ecstasy, ask her again to be your wife. She'll say yes, I guarantee it."

Winn slipped his arms around Melisande's waist. He teased, "I just hope I can remember exactly how I..."

"You can practice on me until you get it right."

Winn chuckled. "You're a good sport, Melly, you know that."

"Bed and wed that silly young woman right away, you hear me? Get that gold for me or you'll find I'm tired of being a good sport. I'll leave you and marry a rich old man back in San Francisco."

Winn's smile fled. He grabbed her hair and forced her head back. "Don't threaten me," he said through clenched teeth.

"Or you'll what?" she taunted, and kissed him.

Thirty

A daunting task lay before them.

That there was an abundance of gold inside the Cavalry Blue was no longer a dream, but a reality. However, bringing the rich deposits out of the mine would call for weeks, months, even years of hard, steady labor.

The rich vein they had uncovered could be extracted without too much difficulty. But well beyond it lay tons of gold ore in deposits of quartz, a hard crystalline mineral in rich veins stretching deep within the mountainside.

The gold would have to be separated from the quartz rock.

Which meant they would first have to hack away at the stubborn rock, haul the heavy ore out of the mine, dump it into a long tom or sluice, and crush it with a sledgehammer to pulverize it. And that was just the beginning. Once the quartz had been mined and crushed, the gold had to be separated from the powdered rock by washing the gold-bearing powder.

When Chang Li had finished building a long, sturdy sluice, he went with Kate into town to purchase a hand-crank pump. They had no choice. They had to have the pump to draw water up from the lake to the mine to wash the quartz rock.

On a bitter cold autumn morning, the two of them walked into town, went directly to the Wilson Livery Stable and hired a sturdy-backed burro, which they hooked up to a two-wheeled cart. Then, with Chang Li leading the animal, they headed for Barton's Emporium.

Chang Li waited outside with the burro while Kate went into the store.

"Morning, Mr. Barton," she said to the owner, who occupied his usual place on a stool behind the counter. He didn't move. Kate smiled at him and said, "A little chilly, isn't it?" And waited for his comment. Clifton Barton always remarked about the weather. It was about the only subject that seemed to interest him.

"Chilly?" He snorted. "Why, it's colder than a witch's tit. Begging your pardon, miss. Now, what brings you out on such a frigid morning?"

As succinctly as possible, Kate told him that she was here to purchase a pump. A hand-crank pump capable of drawing water uphill.

Clifton T. Barton finally came up off his stool. "A pump, you say?" He scratched his chin. "You wanting to pull water uphill, are you?"

"Yes. Do you or do you not carry hand-crank pumps?"

"I carry almost everything a person might ever need or want, Miss VanNam. Follow me."

He came out from behind the counter. Kate motioned Chang Li inside. Chang Li tethered the burro to the hitching rail and hurried in. He and Kate followed Barton as he led the way to the back of the cavernous store.

Ten minutes later Chang Li had picked out a good-size pump capable of siphoning gallons of water out of the lake and uphill. Kate paid for the pump, a substantial sum that took almost all the money she had left. Chang Li loaded the pump onto the cart, and they were ready to head back up to the mine.

"You think our secret will be out now?" Kate asked as she walked along beside Chang Li, who led the burro.

"Not really, missy."

"No? You don't think Clifton T. Barton will tell everyone who comes into the store that we bought the pump?"

"He only interested in weather," Chang Li said with a smile. "But not to worry, I will guard the mine at night."

"Guard the…? You can't do that. You can't work all day and stay awake all night."

"Not stay awake all night. I nap. But if someone come, I wake up and be there to protect property."

Kate thought it over. Finally she said, "I have a revolver."

He smiled. "Yes, I know. Remember how missy fire pistol in air and save me from big bullies."

Both laughed.

A week passed.

Two.

Winn DeLaney was running out of patience. So was his nagging mistress. For two solid weeks now Kate had politely turned him down each time he had extended a dinner invitation. Since the night he had proposed marriage, she had not spent an evening with him.

Tired of the delay, doubting she would ever agree to marry him, Winn decided to try a different tack. He went, late one cold night, into the Bloody Bucket Saloon, ordered a whiskey and looked around at the rough, rowdy crowd.

He spotted, bellied up to the bar, a couple of big, ugly thugs he knew to be town troublemakers. He moved down the bar to where they were and introduced himself.

"Delaney, gentlemen. Winn DeLaney," he said, and extended his hand to the bigger of the two, the one-eyed man.

"Titus Kelton," said the ruffian, who wore badly soiled clothes, "and this here's my friend, Jim Spears."

The red-bearded Spears looked askance at Winn DeLaney and said, "I ain't seen you in here 'afore. You that there dandy what's been squiring that pretty blond girl around town?"

"The very one," confirmed Winn. "May I buy you gents a drink?"

The one-eyed Titus Kelton was already motioning the barkeep over. The two big men downed their shots of whiskey in one swallow and held out their glasses for refills. Winn endured their bad smell, their loud guffaws and their incessant slapping him on the back for the next hour.

Quickly, he cultivated them, and all it took was half a dozen shots of whiskey each. Winn told the pair that he had a proposition to put to them. He suggested that they step outside for a minute and hear what he had to say.

Their breaths vaporizing in the cold mountain air, the three of them stood outside the saloon on the empty sidewalk.

Hunching his shoulders and turning up the lapels of his Chesterfield coat, Winn wasted no time. He explained what he wanted them to do, and told them how much he would pay.

"Ever hear of the Cavalry Blue Mine?" he began.

"Sure, it's that worthless claim up the mountain that—"

Interrupting, Winn said, "I want to hire you two to slip up to the mine late tomorrow night and get me a sample of the tailings so I can have the assayist give me a reading."

"Aw, you're wasting your time, Mr. DeLaney. There ain't no gold in that old mine."

As if Spears hadn't spoken, Winn said, "If the diggings are guarded, which is doubtful, it will probably be only by that little Chinaman, Chang Li." He stopped, smiled, and said, "I understand you boys have had dealings with him before."

Titus Kelton made a face. "That whining little coolie son of a bitch. What you want us to do to him?"

"Nothing much, really. I'm not asking you to harm him. Just to slip up on him—he'll probably be dozing—and knock him unconscious before he gets the chance to identify you. Once you've taken care of him, go inside the mine, light a carbide lantern and fill up a little bag with tailings. Then get out of there fast. Can you do it?"

"Sure, we can," said the red-bearded Jim Spears. "We'll go right now."

"No, you will not," Winn said. "You will go tomorrow night. Further, you will drink nothing stronger than coffee until you have finished the job. Do I make myself clear?"

"Sure, Mr. DeLaney. Now where's our money?"

"Not so fast, Spears. You'll get paid when you hand over the tailings," said Winn. "One last thing."

"What's that, Mr. DeLaney?" asked Kelton.

"Anything goes wrong, I don't know you, understand?"

"Where will we meet you? At your hotel?"

"If either of you sets foot in my hotel, I will kill you," Winn said, his eyes as cold as the freezing night air. "Be out in back of the Whiskey Hill Saloon at exactly 2:00 a.m. I'll be waiting there to meet you. Once you've handed over the tailings, I'll pay you. After that, you're both to forget you've ever met me."

Without another word he turned away and was gone.

"No, I insist." Kate was adamant. "You are going straight to your tent, where you'll get into bed."

"Not that sick, Missy," said the pale, feverish Chang Li as his teeth began to chatter.

It was late the next afternoon.

The two of them had put in a long hard day at the Cavalry Blue. Chang Li had not felt well all afternoon, but he had continued to work, assuring Kate that he was fine. All afternoon she had urged him to leave.

Now, at quitting time, as the weak winter sun was beginning to set, Kate took a good long look at the little man and ordered him to go home at once and get into bed.

"You are running a fever, Chang Li," she said. "I can tell by looking at you."

"Maybe little," he said meekly.

She stepped close and laid her hand on his forehead. "More than a little. You're burning up. Want to go see Doc Ledet?"

"No, no, not need doctor," Chang Li said.

"Very well, but you are not standing guard here tonight," Kate said emphatically.

"But what if somebody…?"

"I will take your place," she said calmly. "I'll guard the mine tonight and you will go home and get well."

Thirty-One

Winn Delaney's henchmen went up to the Cavalry Blue Mine at well past midnight. A full harvest moon shone down from a cloudless sky. Jim Spears spotted the lone sentry at the mine's entrance. The small figure in a dark coat and watch cap could only be the little Chinaman.

Spears motioned to Titus Kelton and pointed. Kelton squinted, nodded. The two men crept as silently as possible up the incline. But the big, lumbering Jim Spears stepped on a loose rock and it skittered down the mountainside.

Alerted, the guard swiftly spun around, yelled "Halt!" and, when they did not, fired a warning shot.

The one-eyed Titus Kelton immediately fired back, hitting the sentry. A loud moan, and the guard staggered. And Kate's cap fell off. Her long blond hair spilled down as she grabbed her bleeding shoulder and sank to the ground.

"We shot the woman!" muttered Jim Spears.

"Son of a bitch!" swore the one-eyed Titus Kelton as the calico cat that was keeping Kate company hissed loudly, streaked down the incline, made a flying leap at the big man and viciously scratched his remaining eye, drawing blood.

Holding his bloody eye, Kelton scrambled away, cursing. Spears was right behind him.

Moaning, Kate tried to rise. But she couldn't quite make it. Cal made soft mewling sounds and gently nudged her, trying to get her up, sensing that she was badly hurt.

"It's okay, Cal," Kate murmured weakly, drawing him down beside her. "I'm all right. I'll just rest a minute and get my strength back."

The cat lay dutifully still against his wounded mistress's side. Losing blood and rapidly growing weaker, Kate thought of Chang Li and how he would berate himself for allowing her to take his place on guard duty because he was sick.

She grimaced and pressed her palm against the bullet wound in an attempt to staunch the flow of blood that was rapidly saturating her woolen wrap. She tried her best to remain conscious, but knew she was losing the battle. She looked up at the cold stars twinkling high overhead in the heavens.

And she smiled foolishly when the face of the man in the moon became that of Sheriff Travis McCloud.

He couldn't sleep.

The feverish Chang Li tossed fitfully, unable to rest. It was more than just his illness. He was worried about Kate up there all by herself in the middle of the night. He should never have left her there.

Finally, Chang Li gave up trying to sleep. He threw back the covers and rose from his narrow cot in the drafty canvas tent he called home. He hurriedly dressed in the darkness and headed to the mine. He knew Kate would laugh and tease him about worrying, but he didn't care.

His teeth chattering from the cold and the fever, he trudged up the mountainside, his lungs laboring in the thin air. When he spotted her lying on the ground with the calico cat meowing plaintively at her side, Chang Li wailed loudly.

He hurried to the unconscious woman and saw the blood staining the fabric of her warm woolen wrap. He fell to his knees and pressed his ear to her chest to see if her heart was beating.

It was.

But barely.

Cursing himself in Chinese, Chang Li carefully lifted her into his arms. With the calico cat racing on ahead, Chang Li carried her down the mountain, wondering where he should take her. Doc Ledet was presently not in Fortune. There had been a mining accident over the hill in Goldbug, and the doctor had gone to help. He might not be back for a week or more.

By the time the exhausted, heavily breathing Chang Li reached town, he knew where he was going. He skirted the rear of the buildings until he was directly behind the city jail.

"Marshal, wake up, wake up!" he called frantically at the door of Travis McCloud's private quarters. "Sheriff, wake up!"

"Hold your horses," Travis shouted, pulling on a pair of trousers and lighting the lamp by his bed. Frowning, his hair disheveled, he yanked open the door, thundering, "What the hell?"

Then his dark face went ghostly white.

"Sheriff, is Missy Kate!" said Chang Li. "She bad shot, may die." And the frightened little man began to cry.

Travis was already taking Kate from Chang Li's arms and carrying her inside to his bed, where he gently laid her down. Not bothering to don a shirt or shoes, he said, without looking at Chang Li, "The bullet must come out now, tonight. Right now! You'll have to help."

Chang Li sniffed away his tears. "Do whatever you tell me."

Travis knelt beside the bed. He swept Kate's blood-soaked wrap open, took it off and tossed it aside.

And he decisively issued orders. "Light all the

lamps. Clean off the dining table. Get a fresh sheet from the shelves in the closet. Spread the sheet out on the table."

Chang Li snapped to, rushing about to do as he was told. When the table was draped with a snowy white sheet, Chang Li gathered clean cloths, bandages and a bottle of tincture of iodine. He heated water on the wood stove. He placed everything on the seats of two straight-backed chairs pulled up near the table.

When Travis carried Kate to the table and laid her on it, he said to Chang Li, "You can either stay here while I remove the bullet, or you can wait in the jail." Travis glanced at the little man and shook his head. "You're feverish. Go on into the jail and stretch out on a bunk in one of the empty cells."

"No, I help you—"

"That's an order, Chang Li."

The man nodded and left.

As soon as he was gone, Travis returned to the bed, reached under the feather mattress and took out his bowie knife. Removing it from its scabbard, he cleaned it, struck a match and ran the tiny flame up and down the length of the sharp blade to sterilize it as best he could. Then he wiped the blade down with a mixture of iodine and warm water. He placed the knife on a clean white towel Chang Li had laid out.

Travis turned his full attention to the unconscious Kate.

But he didn't see a beautiful young woman to

whom he was helplessly attracted. He saw a wounded
patient in need of immediate medical care. He was
no longer the sheriff, but Kate's physician, entrusted
with saving her life. Damn Doc Ledet's hide!

Travis didn't hesitate.

Clinically and devoid of emotion, he stripped
away Kate's bloodstained shirt and batiste camisole.
When she was naked to the waist, he carefully
cleaned and washed the wound.

Then Travis took a deep breath, picked up the knife,
asked the Almighty for guidance and went to work.

Kate remained unconscious while Travis, with his
surgeon's skill, excised the bullet from her left shoulder. It took less than five minutes. He dropped the
bloody bullet into a pan and laid the knife aside. He
carefully cleaned and bandaged the wound.

And only then, when his task was completed and
he'd draped a clean sheet over her, did Travis trem-
ble with fear. Her life was in his hands. The magni-
tude of the responsibility washed over him. He felt
dizzy, and short of breath. He quickly crossed to the
back door, stepped out onto the stoop and took several slow, long breaths of the frigid night air. Seated
on the stoop, meowing sadly, was Kate's cat.

"Hey, boy, it's okay," Travis said as he crouched
down and stroked the cat's head.

When the big calico didn't hiss or try to scratch
him, Travis smiled, scooped him up and took him inside. He carried the cat close to the table where Kate

lay, but kept a firm grip on him lest the calico try to jump up onto the table.

"See, she's all right," Travis soothed, and the nervous cat relaxed and purred softly. Travis lowered him to the floor. The cat yawned and went over to the fireplace, where embers burned low in the grate. Cal stretched out, made soft mewing sounds and went to sleep.

Travis glanced at Kate. He washed his hands thoroughly, then stripped the sheets from his bed and put on fresh ones. He returned to the table, smiling foolishly as he flipped her covering up to her waist and removed her tall rubber boots and stockings. And he bit the inside of his cheek when he unbuttoned her trousers down her flat belly, then struggled to get the pants down past her hips and off.

Travis lifted Kate and carried her to his bed. He placed her in the center of the mattress and drew the clean sheet and warm blanket up over her. He exhaled heavily, reached up and swept his hair back from his temples.

He stared at her.

She had lost a lot of blood. Her face was as white as the sheets she lay on. Her lips—those perfect Cupid's bow lips—were a pale, bloodless pink.

But she would live. He knew she would. She was young and healthy and he would take good care of her. He wouldn't allow her to move from his bed until she was able, no matter how much she objected.

Travis crossed to the fireplace, threw a couple of logs on the low-burning embers and jabbed at them with a poker. Flames shot up, but they did little to warm the chilled room. Then he drew on a clean shirt, pinned on his badge, put on his boots and went to get Chang Li, expecting to find the sick Chinaman sleeping soundly. Chang Li was sitting on the edge of a bunk, wide awake, worrying. Travis allowed him to check on Kate.

"She'll be all right, Chang Li. I'll keep close watch over her. Now go on home and get some rest."

"You send for me if she need me?"

"Yes, I will," Travis promised, and saw the little man to the back door. "Any idea who might have done this?"

Chang Li shook his head. "No, Sheriff. Who would do such a terrible thing? Shoot woman? Not understand."

"I know. Let's keep the shooting to ourselves for a while. Wait until Kate wakes up. Maybe she'll know who her assailant was."

Thirty-Two

Travis blew out all the lamps, save one on the night table by the bed. He pulled up a straight-back chair and sat down.

With a loaded Navy Colt .45 at his elbow, he settled in to spend the long night monitoring Kate's condition.

He tried to recall what he had learned in medical school regarding the care of patients with gunshot wounds. The first step was completed; he had successfully removed the bullet without causing too much additional bleeding. Thank God she had been hit in the shoulder.

A few inches lower and she wouldn't have made it.

Travis shuddered at the thought. His brow furrowed with concern, he leaned close and gently smoothed a wayward lock of hair back off Kate's pale cheek. Just as he'd fancied, that glorious golden hair was the texture of fine imported silk. How many times had he daydreamed about running his hands through her hair?

Travis quickly reminded himself that this woman lying deathly still in his bed was not a beautiful seductress but a helpless patient whose healing had been entrusted to him by a quirk of fate.

Travis tucked the covers more closely around Kate's bare shoulders. He sank back into his chair and laced his fingers over his waist. He never took his eyes off her.

As the hours dragged slowly by, he examined Kate every few minutes. He checked to see if she was running a fever or if her body temperature had dropped dangerously low. She was, he was relieved to discover, neither too hot or too cold. That was an encouraging sign.

Kate remained unconscious throughout his deft ministering. A couple of times she flinched slightly when Travis inspected the wound or replaced the bandage. But she never opened her eyes. And once he was finished with his tasks, she sighed deeply, licked her lips and slumbered on.

Outside, the temperature dropped dramatically.

Inside, a deep chill had set in.

Cold and sleepy, Travis yawned and closed his tired, scratchy eyes. He shifted in his chair, trying to get comfortable. He leaned forward, put his elbows on his knees and his face in his hands. He stayed that way for only a few minutes before he shifted again. He sank down low onto his spine, laid his head back, stretched his long legs out and crossed them at the ankles.

That was no better.

He got up. He paced around the shadowy room. He noticed Kate's cat was awake and seated directly before the door, tail curled around himself, softly meowing to go outside.

"It's cold out there, fellow," Travis said to the calico.

The cat looked up at him and edged closer to the door. Travis let him out, closed the door and returned to the bed. He considered lying down on the floor. But the floor would be cold and hard. He sank back down into the straight-back chair, looked at the soft, warm bed and rubbed his chin thoughtfully.

Then shook his head decisively.

He needed to get some rest if he were to be at his best to take care of this wounded woman.

Travis took off his boots, glanced one last time at Kate's face, rose and very cautiously got onto the bed. He stretched out atop the covers beside Kate. He sighed deeply and turned on his side, facing her. Almost instantly he was asleep.

The two of them slept peacefully side by side in the big feather bed.

Sometime during the night, Kate awakened.

The first thing she saw when she opened her eyes

was a shiny silver badge. A badge that rested on the broad chest of Sheriff Travis McCloud.

Horrified, she screamed, lunged up and immediately winced in pain, waking Travis.

"Why are you in my bed?" she wailed, and tried to hit him when he quickly rolled up into a sitting position.

"Be still!" he ordered, trapping her arms at her sides and holding her immobile against his chest. "Listen to me, Kate! You've been shot. You hear me? Someone shot you in the shoulder. You're injured. You've lost blood."

"Where are my clothes?" she shrieked, horrified that her breasts were bare. She could feel her nipples rubbing against the abrasive fabric of his shirt. "Why did you take my clothes?"

"I had no choice. Your shirt and camisole were soaked with blood. I had to take them off so I could clean the wound and remove the bullet," Travis said, keeping his tone low and soft in an attempt to calm her.

"Let me go," she commanded, though she didn't struggle against him.

Travis continued to hold her in his arms, soothing her, lulling her with the reassurance that she was going to be fine in a few days. When he was satisfied she would put up no further resistance, he gently eased her back down onto the pillow and drew the covers up over her shoulders.

"You'll be okay," he said, "but you must be quiet and rest."

Blushing hotly, embarrassed that he had seen her bare breasts, Kate frantically felt beneath the covers to see if he had removed all of her clothes. She was greatly relieved to find that she still wore her pantalets.

"Do you remember what happened?" Travis asked as he rose from the bed. "Do you know who shot you?"

"I'm thirsty," she replied groggily. Making a face, she added, "I don't feel well."

"I know you don't, and I'm sorry." Travis brought her a cup of water. "Just a few sips," he warned as he helped her take a drink.

Kate shoved his hand away when she felt the covers slipping, exposing her breasts. "Where's my shirt?" she asked, clutching at the sheet. "I want my shirt."

"And I want you to lie down and be still," he said as he set the water aside.

"Where am I?" Kate asked then, her head dropping back onto the pillow. "Where have you taken me?"

"You are in my private quarters behind the jail. But I didn't bring you here," Travis told her. "You were shot last night outside the Cavalry Blue. Chang Li found you and brought you here."

"No. He couldn't have brought me here," she said. "Chang Li was sick. That's why I was standing guard at the mine."

"He got worried and went to check on you," Travis told her. "He found you'd been shot and—"

Frowning, Kate interrupted, "But why would he bring me here?"

"Because you needed immediate medical attention. Doc Ledet's in Goldbug. There was a mining explosion and he went over to help out."

Kate nodded. "Yes, I remember. So you...?"

"I removed the bullet and bandaged the wound."

"I see. Well, I'm grateful to you, Sheriff, but now if you'll kindly fetch my clothes, I'll be going on home."

"You're going nowhere." Travis sat down and pulled his chair close. "I'm keeping you here so I can take care of you."

"I don't need you to—"

"Yes, you do."

Kate sighed, defeated. She was in no position to argue. He had her where he wanted her—in his care, in his quarters, in his bed.

"The minute I get better, I'm leaving," she stated emphatically.

"Fair enough," Travis replied. "Now, suppose you tell me what happened. Any idea who did this to you? And why?"

Kate stared up at the ceiling and thought back to last night. "I know exactly who did it," she said, clenching her jaw. "Those two big brutes that beat up Chang Li last summer. The red bearded man and his one-eyed sidekick."

Travis nodded. "Spears and Kelton."

Kate turned her head and looked at Travis. "Yes, it was them. There's no doubt in my mind."

"Know why they would do such a terrible thing?"

"They're mean men, Marshal," Kate said.

Travis gave no reply, just waited for her to say more. After a long pause, she told him, "Sheriff, there's gold in the Cavalry Blue. Lots and lots of gold. That's what they are after, I'm sure."

"How did they learn about the gold?"

"I don't know. I can't understand it. I didn't tell anyone and I'm sure Chang Li didn't, either."

"When did you discover the gold?"

"After the earthquake. The tremor shifted a wall of rock inside the mine and exposed a rich vein. Once we'd found the gold and had it assayed in Last Chance, Chang Li thought it best to guard the mine at night. But last night he was sick with a fever, so I took his place."

"You sure you didn't mention finding the gold to anyone?"

"No, I just told you, we—"

"Not even to Winn DeLaney?"

Kate immediately took offense. "Winn DeLaney would never harm me!"

"I didn't say he would," Travis replied. "I just asked if perhaps you had mentioned to him that—"

"I did *not* tell Winn about the gold."

Thirty-Three

Winn DeLaney was angry.

With the collar of his Inverness cloak turned up around his ears, he stood out in the cold behind the Whiskey Hill Saloon, gritting his teeth and quietly cursing.

Two o'clock had come and gone with no sign of Spears and Kelton. He had specifically told them to meet him here and hand over the tailings from the Cavalry Blue Mine. It was a simple assignment.

At 2:30 a.m. the night winds rose. The temperature continued to drop. Winn paced back and forth, slapping his hands together, trying to keep warm. It was impossible.

Frozen and furious, he returned to the hotel at ten minutes past three. His mistress, Melisande, was waiting up for him. She was eager to hear what had happened and to examine the bag of gold tailings.

"Damn them both," Winn swore, as he entered the suite. "That pair of fools never showed up."

"No? Why not?"

Cold and short-tempered, Winn snapped, "How the hell should I know? Something must have happened. Maybe that little coolie put up a fight and they're all lying up there dead. Right now, I don't much give a damn. I've been standing out there freezing my ass off and I just want to get in bed." He shrugged out of his cloak and began undressing as he walked into the bedroom.

Frowning, Melisande followed, warning, "This is not good, Winn. Not good at all. I'm worried."

"Well, worry in silence," he said, and crawled into bed. "I'm sleepy." Soon he was slumbering.

Melisande wasn't.

She lay awake in the darkness, feeling uneasy. She knew that something bad would come from this.

Something very bad.

The sun came up and the town of Fortune began slowly stirring to life. Travis checked the sleeping Kate one last time and left his quarters. He was seated behind his desk when Jiggs Gillespie came to work that cold autumn morning.

"Mornin', Trav," Jiggs said cheerily, taking off his warm coat. He immediately frowned when he saw how haggard his boss looked. "God Almighty, Travis, what is it? What's wrong?"

Travis quickly told him of the shooting, concluding with the order, "Organize a posse and go after Spears and Titus. I know there's not much chance of finding them, but we have to try."

"Consider it done," said Jiggs.

By midmorning Jiggs and the mounted posse rode out of Fortune to the cheers of men loitering about on the street. The loud commotion awakened Winn DeLaney. He rushed to the window to look out.

He knew, without being told, that the posse was after Spears and Kelton. Nervous, and cursing under his breath, Winn hurriedly dressed and went down to breakfast to see what he could find out. When he overheard the conversation at the next table, he blanched.

Kate had been shot!

At once he felt ill and lightheaded. What on earth had she been doing at the mine in the middle of the night? How badly had she been hurt? Where were Spears and Kelton? They must have escaped, or by now he'd be clamped in irons.

Winn pushed his breakfast plate away and left. Out on the street, the shooting was all anyone was talking about. Winn joined in their conversations, expressing his outrage. Everyone agreed that the dastardly pair who had shot and wounded Kate VanNam were probably long gone and would never be found.

Winn Delaney was the only man in Fortune who feared the pair might be caught.

Still, he knew it was highly unlikely. And he was *not* leaving Fortune until he got his hands on the gold which he had schemed so long to claim. He was willing to take his chances.

Shortly after the posse had ridden away, Winn, who had seethed when he'd learned that the wounded Kate had been taken to McCloud's quarters, showed up at the city jail.

"Sheriff," he said, stunned to encounter McCloud. "I would have thought you had ridden out with the posse."

"Surprised to see me, are you, DeLaney?"

"A bit. You being the head lawman, hired by the Committee of Vigilance to keep the peace. Shouldn't you be out doing just that?"

"My trusted deputy is leading the posse," Travis said. "I thought it wise to stay here and watch over Miss VanNam."

"I heard the terrible news." Concern clearly written on his smoothly shaved face, Winn said, "I should think Dr. Ledet would be caring for Kate."

Travis didn't bother telling DeLaney that Doc Ledet was not in town. "Hopefully," he said, without rising from his chair, "we'll catch those responsible and bring them to swift justice."

"Yes, yes," Winn said. "Hanging is too good for them."

"I couldn't agree more."

"But Kate? How is my dear sweetheart? I'm here to see her," Winn said. "Perhaps I can offer a degree of comfort and…"

"Sorry, DeLaney, your generous offer will have to wait," Travis said. "She's not receiving visitors."

"I'm not just any visitor, McCloud." Winn fought to contain his irritation. "Perhaps you're unaware that Miss VanNam and I have…well, an understanding. We're planning to be married."

"Comes as news to me." Travis grinned then and asked, "Will it come as news to her?"

Determined to control his temper, Winn said calmly, "Certainly not. As Kate's intended, I insist on seeing her."

Travis pushed back his chair, stood up and hooked his thumbs in his gun belt. "Insist all you like, DeLaney. It's not going to happen. You have to go through me to get to her."

"You can't mean you're actually refusing to let me see her."

"That's exactly what I mean." Travis came around the desk. "There's the door. Don't come back."

"You've overstepped your authority, McCloud. You can't keep me away from Kate."

"Wanna bet?"

* * *

"You had a visitor earlier today," Travis told Kate late that afternoon as he uncovered a steaming bowl of Alice Hester's broth.

"Alice?"

"Make that two visitors," Travis corrected. "Alice brought the broth and a freshly baked loaf of bread. Said she'd be back to see you when you're feeling better. Winn DeLaney stopped by."

Kate glared at Travis. "Let me guess. You refused to let him see me."

"For your own good." He went to the bureau, took a clean nightshirt from the drawer and returned to the bed. "You're not up to tolerating visitors."

"I'm not up to tolerating you," she said, making a mean face at him.

"You'll like me better once you get this nightshirt on and have had something to eat."

"I doubt that. Leave the nightshirt here and go away."

"Sorry, Kate. You can't manage alone. Like it or not, you need my help."

"I don't like it," she told him, but cooperated when he sat down on the edge of the mattress, facing her, and slipped the nightshirt over her head.

Taking care not to hurt her, Travis managed to get her arms through the sleeves, and he dutifully closed his eyes as he pulled the garment down to her waist.

"There!" he said when the task was completed. "Better?"

"Better," she admitted reluctantly.

She even agreed to try a few spoonfuls of the broth Alice had made. But she got angry when, as Travis fed her, and they talked about the shooting, he suggested that Winn DeLaney might be responsible.

"What an asinine thing to imply!" she said, eyes flashing. "That is the most ridiculous statement I have ever heard!"

As if she hadn't spoken, Travis said, "Bert Bost— you've seen him around town on crutches—lost a leg fighting under Scott in the Mexican War. Shortly after DeLaney arrived in Fortune, Bost brought me some disturbing intelligence. He said there was captain at the Battle of Buena Vista who wore distinctive golden spurs." Travis paused, let it sink in. "A cold-blooded killer, scared the Mexican soldiers to death."

"So? Winn's a war hero. That's some slander to his character." Kate rolled her eyes.

"Do you have a brother, Kate?"

The question completely caught her off guard. Travis could tell by the look in her eyes that the answer was yes. He said evenly, "I made some written inquiries to San Francisco. The provost marshal at the Presidio has pay records that show a Gregory Van-Nam was also with Scott at the Battle of Buena Vista."

For a long moment, Kate was silent. Finally she said, "A coincidence at best. If Winn knew my brother, he would have mentioned it. And what does any of this have to do with me being shot?"

"Perhaps nothing," Travis admitted. "Let's hope I'm wrong."

"I told you who shot me! Those two cruel bullies who once beat up Chang Li. A cultured man like Winn DeLaney would not know such men, much less have dealings with them."

"Need sometimes makes for strange bedfellows, Katie."

"Don't call me Katie! And Winn would *never* need them. Why would he?"

"You sure you never mentioned to DeLaney that you'd found the gold?"

"I am absolutely certain I never told him. Or anyone else. Chang Li and I vowed we'd keep it to ourselves, and we did. You know what your problem is? You just can't believe that a man like Winn DeLaney would be interested in me for me alone. And furthermore, I believe you're jealous of Winn. Admit it, Sheriff."

Travis said nothing. Which made her all the more angry.

"Get away from me," she said. "Winn responsible, indeed! You're out of your mind."

But Kate began to have doubts. Did Winn know Gregory? And if so, had Gregory told him about the mine? Could Winn actually be responsible for the shooting? Was he after the gold?

She thought back over the times Winn had asked her countless probing questions about the Cavalry Blue. She hadn't thought anything about it, but maybe he'd had more than a healthy curiosity in the claim.

Was he more interested in the mine than he was in her? Had he known all along that there was gold in the Cavalry Blue?

Thirty-Four

"I want to go home," Kate said, and not for the first time.

"Not a chance," Travis calmly told her.

Forty-eight hours had passed since Chang Li had carried the wounded Kate to the sheriff's quarters. It was just past sunset, the start of another freezing cold night. Travis was stirring the new logs he'd thrown into the fireplace, watching the flames leap high and set shadows to dancing over the big, warm room. When he laid the poker aside, he turned and came to the bed.

"I know you want to go home, Kate, but I can't let you. You've lost blood, you're weak and you need bed rest. Besides, we're not sure who was behind this shooting. You wouldn't be safe alone." His tone was mellow, the look in his dark eyes one of compassion.

"I'm not afraid, Sheriff," Kate said softly, disarmed by his demeanor.

Travis's smile magically changed his handsome face like some inner burst of light from within. His obsidian eyes glittered when he asked, "Is there anything in this world you're afraid of, Kate VanNam?"

They stared at each other.

"You, Sheriff," she finally replied candidly, unnerved by the intimacy that circumstances beyond their control had forced on them.

Travis sank down onto a chair beside the bed. He reached for her hand and held it in both of his own. "Don't be afraid of me, Katie. I could never hurt you." He squeezed her fingers and said, "Do me a favor? Call me by my name, just once. Say it. You never have. Do it now."

Kate gazed into his dark, penetrating eyes and was mesmerized. She drew a shallow breath and said, "Thank you very much for all you've done for me, Travis."

"Again."

"Travis." Kate smiled at him. "Travis," she said once more. "Travis, Travis, Travis. I do like your name, Travis."

"And you'll call me by name from now on."

"Yes, I will, Travis."

He smiled and slowly lifted her hand as he bent his dark head. He placed the softest of kisses in her open palm, then lowered her arm and tucked it back beneath the covers.

"Now, how would you like some of Alice's delicious vegetable stew?" he asked.

"I'd like that." She favored him with a teasing smile before adding softly, "Tra...vis."

He nodded, rose to his feet and turned away, hoping she didn't see the foolish grin on his face. It thrilled him to simply hear her say his name.

Kate turned her head on the pillow and watched as he crossed the room. With his back to her, he stood at the cookstove ladling stew from a pan. She stared at him, wondering if he had any idea how glad she'd been to see him when he'd returned to his quarters at sunset.

Alice had been in and out several times, running over from the bakery across the street, bringing food and good cheer. And Chang Li, now well and worried about her, had stopped by to check on her and to assure her that he was keeping close watch on the mine. And, of course, Cal had spent long hours stretched out on the foot of bed, his mere presence a comfort.

But while she had soundly objected to being left alone with the sheriff at night, Kate found herself looking forward to the moment when, after a long day spent discharging his many duties, Travis returned to his quarters. And her.

Watching him now as his midnight hair gleamed

in the firelight and his wide shoulders strained the fabric of his tan gabardine shirt, Kate felt incredibly safe and content. Travis had taken excellent care of her, serving as both doctor and nurse. To her surprise, he had been unfailingly kind and understanding.

Also, more than once she had awakened from a catnap to catch him gazing at her with an expression of such unguarded tenderness in the depths of his beautiful eyes that she had fought the strong desire to reach out and lay her hand on his tanned face.

Kate sighed now with satisfaction.

Then almost immediately, she frowned.

What was she thinking? Had the bullet that struck her shoulder weakened her brain?

By the time he brought her supper tray to the bed, Kate was no longer speaking to him. She shook her head and refused to let him set the tray across her knees.

Baffled, Travis stood with the tray in his hands, saying, "Won't you try some of the stew?"

Kate stubbornly shook her head.

"But a minute ago you said you were hungry. What's wrong, Katie?"

"I told you not to call me Katie!" she snapped, eyes flashing. "Go away, Sheriff!"

"You need to eat something so that—"

"I am not hungry!"

"Fine." Travis walked over and placed the tray on the table. He sat down, shook out a napkin, draped it over his knee, picked up a spoon and began eating the hot vegetable stew and freshly baked yeast rolls Alice Hester had brought earlier in the day.

Kate had been hungry for the past hour. She had looked forward to enjoying the tasty stew and fresh bread, and now she watched the sheriff devouring it all as if he had forgotten she existed.

Kate grew angrier by the minute. And when, his bowl empty, Travis picked it up and headed back to the stove for a second helping, she could stand it no longer.

"Don't you dare eat all that stew!" she warned.

Over his shoulder he called, "Why not? You're not hungry. No sense letting good food go to waste." He was grinning, but he didn't let her see it. "You hungry now?"

"I...yes, a little."

"Coming right up, Katie."

She gritted her teeth, but said nothing. Travis came directly to the bed, eased her up into a sitting position and plumped the pillows behind her. He returned with the tray and placed it on her lap.

"Want me to feed you?"

"I can manage just fine, thank you." She looked up at him. "Stop hovering over me. I'm not helpless."

"Great," he said, backing away. "I'll go across the street, have a drink, maybe play a hand of poker."

Kate ignored him. She picked up a piece of bread, tore it in two and winced with pain.

Travis was back at her bedside in the blink of an eye. "You okay? Let me have a look."

Over her objections, he unbuttoned the nightshirt, pushed it aside, gingerly lifted the bandage and studied the wound. "No real harm done, but you must be more careful." He put the bandage back in place and rebuttoned the shirt. "Won't you let me help you a little?"

"How can you? You're leaving me alone, heading over to the Golden Nugget."

"Who said anything about the Golden Nugget?"

"Isn't that where you're going?"

"I'm going nowhere. I'm staying here with you," he stated. "All night."

"Thank you." Kate looked into his eyes and murmured softly, "Travis."

Thirty-Five

Travis came home earlier than usual the next evening. The sun had barely set when he walked through the door. Kate was not surprised. She knew the reason he was early. He couldn't wait to see her again. She knew because she felt the same way.

"Hi, Travis," she said with a bright, welcoming smile.

"Hi, Katie," he replied with a slow grin, unstrapping his gun belt and hanging it on the coat tree by the door. He looked around and asked, "Where's your cat?"

"He was restless, so I let him out," she said.

"You shouldn't be up walking," Travis warned as he sat down on the chair beside the bed. Affectionately, he reached out and cupped her cheek.

"You're cold," Kate said with concern, laying her hand atop his.

"It's freezing out there and...and..." Travis stopped speaking. He almost stopped breathing. He swallowed hard as Kate guided his hand from her face down under the covers.

"We have to warm you up," she said, briskly rubbing his hand through the blanket.

Travis cleared his throat. He felt his heart slam against his ribs. His hand was resting on the soft swell of her breasts as she pressed it close.

He said, "I'll, uh, build up the fire."

Carefully, he extracted his hand and rose to his feet. Hoping that she couldn't tell how badly he wanted to take her in his arms, he turned away, closed his eyes for a minute and collected himself.

For the moment he was successful.

But it didn't last.

Not for him, not for her.

The attraction that had been there from the beginning—an attraction both had tried so hard to deny—had quickly grown as Kate recuperated in Travis's care.

Four days had passed since the shooting, and Kate, a healthy young woman, had regained her strength. The color was back in her cheeks. She felt fine, but she was almost sorry that she did. As long as she was weak and helpless, she got to stay here near Travis.

At bedtime that night, she said, "Thanks to you, I'm about well, Travis." She drew a shallow breath. "I should go home tomorrow. Don't you think?"

Travis felt a squeezing in his chest. He came to the bed and sat down on the mattress's edge, facing her. He tried to sound casual when he said, "You don't want to rush it, Katie. Maybe you ought to stay a couple more nights."

"You're the doctor," she replied, barely able to hide her relief.

"I am and it's time you get some sleep." He spread the blanket over her, tucked it in around her shoulders, smiled, leaned down and gave her a very gentle, very brief good-night kiss.

That's all he meant to do.

But her lips were so soft and warm beneath his that he couldn't keep from kissing her again. This time it was not so gentle, not so brief. Travis turned his head slightly, slanted his lips across hers and covered her mouth with his own. He smoothly parted her lips, and Kate's pulse leaped at the first touch of his tongue on hers. Just as it had been that night at the mansion, his kiss was at once invasive, demanding and heart-stoppingly thrilling.

Travis put a hand in her hair and held her head still on the pillow while his mouth hotly plundered hers, taking, giving, swiftly igniting the fires of passion in them both. Kate squirmed and sighed while he kissed her over and over again. His lips were blazing hot and his sleek tongue filled her mouth, tasting, conquering, setting her on fire.

After numerous heated kisses, Travis abruptly

raised his head, hastily released Kate and—apologizing for his behavior—hurried out the back door to cool off in the freezing winds.

It didn't work.

He spent several long minutes out in the cold, taking deep breaths of the frigid air, warning himself to keep his hands off Kate. But when he came back inside, his blood was still scorching through his veins.

Kate sat up in the bed, smiled at him, threw back the covers and opened her arms wide. "Come here, Travis," she commanded.

"You sure, sweetheart?" he replied, his heart hammering.

She nodded. "I've never been more sure of anything in my life."

His legs weak, his pulse racing, Travis crossed to the bed. He again sat down on the edge of mattress and gazed at Kate for a long moment, saying nothing. He wanted this image of her, as she was on this cold autumn night, sitting in his bed and wearing his nightshirt, to be indelibly etched in his memory.

"Ah, Katie," he said at last, and reached for her.

In one swift motion, Travis lifted her from the bed, turned her about and sat her on his lap. He kept one hand around her waist, the other wrapped around the back of her neck. He drew her face down to his, and when her lips were less than an inch from his own, he said, "Kiss me, baby."

Kate kissed him.

She took his handsome face in her hands and pressed her lips to his. Travis quickly took over. He kissed her as he'd been kissing her before he went outside, and soon she was sighing and squirming on his knee. Her arms had gone around his neck and one hand was wound through his hair at the back of his head. The other eagerly explored his back through the fabric of his shirt.

When, breathless, she finally tore her lips from his, she hugged his dark head to her breasts and rested her chin against his forehead. It was then Kate realized that at some time during the onslaught of blazing kisses, as she squirmed on his knee, Travis had deftly removed her lace-trimmed pantalets. They lay on the floor by the bed.

Her face flushed.

She felt Travis's fingers at the buttons of the nightshirt. In seconds it was open to her waist. To Kate's relief, he rose to his feet with her in his arms, kissed her, carefully laid her in the bed and drew the covers up to her waist.

Kate watched as he unbuttoned his shirt midway down his chest, reached up behind his head and drew it up off in one swift movement. He sat down and took off his boots and stockings. He rose to his feet again and his hands went to the fly of his snug gabardine trousers. He shoved them to the floor, but kept his snowy white underwear on.

Then he got into bed with Kate.

"I have wanted," he said, his smooth baritone voice a caress, "to hold you like this in my arms from the first minute I looked out the window of the jail and saw your golden hair blazing in the sunlight."

"You mean it?"

"I mean it and I'll show you that I do." He took her in his arms and once again kissed and caressed her, his warm hand slipping inside the open nightshirt to gently enclose a soft breast. His callused thumb rubbed the rigid nipple and Kate tingled all over. His lips on hers, he gently toyed with the nipple until she was sighing and anxiously thrusting her tongue deep into his mouth.

When he ended the kiss, Kate whimpered in protest at the desertion. But not for long. Travis's burning lips pressed kisses to her chin, to the hollow of her throat, to the swell of her breasts. With his face he moved the open nightshirt out of his way and brushed a kiss on the nipple he had brought to life.

He felt Kate stiffen and exhale. He opened his mouth and warmly enclosed her left breast. Kate's head tossed on the pillow and she clutched handfuls of the sheet when he began to tease her nipple with his tongue, circling it, playfully biting, raking his teeth back and forth. And when finally he began to suck on it, Kate said his name with a sigh.

Travis was such an adroit lover and she was so enraptured, she hardly realized when her nightshirt came off and his underwear vanished. She only knew that she was now wonderfully naked and Travis was, too, and he was doing such incredibly sensual things to her that she might insist neither of them ever get dressed again.

Her eyes opening and closing with bliss as they kissed, Kate felt Travis's hard male flesh pressing against her thigh and his hand on her bare belly, touching, caressing and slowly sliding lower. She emitted a little gasp of excitement when his long fingers raked gently through the crisp curls between her thighs. With his thumb and little finger he gently urged her legs apart. Kate quickly opened them.

And heaven was hers.

Travis separated the golden coils with his middle finger and touched that tiny button of flesh that was wet and swollen and throbbing. Kate began to breathe through her mouth as he dipped the pad of his middle finger into the silky wetness her aroused body provided. He circled the flesh briefly before taking his wet fingers away, spreading the moisture on the head of his throbbing erection, then positioning himself between her legs.

He gripped her pulsing flesh, placed just the gleaming tip inside her and anxiously glanced up at her to see if she was all right. Her beautiful face was aglow and her hair was spread out on the pillow like a gleaming golden waterfall. Travis took his hand away, braced his stiffened arms on either side and easily slid into her.

Kate gasped at the feel of him, hot and hard and heavy, buried deep inside her. She clasped his biceps as he bent and kissed her and began a slow, intoxicating dance of desire. Both gloried in the languid loving. It was as though their bodies had been made for each other. The fit was perfect, the rhythm ideal.

But paradise was short-lived.

The naked pair were so hot for each other, they began to climax almost immediately.

"No…!" Kate murmured, eyes widening, heart pounding.

Travis was relieved she was coming so soon. She was too sweet, too beautiful, too desirable. All his pent-up passion was threatening to explode and come gushing forth. He couldn't hold back much longer. He swiftly speeded his movements, and Kate followed his lead. They moved together in a frenzy of building sexual delirium. They rocked the iron bedstead, its legs thumping loudly on the floor.

Seconds later Kate screamed in ecstasy, and Travis groaned as he joined her in a draining release that left him weak and light-headed.

"Please don't…don't move yet," Kate murmured when she could get her breath, her arms wrapped around his neck.

Travis laughed, turned his face into hers on the pillow and said, "Baby, I couldn't move if I tried."

Thirty-Six

In the sweet afterglow of lovemaking, the sated pair lay in each other's arms, talking, laughing, yawning.

And kissing.

Travis lay flat on his back in the middle of the bed with his arm around Kate. Her head resting on his shoulder, she lay on her side, snuggled close against him, a knee bent and resting on his flat belly. Her hand languidly explored the firm muscles of Travis's chest. "When you went outside, I wanted you to come back in and kiss me again."

"I know," he replied.

"You're conceited, Sheriff," Kate accused, and playfully pinched him.

"No, I'm clairvoyant," he said, sweeping a hand over the curve of her hip and down over her soft rounded buttocks.

"Oh, really," she said, lifting her head to look at him. "What am I thinking right this very minute?"

Travis grinned, then screwed up his face and closed his eyes as if concentrating deeply. "Wait… it's…it's coming to me. I've almost got it. Yes, yes, I have it!" He opened his eyes. "You want me to make love to you again."

"Why, you're a genius," she said with a happy smile.

"What'd I tell you?"

When Travis walked through the door the next evening, Kate tossed off the covers and scrambled up onto her knees to greet him. As soon as he'd hung his hat, heavy jacket and gun belt on the coat tree, he came directly to the bed.

"I thought this day would never end," he said. Putting his arms around Kate, he drew her up into his embrace.

"Me either," she murmured, just before he kissed her.

For a time Travis stood there beside the bed holding her, kissing her, urging the long tail of her nightshirt up. When his eager hands touched bare, warm flesh, he lifted his lips from hers. "Hey, what happened to your underwear?"

Her arms looped around his neck, her blue eyes aglow, Kate said, "I took it off before you got here." She smiled, catlike, and playfully licked at his lips. "Just in case."

"Brazen woman," he accused, "I do believe you're meaning to seduce me."

Travis carefully lifted the nightshirt up over Kate's head and tossed it aside. He lifted the bandage, checked her shoulder wound, asked if it hurt. She shook her head and shivered deliciously. He stepped back and gazed at her pale, slender body for a couple of heartbeats, then wrapped a hand around the back of her neck beneath her hair, drew her to him and kissed her again.

The smoldering sexual fire between them quickly blazed to life. Kate sighed when she felt Travis's warm hand cupping her breast. When his lips left hers and slipped down over her chest, she emitted a shriek of eager anticipation.

With her breath coming in quick little spurts, she continued to kneel on the mattress and watch, entranced, as his dark face joined his caressing hand at her breast. She held her breath when his heated lips enclosed a tingling nipple. Travis harmlessly bit and nibbled on her. It felt so good, but her pleasure increased when his mouth closed more securely over the nipple and his tongue fluttered back and forth and swirled around and around.

"Oh, Travis, Travis," she murmured, holding the back of his bent head and pressing him to her, mindless of her wounded shoulder.

Kate's eyes slid closed with bliss and her sense of touch and hearing increased dramatically. She was intensely aware of the texture of his lustrous hair in her clasping fingers, and the abrasive brush of his gabardine shirt against her naked flesh. The unmistakable pressure of his silver sheriff's badge rubbed against her ribs. The unbelievably pleasurable sensation of his burning lips tugged forcefully on her stinging nipple.

A chorus of pleasing sounds added to the intense delight of the moment. The snapping and crackling of the fire in the grate. The soft purring of Cal as he dozed and dreamed in front of the fireplace. The provocative sound of Travis greedily suckling her.

When at last he released her wet nipple and raised his head, Kate eagerly kissed him and began unbuttoning his shirt. When it was open down his dark chest, she swept it apart, put her arms around his neck and confided, "Since that hot day last summer when you came to my place and hung the front door at the mansion, I have wanted to feel your bare chest against me."

Travis clasped the twin cheeks of her bare bottom and drew her closer. Kate pressed her breasts against his chest, watching as her shiny wet nipples disappeared in the crisp, ticklish raven hair. Playing, brushing back and forth against his muscled torso, Kate smiled and sighed and enjoyed herself immensely.

So did Travis.

While she rubbed her soft breasts against his chest, Travis let his hand glide down her back to her bottom. Grasping the cleft of her buttocks, he reached down and under, to meet his other hand coming from the front. Lean fingers met and quickly began to work their magic.

Kate suddenly stopped her own sexual game to be a willing participant in his. "Travis, what...what are you doing to me?"

"Making love to you, sweetheart," he said, touching and toying with her in such a shockingly carnal way that she momentarily wondered if she was allowing him to do something perverse.

Then all at once she didn't care. This darkly handsome lover was coaxing liquid heat out of her with his stroking, probing fingers. And she was loving it. It was strangely erotic to be kneeling naked on the bed facing the fully clothed sheriff, while he stood there doing such lovely things to her.

With the hand in front, Travis cupped her groin, and his forefinger circled that point of raging desire. At the same time a skilled finger that came from behind was inside her, thrusting rhythmically. Kate gave herself up to the blinding passion.

She grabbed at the strong column of Travis's neck and clung to it while he masterfully caressed her with his lean, artistic hands. While she sighed and gasped and threw her head back, Travis teased and toyed and stroked. And all the while he murmured endearments in low, rich tones that added fuel to the flame.

When Kate felt the dam of desire about to burst,

she grew anxious and frantic, afraid she could wait no longer, and equally afraid she couldn't fully climax. Would she remain in this highly agitated state until pleasure turned to pain?

She needn't have worried.

Travis knew the frantic state she was in. He took loving care of her, and Kate soon cried out with joy and gratitude as he dexterously took her all the way to the top, his magical fingers coaxing her nearer and nearer to sexual nirvana.

And when her powerful orgasm came, she screamed at the intensity of it. Her body spasmed and she tossed her head, her unbound hair whipping into her face and his. When at last the tempest had passed, she weakly collapsed against Travis. He held her against his solid chest, stroking her back, her tangled hair, calming her, telling her everything was all right, that he had her and wouldn't let her go.

When finally she had stopped shaking, Kate raised her head, looked into his dark, flashing eyes and said, "Sheriff, don't ever do that to me again."

"You didn't like it?"

"I liked it too much," she candidly confessed.

Travis grinned. "Now how would you like a nice hot bath?"

"I would," she said. "And then?"

His grin widened, then disappeared, and his expressive dark eyes softened. "There are so many ways I want to make to love you, Kate. So many things I want to do to you. For you. With you."

Awed by the look in his eyes, she said, "Travis, I can hardly wait."

Half an hour later, a serene Kate sat in the suds-filled wooden tub directly in front of the fireplace. Her golden hair was pinned atop her head and a glass of red wine was in her right hand. She sighed with contentment as Travis, on his knees beside the tub, gingerly washed her back.

"You're too good at this," she said. He smiled. She ventured further, "And you're too good, as well, at removing a bullet from a foolish woman who got herself shot." Travis made no reply, but carefully swirled the washcloth along the top of her left shoulder, taking care not to get her bandage wet. "Travis?"

"Yes?"

"I know you're from Virginia. Doc Ledet told me. And he told me that you once studied to become a physician." She stopped speaking and held her breath.

"It's true, I did."

"What happened? Why didn't you become a doctor?"

"Squeamish stomach," Travis said flippantly. "Couldn't stand the sight of blood." He dropped the washcloth and rose to his feet. "How would you like for me to go across the street and pick us up a cou-

ple of sizzling steaks from the Bonanza Hotel dining room?"

Knowing she was not—at the present time—going to get anything further out of him regarding his
past, Kate smiled and said, "Hurry back."

"Fifteen minutes at the outside."

Travis rebuttoned his open shirt, strapped on his
gun belt and thrust his long arms into the sleeves of
his heavy woolen coat. He shoved his hat on his
head, opened the door leading into the jail, then
closed it and stepped back inside. He came to the tub,
laid a hand atop her head, bent from the waist and
brushed a kiss to her lips. "Anybody bangs on either
door, ignore it, you hear me?"

"Who would…?"

"You heard me. I'm locking you in," he said, then
turned and left.

Thirty-Seven

Travis locked the door between the jail and his private quarters. He walked through the darkened space with its empty cells and went on into the front office, where a lone lamp burned atop his scarred desk. Buttoning his heavy jacket, he glanced out the glass-paned windows.

The sun had set more than an hour ago, but it was light as day outside. It was snowing. Hard. And the winds were howling, forcefully blowing the large white flakes in a southerly direction. Travis laughed.

Apparently while he and Kate were making love—oblivious to everything but each other—an early autumn blizzard had roared down out of the Sierras to blanket the town of Fortune.

Travis squinted through the frosty windows. The street was completely covered in white and the sidewalks were deserted. Which suited Travis fine. A raging winter storm generally meant a peaceful night, as miners and hustlers and gamblers alike were more interested in seeking a warm place to escape the elements than causing trouble.

Travis turned up his collar and stepped out into the wind-driven snow. He headed directly toward the Bonanza Hotel. With the icy crust crunching under his boot heels, he started across the street. Before he reached the hotel, he automatically glanced up at the third floor suite of Winn DeLaney.

The window shades were all pulled down, but lights shone inside. Someone was pacing back and forth before the windows. It had to be DeLaney.

Travis frowned.

There was little doubt in his mind that DeLaney had something to do with Kate getting shot. Not that he'd meant for that to happen. The shooting was undoubtedly a screwup on the part of DeLaney's two hired thugs.

Ducking his head against the blinding snow, Travis hurried on. His biggest concern was that DeLaney might pack up and leave town before Jiggs and the posse could find Kelton and Spears. Travis ground his teeth in frustration. He knew if he could have ten short minutes with the despicable pair, he could get the truth out of them.

This wasn't the way they had planned it that night in San Francisco. It had seemed like such a foolproof plan. He had supposed that by now he would be Kate's husband and that she would eagerly sign over the Cavalry Blue to him.

But nothing had gone as planned and now, restless and worried, Winn DeLaney wondered if he should hastily check out and leave town as Melly kept insisting they do. They could just slip away in the midst of this raging snowstorm and give up his dearest dreams. It would be the wise thing to do.

No, damn it! Why should he leave? Why behave as if he had something to hide? With every passing day, the odds of a posse locating Spears and Kelton lessened. Surely they were long gone and would never be brought in.

Winn brightened a little at the thought. His secret was safe. No one had reason to suspect he had anything to do with the shooting. Kate VanNam was his treasured sweetheart, the light of his life. And the whole town knew it.

All he had to do was remain calm and behave as though he was innocent. Then, when Kate was better and back in her mansion, they would pick up where they'd left off. He would ardently court her and marry her as quickly as possible. And once he had properly—or improperly—made love to Kate, his swooning bride would be more than willing to sign over all her property to her adoring husband.

Smiling now as he anticipated the wealth that would soon be his, Winn stopped pacing. He impulsively raised a window shade and looked out to check on the storm. He caught sight of someone crossing the snowy street. He lifted a hand and rubbed at the ice crystals forming on the inside of the glass.

And cursed under his breath.

The sheriff was crossing the street against the wind. Winn quickly sank back, but continued to watch McCloud. How he hated the arrogant, nosey, small-town lawman. The bastard was keeping Kate in his quarters behind the jail, and not allowing anyone in to see her.

Winn scowled. *If that handsome sheriff ever gets his hands on Miss VanNam, we're sunk!* Melly's words came back to him and he involuntarily shuddered as he muttered an oath.

Winn shook his head as if to clear it. He was being foolish. Kate felt nothing for McCloud. She didn't even like the marshal.

Kate reached for a large white towel and rose from the tub. She got out and stood before the fire, languidly drying off. She wrapped the damp towel around her slender body, carefully tucking it in over her breasts.

She pivoted about and stood with her back to the fire. She looked curiously around at the big warm room where she had been for the past five days and nights. Spartan, totally masculine quarters in which she had spent the happiest moments of her life.

Beside the door opening into the jail stood the tall coat tree. A heavy greatcoat hung there, and an old battered straw hat. A black leather vest. A pair of big roweled spurs. A coiled length of rope.

At the center of the room was the table, with a straight-back chair pulled up to it. The chair's twin was beside the bed, where Travis had spent long hours watching over her.

Beside her and just to the left of the fireplace was a much used overstuffed easy chair and matching ottoman. A discarded gabardine shirt was tossed over the chair's back. Directly across from the fireplace was the big double bed with its heavy iron bedstead. The sheets and blanket were badly rumpled from her kneeling there, squirming, as Travis made love to her.

Kate shivered at the vivid recollection of what he had done to her, of the ecstasy she had experienced at Travis's masterful hands. Before this night was over, she wondered, would he make love to her again? She hoped so. He probably would. After all, he hadn't even undressed yet....

Blushing, Kate looked away from the bed and focused on the tall bureau standing against the wall by the back door. In need of a freshly laundered nightshirt, she tiptoed barefoot across the cold wooden floor and stopped before the chest of drawers. She smiled when she saw a small stack of poker chips atop the bureau.

Beside the chips were a couple of thin black cigars and box of sulphur matches. A brush with a comb stuck in its bristles lay on its side. A black silk bandanna was neatly folded. She touched a small pocket knife with a fancy pearl handle. And a leather-bound copy of Alexandre Dumas's *The Count of Monte Cristo.*

Kate glanced at herself in the mirror above the bureau, then opened the top drawer, looked inside and saw only neatly pressed shirts. She closed it, opened the second. Underwear and stockings. She closed that one and opened the middle drawer. She lifted out a white, neatly folded nightshirt, and started to close the drawer.

Kate stopped abruptly, her brow wrinkling. She laid the nightshirt atop the bureau.

She'd spotted the corner of a tintype peeking out from under a stack of nightshirts. Sliding it out from under the garments, she picked it up and stared unblinking at the smiling likeness of a strikingly beautiful woman with pale hair and glowing eyes.

Darling, my heart belongs to you
Your adoring Roxanne

Kate knew immediately knew who the woman was. The aristocratic Southern beauty over whom Travis had fought a duel! He had killed a man for the love of this woman. And he'd kept this tintype all these years.

Kate's initial emotion was jealousy. Then anger. Both were fleeting. *She* had Travis now. Not Roxanne. She didn't hate Roxanne; she was grateful to the foolish woman. If not for the pampered beauty, Travis would never have come out West and she would never have met him.

"Thanks, Roxanne," Kate addressed the woman in the picture. "I'll take good care of Travis. Such good care he'll forget you ever existed."

She shoved the tintype back where she had found it. She returned to the fire, dropped the towel and slipped on the clean nightshirt, but she did not button it.

When Travis returned, Kate was standing with her back to the fire. Her hair was brushed out around her shoulders and held off her face with his black silk bandanna.

"Jesus, baby, what are you doing up?" he asked, snowflakes clinging to his shoulders and raven hair. He set the covered tray atop the table and said proudly, "Got us a couple of the best looking steaks you've ever seen."

Kate came directly to the table. When Travis turned to look at her, she reached up and clasped the lapels of his snow-dampened coat and said, "Great. I'm famished, aren't you?"

Before he could reply, she smiled saucily, rose up on tiptoe, drew his face down to hers and kissed him the way he had kissed her that first time. She wanted to kiss him with such passionate purpose that he'd forget every other woman, including Roxanne.

Thirty-Eight

"The steaks will get cold," Kate laughingly warned when the dazzled Travis shed his jacket where he stood and swept her up into his arms.

"As long as you don't," he said, and carried her to the bed.

He yanked the covers down out of the way and lowered her to the mattress. Sighing, Kate leaned back against the stacked pillows and raised her arms above her head. She winced when Travis grabbed the hem of her nightshirt, flipped it up to her waist, leaned down and pressed a burning kiss to her bare belly.

"Travis," she whispered, flushing hotly. She modestly shoved the nightshirt down.

"Why don't you take that thing off?" he suggested as he stood unbuttoning his shirt.

"I'll let you," she said, and watched, transfixed, as he hastily undressed.

His boots were kicked off, and in seconds Travis had stripped to his skin. In the instant before he climbed into bed, Kate was allowed a fleeting glimpse of him in all his naked glory.

He was a beautiful specimen of potent masculinity, tall and lean and perfectly configured. Conceit and cockiness seemed reasonable in a male with such remarkable good looks and physical ability. His height implied power; his darkness, warmth and passion. His strong sexual magnetism had, from the first time she'd seen him standing at the river landing, both frightened and excited her.

Kate shivered with anticipation now as he got into bed and put his long arm around her. Travis again tossed her nightshirt up to her waist. This time she made no move to lower it. His dark eyes smoldered when he leaned close and kissed her mouth. While they kissed, Kate could feel the heat and hardness of his heavy erection surging against her hip. With his lips fused to hers, Travis took her hand and guided it down to him.

After a long, invasive kiss, his lips left hers. So did his hand.

Travis looked into her eyes. "Touch me, sweetheart. Love me."

Kate curiously glanced down at the surging male flesh rising from a dense growth of raven curls. She gently tightened her fingers around him. She looked back up his face and saw the fire in his beautiful dark eyes. Their gazes locked and held as Kate caressed him with an expertise born of passion. It was a riveting moment for them both.

Travis enjoyed the sweet agony as if it was the first time a woman had ever touched him. To have this beautiful blond angel's soft hand warmly stroking him while he gazed into her glowing blue eyes was a pleasure beyond compare. His belly tight, his heart hammering, Travis wanted time to stand still. To stop this minute. To have this beautiful young woman with whom he was falling in love hold him in her loving hand forever.

To never let him go.

Kate knew exactly what was running through his mind, and she experienced a quick surge of heady female power. It was thrilling to know that this big, strong man was, at this moment, enslaved by her. She dominated him with the mere stroking of her fingers. Conquered him by looking steadily into his eyes. Highly erotic. Exciting beyond compare. She could, if she wished, lead him anywhere...

Travis abruptly tore Kate's hand away, sat her back against the stacked pillows and pushed her nightshirt up over her breasts. He gently urged her legs apart, wrapped a hand around the back of her left knee, raised it slightly and cocked it outward.

And then it was his turn to master her with only the touch of his hand.

Kate watched with held breath as his lean brown fingers caressed her pale white belly. She sucked her bottom lip between her teeth as he raked the tips of his fingers through the crisp coils of golden hair between her thighs.

And when he touched that spot where all her burning desire was centered, Kate lifted her eyes to meet his. As it had been when she caressed him, their gazes locked and held. They looked steadily into each other's eyes while Travis's long, tapered fingers explored and circled and teased the wet throbbing flesh she so willingly allowed him to claim.

Kate enjoyed this lovely torture as if it were not simply the pleasurable prelude to total lovemaking. To have this man's artistic hand touching her in that most intimate of all places while she gazed into his smoldering eyes was pure joy. Her stomach fluttering, her nipples stinging, she wanted time to stand still. To stop ticking away. She wanted this gentle man with whom she was falling in love to keep his loving hand on her forever.

Travis knew exactly what was running through Kate's mind, and he was supremely confident of his masculine power. It was arousing to know that this slender, fragile woman was, at this moment, ruled by him. He controlled her with the stroke of his fingers. Mastered her by looking into her eyes. He could, if he so chose, have her do anything he wanted...

Burning up, wanting her as he'd never wanted a

woman, he took his hand from Kate and agilely moved between her legs. He slid down and carefully positioned himself so that only the smooth tip of his engorged shaft was touching her slick swollen sweetness.

With his weight supported on a stiffened arm, he kissed her and said, "Let's quit torturing each other, sweetheart."

"Yes, let's," she whispered breathlessly, and sighed with bliss when he slid easily into her.

Knowing she was as aroused as he, Travis waited only a few seconds before he began the deep, rhythmic thrusting both their bodies demanded. Instantly the passion they thought couldn't get any hotter escalated. Kate clung to Travis and eagerly tilted her pelvis up to meet each deep driving plunge of his hard male flesh. She bucked and thrust wildly against him, her feverish body gripping the throbbing flesh that impaled her, filled her, stretched her.

Both wanted the pleasure to last; both knew it wouldn't. They couldn't hold back much longer. They were too hot for each other, their bodies too aroused by the teasing foreplay.

In minutes they were gripped in a spiraling explosion of heat, swept into a vortex of intense carnal gratification. It buffeted the joined pair with an ecstasy so intense it was frightening. They moaned and gasped and went at each other with an animalistic ardor that rocked the bed and twisted the sheets.

"Travis!" Kate screamed his name as she wrapped

her arms around his neck, her legs around his back, and held on for dear life.

She knew that he was following her into paradise when she felt the hot liquid gushing high up inside her.

When it was finished, Travis fell tiredly onto his back beside Kate. Their hearts racing, their bodies perspiring, they lay limp and immobile for several long minutes, fighting to get their breath. It was Travis who stirred first.

"You okay? Did I hurt you, baby?" he asked.

"No," she assured him. Then she laughed musically and said, "I suppose the steaks are cold."

Travis lifted one of her hands to his lips, turned it over, kissed the palm, and said, "I'll warm 'em up."

Hours later, after they'd devoured the juicy steaks, they again lay in bed, sated, happy, reluctant to go to sleep despite the lateness of the hour. Gripped in the first sweet blush of falling in love, they felt that every moment was precious, golden, not to be missed. The simple act of lying in bed together and knowing that come morning they would awaken together, was delightful beyond their wildest dreams.

Wise enough to suppose that this was an opportune time to learn more about this man in whose arms she lay, Kate broached the subject of the mysterious woman whose tintype she had seen beneath the folded nightshirts.

"Travis, am I the only woman in your life?"

"The only one," he said with a yawn.

Kate traced the line of dark hair going down the center of his stomach with her fingertip. "I heard a rumor that you once fought a duel over a beautiful woman." She waited.

"You heard correctly."

"Were you terribly in love with her?"

"I thought I was," Travis said.

"And?" she gently prodded.

Travis smiled. "Katie, it was a long time ago."

"I don't care. I want you to tell me about it. Please."

Travis nodded. And told her everything.

He calmly revealed how a decade ago a beautiful, conniving thirty-one-year-old Richmond divorcée had captivated him when he was a green twenty-two-year-old. The woman, Mrs. Roxanne Bond, had played him for a fool and had, for sport, goaded one of her many lovers into challenging him to a duel for her affections. A duel in which he had killed a man. He had taken a man's life and the deed had ended his hopes of a medical career. And then Roxanne had coolly informed him that if he was not going to be a successful physician, he couldn't expect her to waste any more time on him.

"Within twenty-four hours I left Virginia, heading west," Travis concluded "And here I am, sheriff of Fortune." He paused, then said, "Now I've done my bit. It's your turn."

Kate was dying to ask a million questions, but she

refrained. She began to talk about her life back in Boston, telling Travis how she and her older brother had been raised by her dear uncle as children of privilege before the vast family fortune had been lost.

"So you *do* have a brother?" Travis interrupted. "Where is he now, Kate?"

"I honestly don't know. I no longer consider him a brother."

"What happened?"

"Once the family fortune was gone, Gregory left, giving no thought to the welfare of my uncle Nelson and me. We never heard from him again." She fell silent.

"Go on," Travis urged.

Kate picked up the story, telling of how she had inherited the run-down mansion and the Cavalry Blue from her great-aunt Arielle VanNam Colfax on the very day her dear uncle passed away. Her uncle had managed to save a little cash, bless him, and she had used it to come to California.

"And the once great VanNam fortune?" Travis asked when she had finished the story.

"Flowers." Kate's voice was expressionless.

"Of course." A smile lit Travis's face. "The tulip craze."

"Worse yet," Kate said.

"Poppies?" He was frowning now. "The opium trade?"

"Heavens no!" She laughed at such an absurd

idea. "We'd still be rich were that the case." She sighed then and said, "The VanNams made and lost a great fortune in Dutch hyacinth bulbs."

"I'm sorry, sweetheart," Travis said.

"Don't be. Everything has worked out for the best. If the fortune hadn't been lost, I would never have come to California." She raised herself up onto an elbow and said, "And now I've found the gold."

"You're wealthy again."

"Yes, but that's not enough. I want it all."

"All?"

"I want you," she said, and placed two fingers on his sensuous lips. "I want your heart."

Travis grinned. "Baby, if you can find it, you can have it."

Thirty-Nine

The lovers remained awake far into the night.

With each passing hour they explored each other fully, both physically and mentally. It was not just Travis's bare brown body that Kate so eagerly examined. She was intent on learning what went on in his keen mind, as well.

It was the same with Travis. Not satisfied to simply explore every silky inch of Kate's pale, naked form, he urged her to tell him her deepest secrets, to never hide her feelings from him.

Neither had shared their innermost thoughts with anyone else before. It was a brand-new world for the determined, independent Kate and the dauntless, stoic Travis.

In the short time she'd been in his care, Kate had learned about passion from the patient, experienced

Virginian. And Travis, who knew all about passion, had learned about love from the sweet, guileless Bostonian.

She was, he happily realized, nothing like the worldly thirty-one-year-old divorcée who had played him for a fool a decade ago. To this kind, caring young beauty he could entrust his heart with no fear of her breaking it. She was not that kind of woman.

As if she had read his thoughts, a sleepy Kate said softly, "Don't be afraid to love me, Travis."

"I won't be."

After a pause, she asked, "Should I be jealous of Roxanne?"

"No. I was a boy then, sweetheart. I'm not now."

"Should I be jealous of any other woman or women who—"

"I love you, Kate VanNam. You and nobody else."

"That's the right answer, Sheriff."

At seven the next morning Travis slipped out of bed while Kate slept on. He built a fire in the grate, washed up, shaved, dressed and came to the bed to kiss her goodbye.

"What are you doing up?" she asked with a yawn.

"I work here, remember."

"Mmm. So you'll be just inside in the jail?"

"Yes. If I have to leave for any length of time, I'll let you know. Now go back to sleep, honey. I'll check on you later this morning."

"Okay," she said, her eyes closing. Then all at

once she lunged up, a frown on her face, the covers falling to her waist. "Where's Cal? Is he outside in the cold? He'll freeze to death!"

Travis laughed. "Relax! He's in the jail, remember? I put him in there the minute I got home yesterday afternoon. And I fed him the leftover steak last night, after you fell asleep. Want me to bring him in here?"

"No, not really," she said, wanting only to go back to sleep. "You'll look after him?"

Travis grinned. "You know I will."

Kate smiled. "And you'll look after me?"

"For the rest of my life, sweetheart."

With a steaming-hot cup of coffee in his hand, Travis went into the jail. He looked about for Cal and saw the big calico stretched out, sound asleep, on a cot in one of the empty cells. Travis didn't disturb him.

He went on into the front office and stood looking out the windows as he drank his black coffee. The snow had stopped falling. At this early hour the streets were still deserted. The town had not yet stirred to life.

Travis circled his desk, sat down and leaned back in his chair. He glanced across the street at the Bonanza Hotel, automatically focusing on the third floor suite of Winn DeLaney. Travis clenched his jaw. He was still afraid Delaney would sneak out of town before Jiggs could bring in Kelton and Spears.

While Travis sat at his desk, a bright alpine sun rose, and with it the temperature. By nine o'clock the snow had begun to melt and the town to bustle. Miners with their axes were heading to their diggings. Merchants were wheeling out carts to display their wares. The ping of a blacksmith's hammer rang out from his shop past the livery stable.

Across the street at the Bonanza Hotel, a light came on in the third floor corner suite.

And Travis's dark eyes narrowed.

Winn DeLaney got out of bed, drew on his black silk robe and crossed to the front windows. He raised a shade and peered curiously out. The storm had passed. The sun was shining brightly, the snow quickly melting.

Winn looked across the street to the city jail. He scowled when he saw Sheriff McCloud seated behind his desk. For a man who the Committee of Vigilance paid to get out on the streets and keep the peace, McCloud sure spent a lot of time sitting behind his desk, doing nothing.

Winn irritably yanked the shade down and turned away.

"Is it still snowing?" asked the voluptuous darkhaired woman in his bed.

"No. The sun's out, the snow's melting."

Melisande sat up, pushed her hair back from her eyes. "So we could get out if we wanted to? Winn, let's go. Let's leave right now while we still have the chance."

"We're not leaving," he said, pacing restlessly

back and forth. "How many times do I have to say it? We are not going without the gold!"

Melisande threw back the covers and rose from the bed. Hands on her hips, she said, "Damn you, Winn! It is too dangerous. We are going to get caught if we stay. Any minute that posse could ride back into town and—"

"Doesn't matter if they do. They'll come back empty-handed and that will be the end of it. Spears and Kelton will get lost in some other primitive mining camp and no longer pose a threat." He paused, took a deep breath and said, "Then as soon as the girl is feeling better and is back home in her mansion, I'll go up and successfully seduce her."

"Oh, really?" Melisande snorted derisively. "That woman's been shut up over there with that handsome lawman for the past five days. I'll wager eight to five she's already been 'successfully seduced.'"

"Kate VanNam is a naive, well-bred young lady who would never—"

"Wouldn't she? She's a woman first and Mc-Cloud's one magnetic male." Melisande lifted bare shoulders and hugged herself. "He exudes potent sexuality from every pore, so I wouldn't be a bit surprised if—"

"Will you kindly shut up and let me think!"

Well before noon most of the snow had melted. Only a few traces remained on the shady sides of buildings. The town was humming with life. Travis had ventured out a half-dozen times, stopping in here and there, saying good-morning, checking on people, keeping the peace with his presence. But he never went far enough away that he couldn't keep an eye on the jail's front entrance.

Until a sudden occurrence demanded his attention. He'd been back inside only long enough to take off his coat when an upset man in a bartender's apron came running in, calling his name. "Sheriff McCloud! Sheriff McCloud! Come quick! Spanish Rose and Bad Bertha are going at it again down at Tillie's. Rose is pulling Bertha's hair and Bertha's threatening to slit Rose's throat."

"Be right there," Travis said, already rising from his chair. Not bothering to grab his coat, he was to the door when he caught sight of the stick-thin, toothless H. Q. Blankenship coming across the street. Travis called out to the old sourdough.

"What do you need, Sheriff?" Blankenship hurried over.

"I'm deputizing you, H.Q.," he said, and pinned his silver star to the man's narrow chest. Travis took a weapon from his gun belt and handed it, butt first, to the surprised man. "Take this loaded Colt and stand guard here in the jail. Anybody tries to get back there to Miss VanNam, stop them."

"Yes, sir, Marshal," said the flattered H.Q., his

pale eyes brightening with excitement. "I'm not to let anyone visit her?"

"Alice Hester or Chang Li, nobody else," Travis said, and was gone.

Winn DeLaney had finished a late breakfast in the Bonanza dining room. He was entering the lobby, where he liked to sit and keep watch on the city jail, just as Sheriff McCloud came hurrying on the heels of an excited little man in a white bartender's apron.

Winn quickly crossed to the hotel's front windows and watched as the coatless sheriff trotted down the sidewalk toward the southern end of town.

He smiled. This would be, he decided, the opportune time to visit his wounded sweetheart. There'd be nobody there to keep him away from Kate. He'd get the chance to explain that the big, bullying sheriff was responsible for him not visiting sooner. He had wanted to come to her at once, to comfort and care for her. He had worried himself sick over her.

Winn exited the hotel. He looked far down the street, where a group of men, shouting and whistling, had gathered outside Tillie's bordello. He stared unblinking as the sheriff waded into the mob, pushed men out of the way and disappeared inside.

Barely able to hide his glee, Winn strolled as casually as possible to the hotel's entryway. He stepped outside and looked across the street to the jail. And he promptly frowned. A woman was going in the

front door. Damn it to hell! No doubt it was that widowed bakery owner, the chirpy, cheerful Alice Hester. What a nuisance. But she was a good friend of
Kate's. No telling how long Mrs. Hester would stay.

Winn muttered an oath and went back inside.

"Good Morning, H.Q."

"Morning, Miss Knight," he said, his eyes round
with surprise when he looked up to see who was
coming in the door. "What brings you out at this
early hour?"

Valentina smiled and held up a fancy oval box
covered in shimmering gold paper and tied with a
purple ribbon. "The wounded patient, of course. How
is Miss VanNam today?"

"I don't rightly know," H.Q. said, and shook his
head. "I'm not allowed back there. And, I'm sorry to
say, you're not either, Miss Knight."

"No? Why on earth not?"

"Sheriff McCloud deputized me," H.Q. said
proudly, sticking out his bony chest. "Made me vow
I'd not let anyone in to see her, saving that little Chinaman what works for her and Mrs. Hester from the
bakery."

Valentina laughed gaily, waved a gloved hand in the
air and said, "I'm certain the sheriff didn't mean me."

"Alls I know is Travis said 'keep everybody out
'cept Chang Li and Mrs. Hester.'"

"Be reasonable, H.Q. I've come as a good neigh-

bor and have brought the poor dear a box of chocolates to brighten her spirits. Now, stay where you are
and keep an eye out for mischief makers."

With the worried little man frowning after her, Valentina went on into the back of the jail. All the cells
were empty. Not a single prisoner inhabited the place,
only a big calico cat dozing peacefully on a bunk.

Valentina walked down the corridor between the
cells. She stopped before the closed door leading
into Travis's private quarters, drew a deep breath and
knocked.

"Just a minute," Kate called out, and frantically
looked about for her discarded nightshirt. She spotted it across the room, draped over a chair. She
bounded out of bed, dashed over and grabbed up the
garment. She yanked it over her head, winced in pain
from the quick jerky movement, stuck her arms
through the sleeves and went back to the bed.

"Who is it?" she called. "Alice, is that you?
Chang Li?"

Valentina opened the door and stepped inside.
Kate's eyes widened when she saw the handsome,
dark-haired woman who was splendidly attired in a
Cossack-style hat, with an ermine wrap slung across
a black tunic and black stockings.

Closing the door, Valentina said, "You don't know
me, Miss VanNam. I'm Valentina Knight."

"A pleasure to meet you, Miss Knight," Kate replied with a genuine smile.

"Is it?" Valentina asked, venturing closer. "I think it only fair to tell you that I own and operate the Golden Nugget saloon. I sing there every night. It is not the kind of place young ladies like you... So if you don't want to associate with my kind, I'll turn around and leave."

"No, no, please, take off your wrap and sit down. You're very welcome here, Miss Knight."

Valentina smiled then and approached the bed. "In that case, I brought you some Belgian chocolates and I'd bet anything that you have a sweet tooth."

"You've found me out," Kate said with a laugh. "Thank you so much for coming to visit, Valentina. Please, do sit down. Let's get acquainted."

The woman nodded, took off her gloves, hat and wrap, tossed them all across the foot of the bed. She then took the offered chair. She looked curiously around and mused aloud, "I've never been in this room and..." She caught herself and said no more. "You feeling better? I trust the sheriff is taking good care of you."

"Yes, he is," Kate said, hoping her face was not red. "How fortunate for me that Chang Li thought to bring me here to the marshal, since Doc Ledet was out of town."

"Indeed. It was quick thinking on Chang Li's part," said Valentina.

The two women, carefully examining one another, at first made stilted small talk. But in no time, they were becoming comfortable with each other. They exchanged stories about their respective homes. Kate talked about her life back in Boston, very different from the one she now lived in Fortune. Valentina spoke fondly of her New Orleans home. Said she missed the charming old city as well as the mild, semitropical climate.

"I've stayed too long," she announced after twenty minutes. "I'll tire you."

"No, not at all," Kate assured her. "I feel fine. Really."

Valentina got to her feet. She picked up her discarded hat, wrap and gloves. "Nevertheless, I must go now."

"Come back real soon," Kate said.

Valentina laid a hand on Kate's shoulder and patted gently. "You're a wise and very kind young lady, Kate. No wonder..." Again her words trailed away. "Thank you for your hospitality."

"Thank you for coming. And for the chocolates." Kate knew, after only this brief, cordial visit, that Valentina Knight was in love with Travis. She felt a surge of compassion for the other woman. "Does he know?" she softly asked.

Valentina knew exactly what she meant. She gave no reply, just shook her head, turned and walked away. When she reached the door, Kate said her name. Valentina turned to look at her.

Kate said, "If it's any consolation, I'll take good care of him, I promise."

"You'd better," she warned with a smile. "If you don't, you'll answer to me." She quickly turned away before Kate could see the shimmer of tears that sprang to her eyes.

Forty

"Out of the way, Sacramento Slim," Sheriff Mc-Cloud ordered the tall, slender man with a slashing zigzag scar across his forehead. "Move it," he said to Two Fingers Johnson and Rattlesnake Jack.

Travis pushed his way through the whooping crowd and into Tillie's two-story establishment. In the receiving parlor a couple of furious women were standing toe to toe, gouging and biting and cursing each other.

The pretty young spitfire, Spanish Rose, was viciously pulling Bad Bertha's long, dyed-red hair. Bad Bertha was squealing like a stuck pig and desperately trying to get to the jewel-handled dagger she kept in the satin garter that encircled her fleshy thigh. Both women were bleeding from scratches to their faces, bosoms and arms.

"Ladies, ladies," Travis said, and rushed into the fray.

He stepped up behind the red-haired Bad Bertha, wrapped a long arm around her thickening waist and held on for dear life as he reached down and deliberately relieved her of the dagger. He handed the weapon over his shoulder to an anxious Tillie, whose major concern was for the parlor's fine imported furniture. The fighting women had already smashed a pair of priceless porcelain vases and turned a cherrywood table into a worthless pile of splinters.

Bad Bertha, the angered redhead, shoved a sharp elbow into Travis's chest and tried to shake him off. He hung on, despite the pain. Spanish Rose pressed her advantage, yanking her opponent's hair forcefully and pulling her down. Bad Bertha slammed against the square-carved piano, her shoulder striking the ivory keys, her knees hitting the carpet. She dragged Travis down with her and then fell over backward atop him.

Summoning all his strength, Travis squirmed out from under her and went after Spanish Rose. Rose spat and cursed and threatened to kill him. Travis yanked her up, tossed her, kicking and screaming, over his shoulder, and almost made it out of the room.

But not quite.

Bad Bertha quickly recovered, charged and knocked both Travis and Rose to the floor in the arched doorway leading into the corridor. Bertha screamed like a panther and jumped right on top of the downed pair. Most of the crowd outside had shoved their way in, determined not to miss the fun. Cheers and whistles and applause reigned and bets were taken on who the winner of the three-way brawl would be.

Travis McCloud was the heavy favorite, though clearly he was currently at a disadvantage.

The sheriff was outnumbered, and once the two women declared a truce, they turned their wrath on him. And, while they could and did kick and bite and scratch and try their best to hurt him, Travis had never, would never, hit a woman. Nor harm one in any way. His role was that of peacemaker—to subdue the combatants and quell the disturbance.

That's just what he did.

After fifteen minutes that seemed like an hour to him, Travis came out the victor. But not before he'd suffered a bitten ear, kneed groin, scratched cheek, torn shirt and bruised chest.

Struggling to catch his breath, he lay flat on his back on the floor. On either side of him, a restraining arm clamped firmly over her waist, lay a weak, winded woman. Spanish Rose had a bloody nose, plus her red-satin dress was torn, her fishnet stockings in ruins. And Bad Bertha had a black, swollen eye, scrapes and contusions, and badly tangled hair.

Travis turned his head, looked at one, then the

other. Both smiled sheepishly at him. Then they giggled. In seconds everyone, including the town sheriff, was laughing, and the relieved Tillie shouted to be heard, saying, "Champagne on the house for everyone!"

Winn DeLaney couldn't believe his eyes.

He had been wrong when he'd assumed Kate's visitor was the widow Hester. It was Valentina Knight who walked out of the jail. He wouldn't have thought the two would have known each other.

Miss Knight was leaving now and the sheriff was still absent from the jail. Winn knew this was his opportunity to see Kate. He brushed imaginary lint from his lapels, smoothed his hair back off his temples and stepped out onto the sidewalk. He cautiously looked three blocks down the street to Tillie's Pleasure Palace. The crowd was still packed in there. He could safely assume that the sheriff was, too.

Winn smiled, pleased, and started to step down into the street. He stopped abruptly and cursed. Another woman was entering the city jail. This time it was Alice Hester. Winn shook his head. For God sake, who else would be running in and out of there? How could Kate be expected to recuperate if she was never allowed to get any rest?

Exhaling with growing frustration, he turned and went back inside the Bonanza Hotel.

* * *

"Thank you so much, Sheriff McCloud," said the grateful Tillie, nodding and setting the feather in her upswept hair to dancing.

"Don't mention it," Travis said, taking the perfumed handkerchief she offered and blotting the blood away from his scratched cheek.

"You don't mean to take Bertha and Rose in, do you, Marshal? It surely won't be necessary to toss them in jail, will it?" asked Tillie, concerned that their absence would hurt business.

"No, but I'm holding you responsible for them, Tillie," Travis warned.

"Bless you, Sheriff. I'll see to it they cause no more trouble."

"You better. If I have come back down here…"

"You won't," Tillie assured him. "Tell him, girls," she prompted them.

"We'll behave, Sheriff," said Spanish Rose.

"If I hurt you, Marshal, I apologize," offered Bad Bertha.

"I'm fine, but if you two keep fighting, somebody's really going to get hurt."

"It won't happen again," Tillie said, and rushed him out the door.

Winn watched and waited.

He was overjoyed when Alice Hester stayed inside the jail for less than five minutes. Apparently, she needed to get back to the bakery, and had only come over to bring Kate something to eat.

Winn waited until the widow was back inside her shop. Then he exited the hotel, looked up the street and down. He saw nobody who might conceivably be going to visit Kate. No doubt the little Chinaman was at the mine.

Winn crossed the street, rehearsing what he would say to Kate. He would tell her how he'd been worried sick about her and how the tyrannical sheriff had refused to let him in to visit. By the time he reached the sidewalk outside the jail, Winn had a touching speech all thought out and ready to deliver in his most sincere tone of voice.

He stepped into the door of the jail and frowned when he saw, seated behind the sheriff's desk, a skinny, toothless old man.

"Don't get up," Winn said, waving a dismissive hand. "I'm just going in to visit Miss VanNam."

Already on his feet, H.Q. said, "Sorry, you can't go back there, mister."

Winn said, "Perhaps you don't know who I am. I'm Winn DeLaney and I'm engaged to Miss Van-Nam. She's my fiancée."

"That may be, Mr. DeLaney, but the sheriff deputized me and left me in charge," said H.Q. He reached for the Navy Colt that lay on the desk. "I have my orders. You're not to go back there."

"Is that a fact?" Winn said sarcastically.

"'Fraid so, sir."

Winn grinned. "And just who's going to stop me?"

"I am," H.Q. said calmly, raising the gun and aiming it squarely at Winn's chest.

"Jesus, put that thing away before you hurt somebody," Winn cautioned, but he continued to advance.

H.Q. came out from behind the desk. "Take another step and I'll fire."

Winn stopped abruptly. He frowned nervously. "Are you daft, old man? The sheriff never meant for you to—"

"Yes, I did," came a low, modulated voice from just behind him. Winn spun about to see Travis standing in the doorway, his hair disheveled, face scratched and shirt torn. Travis said, "My deputy has asked you to leave. Were I you, I'd go." He crossed his arms over his chest.

Flushing with anger, Winn said, "Overstepping your bounds a bit, aren't you, Sheriff?"

"Am I?"

"Yes, you are. You know you are."

"What are you going to do about it, DeLaney?"

"I'll tell you what I'm going to do about it, McCloud. You were hired by the Committee of Vigilance to keep the peace in Fortune, not to harass its citizens. I believe the committee should hear about this outrage."

"Why don't you tell 'em?" Travis said with a grin.

Forty-One

"Travis, what on earth happened to you?" Kate asked, worriedly eyeing his torn shirt and scratched face.

"Just the usual. A couple of ladies fighting over me," he said with a straight face, and came to the bed unbuttoning his ruined shirt. "I'm used to it," he added with a twinkle in his eyes.

"But you're really hurt," Kate said when he took off his shirt and she saw his bruised ribs.

"Don't worry about it. I'm fine, baby," he said, before he leaned down and kissed her.

Kate didn't believe him. She got out of bed and followed when he went to the stove to put on a kettle of water. "Sit down and let me do that," she ordered. "It's my turn to care for you."

"With pleasure," Travis said, pulling out a chair and sitting down. While the water heated, Kate carefully examined his scratched face, bloodied ear and bruised ribs. She got out a couple of clean cloths, laid them on the table, and once the water had heated, poured some into a pan.

She gently bathed Travis's scratched face, red ear and bruised ribs. Standing between his spread knees, she asked, "Should I bandage the ribs?"

"No. Not necessary. I'm used to getting a few scrapes and sprains. This stuff is minor."

"Nevertheless…" Kate dropped the cloth into the pan of water and sank to her knees before him. She leaned close and began brushing the lightest of kisses to his ribs. With her soft lips against his flesh, she said, "Now, tell me exactly what happened. Leave nothing out."

Cupping her golden head, Travis laughed and recounted the drama that had taken place down at Tillie's. Kate's head came up. "Females actually did this to you?"

"They did," he said. "And it's not the first time."

"But how can you defend yourself against a woman?"

"Not very well." Travis grinned. "You should know that better than anybody. I have no defense against you." He kissed her and said, "Anything you want from me, you know I'll give to you. Anything you want me to do, I'll do it."

Kate pulled back a little. "You mean it?"

"Try me."

"Well, there is something," she said, clasping his wrists in her hands. "I'm awfully tired of lying in bed."

"So, get up if you feel like it."

"Well, that's just it. If I'm to get out of bed, I need clothes and things." She released his wrists and draped her forearms over his knees. "I was hoping maybe we could go up to the mansion this afternoon and I could pick up a few things."

"Tell me what you need and I'll go up and—"

"No, I want to go myself. You wouldn't know what to get."

"Why not wait a couple more days?"

"But I feel fine, Travis. Really I do, and if I could put on some clothes, I'd feel even better. Please, it wouldn't take long, we could just walk up there and stay a few minutes while I gather up some clothes." She looked into his dark expressive eyes and knew he was weakening. "Wouldn't you like to see me in a dress, with my hair washed and brushed?"

"You couldn't be any prettier than you are right now."

"It means a lot to me, Travis."

He shrugged his bare shoulders. "As I said, I have no defense against you. If it'll make you happy, we'll go. But only for a few minutes. And we're not walking."

"We're not?" she said, and shot to her feet.

"No. I'll bring my stallion around to the back door

and we'll ride up." He clasped her narrow waist and added, "But we can't be gone long."

"Twenty minutes at the outside," she said, and automatically went to change clothes. Then quickly realized she had no clothes to change into. She grabbed at her nightshirt and said, "What will I wear? I can't go out like this!"

"See the heavy greatcoat hanging on the coat tree?" he asked, rising to his feet. "Wear that over your nightshirt. And put on those rubber boots you were wearing when Chang Li brought you here."

Kate was as excited as a child when, minutes after leaving, Travis knocked on the back door. Swirling the greatcoat around her shoulders, she opened the door and stepped out into the bright alpine sunshine.

Directly behind Travis stood a saddled Appaloosa stallion, its reins dangling to the ground. Travis plucked her from the stoop and lifted her up to sit across the saddle. He picked up the reins, looped them over the stallion's neck and swung up behind her, enclosing her in his arms.

They skirted the backs of the buildings and soon left the town of Fortune, unobserved. In minutes they were at the mansion. Once they'd dismounted, Travis again tossed the reins to the ground.

"Aren't you afraid he'll wander off?" Kate asked as Travis helped her in the front gate.

"No. I trained him myself," he said. "He won't leave without us. He knows better."

On the front veranda, Kate handed Travis the key he had given to her when she'd first moved in last summer. He put it in the lock, turned the knob and opened the door. He didn't return the key to Kate, but put it in his breast pocket.

The big house was chilly, and Travis was immediately sorry he'd allowed Kate to come. The last thing she needed was to catch a cold.

"Wait," he said, when she started to go into one of the rooms to start collecting her things. "Let me build a fire. Sit down there on the sofa and wait until it warms up a little."

Kate was agreeable. She kept on the heavy coat, and sat down while Travis tossed a couple of logs into the fireplace. In no time he had a healthy blaze going, and the big room began to lose its chill.

Soon Kate threw off the coat and went about gathering up needed articles. Travis offered to help, but she declined. He sat on sofa and watched as she came in and out of the room, placing items of clothing and sundries in a stack near the arched doorway. She was totally preoccupied with her task. And Travis was totally preoccupied with her.

Even in the nightshirt and tall rubber boots, she was without doubt the most irresistible female he had ever known. She was a tempting seductress. She was thoughtful and kind. She was playful and tormenting. She was innocence and purity. She was cunning and wanton. She was all these things.

And she was his.

The room was now warm.

So was he.

Travis rose.

He went directly to the painting of Arielle Van-Nam Colfax, carefully lifting the picture and turning it to face the wall. He returned to the sofa, which he moved at an angle so that it faced the fireplace.

He adjusted the tall mirror that leaned against the wall beside the fire. Then he picked up his greatcoat from the back of the sofa and carefully spread it out in front of the flames.

Travis straightened and ran a hand through his hair. He went out into the corridor and locked the front door. He came back into the drawing room and called out, "Kate, can you come in here a minute, sweetheart?"

Forty-Two

"Be right there," Kate answered. Shortly, she came into the room. She had a dress thrown over her arm and a pair of shoes in her hand. Curious, she crossed to where Travis stood before the fireplace, and looked up at him. "What? What is it?"

Travis reached for her. "I missed you," he said, drawing her into his embrace. "Let your chores go for a while. Stay here with me."

"Is that all you wanted?" Kate said with an indulgent smile.

"No, that's not quite all." He took hold of her upper arms, bent his dark head and kissed her.

In seconds Kate was lost in the steamy kiss. She sighed and dropped the shoes and dress. Soon she felt the nightshirt being eased up her thighs, and knew that Travis was going to make love to her here in the mansion in the middle of the afternoon. Once the nightshirt was up past her waist Kate helpfully lifted her arms so that Travis could slip the sleeves off and get the garment over her head.

Once it was off, he held the nightshirt for a minute, then dropped it to the floor and reached for her.

For several thrilling minutes they stood there before the warming fire, kissing urgently. His hands gently caressing her exquisite back and flaring hips, Travis murmured endearments and continued to kiss her until he knew she was aroused.

Finally he tore his burning lips from hers, and Kate sighed and laid her head on his shoulder. It was then she glimpsed the two of them in the tall, massive mirror. She blinked in surprise, then blushed with embarrassment. And lastly stared, fascinated. It was an oddly erotic vision: Travis fully clothed, she totally naked, save for the tall rubber boots.

"I want," he said against her hair, "to make love to you here in this room, on that sofa, in front of this mirror."

Kate shivered at the naughty suggestion. She buried her face against his shoulder. "Should we?" she whispered, intrigued, but apprehensive.

"You can close your eyes, sweetheart," he told her. "You don't have to look. Unless you decide you want to."

Travis kissed her again and sat her down on the sofa. He knelt before her and removed her boots. Kate took the opportunity to again glance into the mirror. Her stomach contracted sharply and she quickly looked away, feeling as if her cheeks were on fire.

Once her boots were off he rose and began unbuttoning his shirt. When he whipped it off and tossed it aside, Kate stood up. She licked her lips as her hands went to his belt buckle. Together they anxiously undressed him. When he was as naked as she, Travis was facing the mirror and Kate's back was to it.

Travis looked over her head to gaze at their reflection. He shuddered with ecstasy. This pale, beautiful woman whose golden hair spilled down around her bare shoulders was gently gripping his ribs and kissing his chest. And in the mirror he could see the tempting view of her fragile back, flaring hips, rounded bottom, shapely legs and slender ankles.

Nature's finest masterpiece.

Travis's hands remained at his sides. As much as he wanted to touch her, he was more intent on gazing at her tall slender form in the mirror, unblemished by clothing or his own caressing hands. Looking at her, he balled his hands into tight fists and felt his belly tighten. Suddenly, he became aware of her tongue teasing at a flat brown nipple.

Travis lifted his hands, cupped her face and urged her head up. He bent and kissed her, his tongue sliding into her mouth to toy and tangle with hers. While he was kissing her, he slowly, adroitly began turning her about. When the prolonged kiss ended and he raised his head, his back was to the mirror.

Just as he'd intended.

Still, he knew she couldn't see their seductive reflection because he was much taller than she. So he slowly sank to his knees before her, and Kate immediately saw them framed in the mirror. She stared, entranced, and trembled with ecstasy. This dark, handsome man with the gleaming midnight hair was gently clasping her waist and kissing her breasts. And in the mirror she saw the tantalizing image of his beautiful, deeply clefted back, his trim waist, slim hips, firm buttocks and powerful thighs.

God's finest creation.

Kate's hands were at her sides. While she yearned to touch him, she was too engrossed by simply staring at his perfect physique in the mirror, unmarred by clothing or her own grasping hands. Gazing upon him, she clenched her fingers into tight fists at her sides. Suddenly Kate became aware of his tongue lightly teasing a tingling nipple.

She lifted her hands, tunneled her fingers into his dark, lustrous hair and pressed his face closer. She drew a quick breath of air as his mouth closed over the aching nipple. He began to suck vigorously, his jaws flexing, his eyes closed, long dark lashes touching her, tickling her.

Kate's inhibitions fell away as her passions rose and she fully surrendered to the carnal pleasure of the moment. She found it incredibly thrilling to have her dark lover's heated lips at her breasts while she unashamedly watched in the mirror.

Kate became intensely aware of her surroundings. She dreamily glanced around, wanting to remember everything exactly as it was on this unforgettable autumn afternoon. The large drawing room where one day they would entertain invited guests was today their private sexual playground where only the two of them could enter. The blazing fire in the grate licked lovingly at their bodies and bathed their bare flesh with a soft rosy hue.

She again looked directly into the mirror, at the pair of naked lovers reflected there—the dark, compelling man and the pale, enchanted woman. She sighed deeply, took her hands from Travis's raven hair and let her fingertips dance nervously along his broad shoulders.

When his lips released a wet nipple, Kate supposed that he would swiftly rise to his feet and take her to the sofa. She bit her lip when, instead, he remained on his knees. Her heart raced when he wrapped his arms around her, laid his cheek against her stomach and said, "I want to kiss you all over, sweetheart." He brushed a kiss to her fluttering belly. "And you can watch while I do."

Forty-Three

Kate felt her heart beating in her ears when Travis lifted his head and looked up at her with his dark, sultry eyes that had the power to mesmerize.

Steadily holding her anxious gaze, he urged her down to her knees before him. For a long, tense moment, they remained in front of the mirror, the only sounds those of the snapping, crackling fire and their own rapid breaths.

Travis lifted a hand, swept Kate's long golden hair back off her shoulders, wrapped an arm around her waist and drew her up against him. When he bent his head to kiss her, he hesitated.

And he said softly, "I'll never do anything you don't want me to do, Kate. Never."

Then his mouth closed over hers in a kiss that made her heart race and her bones melt. Kate's weak arms came up around his neck and she anxiously clung to him as he kissed her over and over again. At some point during the heated exchange, Travis put an arm out and gently lowered Kate to the floor, following her down.

When at last his lips released hers, she was on her back with Travis lying on his side against her. Kate didn't question him when he said in that slow Southern drawl she'd come to adore, "Turn over onto your stomach, darlin'."

Kate turned over, but raised up onto her elbows and rested her chin in her hands. At once she became aware of the slightly abrasive texture of the greatcoat beneath her bare body. In her heightened state of arousal, it felt good.

But not as good as the heated lips that began scattering kisses over her shoulders. Then over her back and waist. Kate soon lay down flat, sighing and folding an arm beneath her cheek. She had, by design, turned her face toward the mirror. She lay there and watched as Travis kissed her "all over" just as he'd promised.

She snuggled comfortably against the spread greatcoat while Travis kissed the twin dimples at the base of her spine, then up and over her rounded buttocks and down her thighs, to behind her knees and her calves and ankles.

It was electrifying.

She purred like a cat.

When he eased her over onto her back, she looked up at him and trembled. In his beautiful eyes was all his love, all his passion, plus his promise to cherish her for a lifetime. He leaned down and softly kissed her parted lips, then her throat and her shoulders, his hair ruffling against her chin. He trailed open-mouthed kisses down the center of her chest, around each breast, then enclosed a pebble-hard nipple in his mouth and briefly sucked on it.

Kate again turned her head and gazed into the mirror. She saw Travis's handsome face and raised a hand to touch his dark head. But before she could place her fingers in his hair, his lips released the nipple and moved on.

Sliding downward.

His hand at her waist, Travis kissed her flat belly. Kate whispered his name as she watched his dark face slowly slip lower. She continued to gaze into the mirror while he probed her navel with the tip of his tongue and then licked the faint line of pale fine hair going down the center of her belly to the blond triangle of curls between her thighs.

Kate held her breath.

Travis brushed a kiss to her hipbone. And then, in one swift, fluid movement, he reached for her hand and drew her up into a sitting position. He clasped her waist in both hands, pushed her to feet and maneuvered her about so that she felt the sofa's edge touch the backs of her legs. She weakly sank down onto the couch and shivered when Travis knelt before her.

His hands gripped her knees, and he gently urged them apart and drew her to the edge of the cushion.

He looked directly into her eyes and said softly, "Tell me to stop and you know I will."

She could barely breathe. As his dark head slowly lowered to her, Kate automatically lifted her eyes to the mirror. She felt his hands gently clasping her hips, felt his glossy hair tickle her belly. Then she felt his mouth, burning hot, on the inside of her right knee. He kissed the skin there and then, his lips never leaving her flesh, kissed a slow, deliberate path up the warm length of her thigh.

An eyelash away from the golden curls of her groin, he stopped, raised his head and said huskily, "Kiss me. Kiss me, sweetheart."

"Yes," Kate whispered. She put her trembling hands to his tanned jaws, leaned down and aggressively kissed him, thrusting her tongue deep into his mouth. When their lips separated, Travis again bent to her. He kissed her left knee and, as he'd done before, teasingly nipped and licked and his way up to the edge of the springy golden coils.

Kate was on fire.

She arched her back and gripped the edge of the sofa's cushion. Her breath was coming in short little gulps. Her breasts were swelling, the nipples standing out in twin points of desire. Her belly was contracting sharply. And between her trembling thighs, now open to him, the slick female flesh was pulsing with passion and wet with need.

Kate tensed when at last she felt Travis's breath stir the curls there. She raised her eyes to the mirror. Her back arched again as she waited, her whole body vibrating, her throat dry, her eyes glazed with passion.

Travis nuzzled his nose and mouth in the golden curls, then dabbed playfully with his tongue. Lightly he teased the burning flesh beneath, blowing his breath over it. He tormented her until Kate murmured, "Please. Please."

"Please what?"

"Kiss me."

"Show me where, baby."

Feverish, all her inhibitions burned away in the sexual heat, Kate put her hand between her legs and touched her fingers to the slick, pulsing flesh between her kiss-dampened curls.

"Here. Kiss me here," she whispered, feeling as though she would die if he did not.

He did.

Travis's hot mouth immediately covered her fingertips, and for a second, Kate didn't move her hand. It was tremendously arousing to have his tongue licking her fingers while she touched herself. When she started to take her hand away, he stopped her, swiftly grasping her wrist.

"No, sweetheart. Let's play awhile," he coaxed. "Make the pleasure last."

"Show me how."

He did just that. And it proved to be a highly exciting diversion. With his tongue, Travis pressed against her slender fingers, and in turn those fingers pressed against the pulsating point of ultrasensitive female flesh. The joy intensified when Travis forced her fingers apart with the tip of his tongue in pursuit of the sweetness beneath.

Kate found this erotic exercise to be unbearably exciting. It didn't seem depraved or shocking, but merely a delightful sexual game she was more than pleased to play with her trusted lover. She understood that her opponent's objective was to get his tongue between her protective fingers. Hers was to prevent that marvelous tongue from gaining access. It was fun, it was bawdy, it was terribly exciting.

But it was fleeting.

Kate's opponent was too talented and she was too incredibly hot to outlast him. The prize for which she could wait no longer was Travis's burning mouth and stroking tongue on her throbbing flesh.

Attuned to her every wish, Travis immediately let go of her wrist. She stifled a near sob of bliss when his hot, open mouth took the place of her fingers.

The first stroke of his tongue brought an incendiary shock of ecstasy unlike anything she'd ever experienced. That awesome joy intensified when she looked into the mirror and watched. She moaned as his tongue spread a sexual fire that threatened to blaze out of control and totally consume her.

"Travis, Travis!" She called his name, thrust her hands in his hair at the sides of his head and anxiously drew him closer.

Wild and wanton, she tilted her pelvis up as she opened her legs wider. Her breath was coming in labored pants. Her eyes opened and closed, affording dazed glimpses of them in the mirror. A shuddering climax was imminent; she felt the frightening release coming.

So did Travis.

He slid his hands beneath her and clasped the twin cheeks of her bottom. He lifted her slightly and his dark face sank more fully into her. When she began to frantically call his name, he licked and lashed and loved her, giving her all she needed.

Kate frantically moaned and bucked and writhed. She begged him to stop, then begged him to never stop. She felt that she would surely die if he took his hot mouth from her.

Then it began. Her climax was so wrenching, so intense that she clung to his dark head, frantically pulling his hair and pressing him closer.

The orgasm went on and on, and Kate gasped his name as she looked into the mirror and saw his handsome face buried in her flesh, coaxing the eruptions of ecstasy from her with his masterful mouth.

When the final explosion happened, she screamed and shuddered, and Travis kept his mouth tightly fused to her until she finally collapsed, shaken and gasping for breath, against the sofa's high back.

Only then did he raise his head.

He came up onto the sofa, put his arms around her and held her close against his chest.

Forty-Four

A patient lover, Travis suppressed the natural impulse to swiftly seek his own release. Had she been only a beautiful courtesan with whom he could slake his lust, he wouldn't have waited. He would have already been buried deep inside her.

But this was Kate.

His Kate. The woman he loved.

So he waited.

And he contented himself with gazing at the two of them in the mirror. It was a vision he knew he would never forget. Kate's head on his shoulder, her cheek against his chest, her eyes closed. A slender arm was draped across his waist and her pale, limp body was pressed warmly against his side.

It would have a been sweet, peaceful moment in time if not for the fact that he was so achingly aroused it was painful. Still, he was not going to rush her.

Travis was looking into the mirror when, without opening her eyes, she laid a gentle hand on his straining masculinity. He jumped, startled, then tensed and held his breath as she eagerly, but ineptly, toyed with him.

When finally she opened her eyes and lifted her head, she said with childlike innocence, "Show me, Travis. I don't know how to…"

His hand quickly covered hers. "Something more like this, sweetheart." He guided her fingers slowly up and down the length of his erection, from base to head and back again. "It's easy. Nothing to it, really."

Kate quickly caught on. "I've mastered it," she said. "Now take your hand away and let me show you." He reluctantly obeyed. Stroking him, exciting him, she repeated his own words back to him, "I'd never do anything you don't want to do."

"Now, Kate…"

"Shh," she warned. Releasing her hold on him, she slipped down off the sofa in one swift, agile movement and turned about to kneel before him.

Her eyes flashing blue fire, she gripped his knees and pushed them apart. She looked up at him with a mischievous smile and said, "Tell me to stop and I will."

Travis didn't tell her stop. He didn't trust his voice. It was hard to breathe, much less speak. As Kate's golden head slowly lowered to him, Travis couldn't keep from lifting his eyes and glancing into the mirror. He watched like a captivated voyeur.

He felt Kate's hands clasping his thighs, felt her silky hair tickling his bare belly. Felt her soft lips, burning hot, on the inside of his right knee. Kate kissed him there, then moved her mouth in a deliberate path up the inside of his steely, hair-dusted thigh.

And all the while Travis watched in the mirror.

An inch away from the raven curls of his groin, she stopped, raised her head, tossed her hair back from her face and said, "Kiss me, Travis."

He leaned down and kissed her, but when he tried to draw her up onto the sofa, Kate tore her lips from his and again bent to him. She kissed his left knee and teasingly nipped and licked her way up to the edge of the crisp midnight coils.

Travis's entire body became rigid with eager expectancy when he felt Kate's breath against his surging erection. She blew that warm, moist breath on him and his passion-glazed eyes again lifted to the mirror. He almost had a coronary when he felt Kate's soft lips tentatively settle on the throbbing tip of his erection.

He allowed himself only a few fleeting seconds to enjoy the erotic sight of her kneeling between his spread knees, her head bent to him, the glorious golden hair spilling over his lap and thighs. When he felt her mouth begin to slide hesitantly down over him, Travis groaned, bit the inside of his cheek and urged her head up.

"Stop, sweetheart. I want you to stop."

"I want to love you like you loved me," she said.

"Another time."

"But you're still…you haven't…"

"No, but I will once I'm inside you," he said. Taking hold of her upper arms, he pushed her to her feet, then drew her astride his lap.

She cupped his tanned cheeks in her hands. "If that's what you want."

"It is, sweetheart."

She kissed him and said against his lips, "Know what I want?"

"Tell me."

She lifted her head. "I want to do this myself. You're not to make a move to help. Let me put…" Her words trailed away.

"It—and I—are all yours. Do with us what you will."

Kate nodded, pushed her tangled hair behind her ears, scooted back on his hard thighs and again gently took him in hand. Then, biting her lip in fierce concentration, she carefully guided the swollen tip up inside her.

Resting her hands atop his shoulders, she looked steadily into his eyes as she slowly, surely slid down onto him.

"May I move a little now?" he asked when she was fully impaled upon him.

"Mmm," she replied in a silky voice as she looped her arms around his neck and pressed her cheek to his.

At first his movements were slow, deliberate, the languid flexing of his buttocks, the leisurely surging of his pelvis. His hands filled with the pale cheeks of her bottom, he rhythmically drew her down on him as he rose to meet her.

But her soft, yielding body was too sweet and he had waited too long for release. He couldn't hold out much longer. He increased the tempo of his thrusts and, blinded by passion, he no longer looked into the mirror. His eyes closed, his heart hammering, he pumped into Kate with an almost savage hunger. Fearful he would hurt her, but unable to slow the pace of his fevered lovemaking, he slipped his arms under her bent knees to clasp her more firmly to him.

The position more fully tilted her pelvis and afforded deeper penetration. At once the pleasure, both his and hers, spiraled upward, and they gasped at the escalation of ecstasy.

For a few frenzied seconds more they made primitive, passionate love this way, their enjoined bodies damp with sexual perspiration, flesh slapping against flesh in a wild, exhilarating ride.

It might have lasted a few moments longer if Kate hadn't asked breathlessly, "Can you see us in the mirror?"

Travis's dark eyes lifted.

He saw them.

And it brought on a draining, pulse-pounding climax unlike anything he'd ever experienced. It was the same for Kate. An orgasm so powerful overtook her that she screamed and clung to him as wave after wave of ecstasy washed over her.

When the tempest finally passed, she sagged against him, too weak to move. They stayed like that for several long minutes, warmed by the afterglow of incredible lovemaking.

Finally Travis said, "You're gonna be the death of me yet, baby."

"But you'll die happy."

Laughing, they hurriedly dressed.

The fire had gone completely out. The big room was chilly. They realized they had stayed at the mansion much longer than intended. Twenty minutes had turned into two hours.

"You ought to be ashamed of yourself. Leaving the citizens of Fortune unprotected all this time," Kate teased as she drew a woolen dress over her head. "You might lose your job over this, Sheriff."

"Could be," he replied, unconcerned. "I might very well get booted out of town."

"I wouldn't be a bit surprised," she said with a smile.

"If so, will you come with me?"

"When you like. Where you like."

Forty-Five

"When did you get back, Doc?"

His white eyebrows lifting, Dr. Ledet replied, "I might ask you the same question, Sheriff."

The doctor had arrived in Fortune while Travis and Kate were at the mansion. He'd hardly had time to unlock his office and put down his black bag before hearing the shocking news that Kate had been shot and the sheriff had removed the bullet. She was, he was told, convalescing in the sheriff's quarters.

Deeply concerned, the doctor had immediately hurried to the jail. And found it empty, save for a big calico cat dozing on a bunk in one of the cells. He had hurried on through the jail and pounded on the door of Travis's private quarters. No answer. Really getting worried then, wondering if Travis had been called away to handle a disturbance, leaving the in-

jured Kate alone, the doctor went directly to the sheriff's desk. He pulled out a drawer, hoping to find a
key to Travis's quarters.

He found no key.

Growing increasingly frustrated, he had hurried
back outside and slipped through the alley to the rear
of the building to bang on the back door and call
Kate's name. To no avail. Finally he returned to his
own office, where he had paced the floor, imagining
all kinds of dire possibilities.

Two long hours had passed when finally he saw
Travis step out onto the sidewalk in front of the jail.
Muttering under his breath, the doctor snatched up
his black bag and rushed right over.

Now, as the two men faced each other, the frowning physician told Travis, "Soon as I got back, I
heard about the shooting and came over, but nobody
was here."

Travis looked a little sheepish. "Yes, well, Miss
VanNam was feeling so much better she insisted I
take her up to the mansion to get some clothes."

"You couldn't have gone up by yourself and..."

"She wanted to go, Doc." Travis shrugged broad
shoulders. "You know how women are."

"So you took it upon yourself to pronounce her
able to walk all the way—"

"Keep your shirt on, we didn't walk. We rode my
stallion up."

Dr. Ledet again shook his head. "I want to see the

patient immediately! Who knows what lasting harm
may come from her being jolted up and down on the
back of a horse!"

Thankful the scolding physician didn't know what
he and Kate had really been up to, Travis said, "You'll
see for yourself that she's mending remarkably well."

"Let me be the judge of that," the doctor replied
testily. He stepped inside and started toward the back
quarters.

"Fine, but wait here a minute," Travis said, following on his heels. "I'll just check to see if she's awake.
She might be napping, and we wouldn't want to disturb her."

"She's likely worn out from you allowing her
to—"

"Have a seat, Doc," Travis interrupted, indicating
a chair.

Travis went to the rear and, opening the door just
wide enough to slip through, quickly put his finger
to his lips when Kate looked up, smiled and started
to speak.

Fresh out of a bath, she was seated cross-legged
on the floor in front the fire, brushing her long golden
hair. She wore only her lace-trimmed pantelets.
Travis came to her, crouched down and whispered,
"Doc Ledet is here."

"Here in Fortune? Or here at the jail?" she whispered back, brush poised in her hand.

"Both," he said, helping her to her feet. "He wants

to have a look at your shoulder. Now, hurry and get in bed while I fetch you a nightshirt."

Nodding, Kate anxiously crossed the room while Travis briefed her on the fact that the doctor had come by the jail earlier and found them both gone. "I told him you insisted on going up to the mansion to get some clothes."

Kate nodded again. Once she was in bed, Travis helped her into the nightshirt, then drew the covers up over her. "Ready?"

"Yes. Send him in."

"Don't let anybody know what a good job Travis did," Doc Ledet said, after carefully examining the healing bullet wound. His eyes twinkled when he added, "You do and I'll be out of a job."

"It'll be our secret," Kate assured him.

After ten minutes with his patient, the physician closed his black bag. "I might as well go," he said. "Obviously, you don't need me."

"I'm glad you're back, Doctor, and I appreciate you looking in on me."

The physician smiled, patted her good shoulder and glanced curiously around the room. He noticed the wooden tub of soapy water, with a couple of damp towels and a hairbrush beside it. A blue woolen dress was tossed over the arm of Travis's easy chair. Other articles of feminine attire were scattered about the spacious room.

He didn't comment, but he wasn't fooled. When he rejoined Travis, he said, "You did an excellent job, Sheriff." His eyes twinkled with mischief when he added, "In fact, Kate's in good enough shape to go on home." He looked at Travis and waited for a response. He got none. "I see no need for her to stay at your place any longer. I'm sure you must be tired of sleeping in the jail."

Travis didn't take the bait. As enigmatic as ever, he ushered Doc Ledet to the door, following him out. They stood for a few minutes on the sidewalk in the fading autumn sunshine, talking about the sudden snowstorm and how quickly it had melted. About the Goldbug mining accident. About the chances of Jiggs and the posse finding Kelton and Spears.

Finally Doc Ledet said, "Well, I'm tired and I'm hungry, so I'll be getting on home, Travis."

"Thanks for coming."

"Don't mention it. I'll likely stop by tomorrow, check on Kate. That is, if she's going to be here at your place." Again he quizzically lifted his eyebrows.

"Good evening, Doc."

Travis stayed where he was for a couple of minutes after the doctor had gone. He was just turning to go back inside when the muscular, mustachioed Sam Barkley, bartender and bouncer at the Golden Nugget, came out of the saloon carrying a large wooden sign.

Travis squinted as Sam leaned the big placard

against the wall just right of the bat-wing doors. He began hammering it in place, and Travis read the two-word sign: For Sale.

As Sam was finishing up, Valentina Knight walked through the saloon's swinging doors. She stood before the sign, examining it. She said something to Sam and shook her head approvingly. The big man went back inside while Valentina stayed a moment longer.

Travis stepped down off the sidewalk.

He crossed the street. Valentina turned as he approached.

"Evenin', Val."

"Travis."

"What's all this?" he indicated the sign. "You actually meaning to sell the Nugget?"

"I am." She smiled. "Want to buy it?"

"Why sell? You told me yourself you're making a fortune."

"Ah, well that's just it. I have all the money I need so there's no reason for me to stay." She looked at him half hopefully. "Is there, Travis?" When he gave no reply, she quickly added, "The truth is I've grown tired of these backward gold camp towns. I miss the elegance of New Orleans. I'm going home."

"I wish you all the best, Val," he said. "You'll say good-bye before you leave?"

"Why you know I will."

Both knew she would not.

Forty-Six

Midnight.

Travis was awake. Kate was not. Cal the cat dozed before the dying fire. Travis lay on his back, an arm folded beneath his head. Kate was curled up on her side, facing him. Cal was sprawled on his belly, paws out before him.

Travis was tired, but not sleepy. He was intrigued with the sleeping beauty beside him. He gazed fondly at her golden hair spilling across the pillow and at the angelic face in repose, those striking blue eyes closed, her long lashes stilled. Above the sheet's top edge, her pale silky shoulders were a bedeviling reminder that beneath the sheet she was as naked as he was.

At bedtime she had shed her clothes, and, to his surprised delight, had not donned a nightshirt. She had winked at him, smiled and saucily climbed into bed, beautifully bare. It was the first time that had happened. Excited by the gesture, he had anxiously shed his own clothes, supposing she was ready to make love again.

But once he'd slid into bed and reached for her, she'd kissed him quickly and said, "Are you as sleepy as I am?"

Before he could answer, her eyes had closed and she was asleep.

Two hours had passed since then.

And still Travis was wide awake. He couldn't relax, couldn't unwind. And it was her fault. Try as he might, he couldn't forget for a moment that this exquisite young goddess was naked in his bed. It was so disturbing, so unsettling, he was half tempted to wake her and insist she put on a nightshirt so that he could get some rest.

Kate stirred in her sleep and Travis tensed. Her knee slid up his leg and a soft hand fell across his chest. But she slept on. He gritted his teeth. And then very carefully, very slowly, he edged closer to her until their bodies were touching. He eased over onto his side to face her, gently drawing her leg up over his hip.

Travis lifted his head off the pillow. Resting his weight on an elbow, he cautiously leaned over and lowered his lips to hers. His mouth settled gently over hers in what he promised himself would be one brief, closemouthed kiss. But once he felt her warm lips beneath his own, his mouth opened ever so slightly.

And his heart thudded in his chest when he felt the

fluttering tip of her tongue against his open lips. She was asleep, but she was kissing him. Incredibly erotic! He wondered how long they could kiss before she awakened and realized what was happening. Shudders of excitement surged through him, Travis kept his mouth on hers while she sweetly responded.

He was never quite sure when Kate woke up. Not a word was spoken between them. Their bodies said everything. Silently, they kissed and touched and embraced. And sometime during all that enjoyable play, the covers were kicked to the foot of the bed.

The fire in the grate had burned low and the room was chilly. But they were not. They were feverish with desire, their bare skin hot to the touch. And to the taste. It was the oddest of sensations for them both. They were highly aroused, but at the same time languid in their lovemaking. They changed positions again and again, tumbling about on the rumpled bed, taking turns at being conqueror and conquered.

Tingling with arousal, a deliciously lazy Kate soon found herself backed up spoon fashion against Travis. His strong arms were around her and his solid chest was pressed against her back. She sighed when a dark hand drifted up to fondle a bare breast, lean fingers plucking at the awakened nipple. Kate squirmed when that hand slipped down her belly and through the golden triangle of hair to touch that tiny bud of passion.

She sighed and shivered and felt Travis's powerful erection throbbing against her bare bottom. Instinctively, she knew his intent and didn't object. He was going to make love to her in this position, and she found the prospect incredibly tantalizing.

Kate arched her back, leaned a little forward on the pillow, opened her legs and pressed her buttocks more firmly against him. Travis did the rest. She bit her lip when she felt the hard, heavy flesh enter her from behind and inch cautiously into her. His lips pressing burning kisses to her shoulder, Travis waited only a few heartbeats before thrusting farther.

Guiding her movements with his hands, teaching her how, he urged her hips back against him as he drove into her, plunging slowly, warily, taking care not to hurt her. Until at last his full, throbbing length was inside her.

For a long moment he stayed completely still, waiting for her, making sure she was relaxed and ready. When she began the subtle, sensual grinding of her hips, he flexed his buttocks and surged to meet her, keeping the tempo slow and easy.

After several pleasing moments of making love this way, their enjoined bodies cried out for more. Travis sped up his movements. Her wild golden hair slapping him in the face, Kate gasped and writhed and quickly caught his rhythm. His arms came back around her. One hand caressed her breasts; the other went between her legs.

His talented hands added to Kate's escalating ecstasy. She liked this way of making love. It was thrilling to have him buried deep inside her while at the same time his magical fingers were doing such wonderful things to her. The naughty thought struck her that she wanted Travis to do it just like this every time he made love to her. She would insist that he take her from behind so that his marvelous hands could...could...

Kate gasped and her body spasmed as the first blinding wave of a wrenching orgasm washed over her. Travis groaned as his own release began. They came together, sharing a climax so intense it was frightening. The deep tremors of ecstasy buffeted them for several seconds before finally leaving them totally spent.

And blissfully happy.

Deeply content, both sighed tiredly and fell asleep, lying there just as they were, having uttered not a single word throughout the impetuous lovemaking.

Forty-Seven

It happened at high noon.

Five days after the shooting, Winn DeLaney walked into the lobby of the Bonanza Hotel. He was about to enter the dining room for a leisurely midday meal, but the sudden thunder of horses' hooves caused him to stop in midstride and turn. His pulse became erratic as he crossed the lobby and stepped outside to investigate.

Squinting, he looked down the street and, to his horror, saw Deputy Jiggs Gillespie and the posse ride into town. With them were the apprehended Titus Kelton and Jim Spears. In a great cloud of dust, the mounted men came to a halt before the city jail. Winn swallowed convulsively when Sheriff Travis McCloud stepped out of the building to take possession of the cuffed prisoners.

Panic seized DeLaney.

For a dreadful moment he stood there immobile, unable to think or to move.

Then it became crystal clear what he should do. He had to get out of Fortune before those two brawny thugs told on him.

Winn hurried back inside. With a shaking hand, he reached into his trouser pocket and peeled off a couple of bills. He hurried over to Dwayne, handed him the bills and instructed the puzzled room clerk to send a messenger to the Whiskey Hill Saloon to fetch a dark-haired young lady who worked there.

"Her name is Melisande," Winn said. "Have Melisande come here at once." When Dwayne hesitated, looked at the bills, then back at him, Winn shouted, "Now!"

"Yes, sir, Mr. DeLaney," said the startled clerk.

Winn rushed back upstairs to start packing. In minutes a worried Melisande joined him. Out of breath, she gasped, "Winn, what are we going to do? They've brought in Kelton and Spears and—"

"I know that!" Winn yelled at her. "They're sure to implicate me in Kate's shooting. We have to get out of Fortune right now, today!"

Nodding, Melisande began anxiously tossing clothes on the bed, where a large valise was open. She was starting to change out of her gaudy satin costume when a loud knock came on the door. She and Winn exchanged looks of alarm. Winn motioned for her to keep silent. He reached for his revolver.

"Open up, DeLaney," Sheriff McCloud calmly ordered.

His jaw ridged, Winn raised his revolver and fired through the door. The bullet missed Travis by an inch and lodged in the hallway wall. The sheriff again ordered DeLaney to open the door. When he refused, Travis warned him to stand back, then he kicked the door open.

Delaney took aim, but Melisande screamed, "No, Winn, no!" and threw herself between the two men just as DeLaney fired.

She slumped to the floor, hit in the back.

"Put the gun down, DeLaney," the sheriff warned.

But Winn again took aim. Travis, having no choice, shot and killed him.

Travis holstered his Navy Colt and hurried to the wounded woman. He sank to his knees beside her. Her eyes, filling with tears, were open, and she was clutching her bloodstained bodice.

"Winn," she gasped. "Is Winn all right?"

Travis gave no reply. He gingerly lifted her and carried her downstairs, then directly across the street to Doc Ledet's office. The doctor saw them coming and rushed into the back room to wash up and ready his instruments.

"Lay her there on the table, Sheriff," he instructed when they came through the curtained doorway.

Travis nodded and gently lowered the woman to the sheet-draped examining table. He immediately turned and went into the front office as the doctor began cutting the woman's bloody clothes away.

Travis paced as the minutes ticked away. After half an hour, he looked up as Doc Ledet came through the curtains.

Travis gave him a questioning look.

The doctor shook his head. "The woman's mortally wounded, Sheriff. She won't live till sundown."

Travis nodded. "She conscious?"

"No. No, she's not." The physician rolled down his shirtsleeves. "What happened?"

Travis related exactly what had taken place at the Bonanza. When he concluded, Doc Ledet rubbed his chin thoughtfully and said, "Looks like you were right all along about DeLaney."

"Unfortunately."

"I'll go on over to the hotel and pronounce DeLaney dead, then summon Clarence, the undertaker."

"I'll stay here. Maybe the woman will regain consciousness."

"Good enough. I should be back in fifteen minutes."

The sun was sinking in the west when Doc Ledet came hurrying into the jail. "She's awake, Trav. The woman's awake."

Travis was up out of his chair in an instant. He trotted to the doctor's office ahead of the puffing physician. While Doc Ledet waited just outside the curtained doorway, Travis stepped up to the table. The woman looked up at him, her eyes filled with tears.

Travis gently took her hand in both of his. "Is there anything I can do? Anything I can get you?" His voice was low, soft.

"Is Winn…is he dead?" she asked.

"I'm sorry," Travis replied.

Tears spilled over and ran down her cheeks as she said, "I'm going to die, too."

"Doc Ledet will do everything he can to…"

"Sheriff, I am not going to make it, and there are some things I must tell you to…to ease my conscience."

Travis lightly squeezed her hand. "That's what I'm here for, miss."

Melisande began to talk, to tell Travis everything. "Winn wanted the gold."

"How did he know about the gold?"

Melisande swallowed with difficulty. "Winn fought alongside Kate VanNam's brother, Gregory, under General Scott in the Mexican War. Later both Winn and Gregory turned up in San Francisco and renewed their acquaintance. Gregory bragged to Winn about the Cavalry Blue Mine and how one day he would inherit it and be a very rich man. But when his great-aunt Arielle Colfax died, Gregory learned that she had cut him out of her will. She left every-thing—including the gold mine—to his sister." Mel-isande grimaced in pain.

"Rest awhile," Travis coaxed. "We'll talk later."

As if he hadn't spoken, Melisande confided, "After learning that Kate VanNam had inherited the mine, Winn killed Gregory to get him out of the way. You see, we had proof that there was gold in the Cavalry Blue. We stole the report from a noted San Franciscan assayist and then...then I—I killed the poor man while he was in the hospital. And I took the assay from his files."

Travis said nothing. He showed no emotion. But he recalled reading about the murder of a prominent assayist in the crime journal.

The dying woman continued, "Winn's plan was to come here to Fortune and marry Kate VanNam. When she was his wife, he would have her sign the mine over to him. Once he legally had his hands on the gold, he would divorce her and marry me." She began to sob, "I was in love with Winn. I'd have done anything he asked."

Feeling compassionate, Travis placed her hand back on the table at her side and patted her shoulder. "You get some rest. You'll feel better tomorrow."

But the woman's wounds were fatal.

She died with the last glimmer of light.

Travis returned to his quarters and the anxious Kate. He told her of the pair's failed scheme to get their hands on the gold.

Then he took her in his arms and, as gently as possible, informed her that her brother, Gregory, was dead.

Forty-Eight

"We'll get the executioner over from Hangtown to take care of Kelton and Spears," Doc Ledet said the next day.

Travis nodded, but frowned slightly. The doctor caught Travis's expression and said, "Kate doesn't want to see them hanged, does she?"

Travis shook his head. "She's a sweet, charitable soul, Doc. She hates to have any more bloodshed."

Doc Ledet rubbed his chin thoughtfully. "You could let the pair go. Warn them, under the Committee of Vigilance's threat of death, never to set foot in California again."

Travis looked at the white-haired doctor. Doc Ledet smiled and said, "Have Jiggs guard them tonight. He'll fall asleep. He always does."

Travis frowned and said, "The town's expecting a hanging. They'll be disappointed if there isn't one."

Eyes twinkling, the physician said, "Not if there's a wedding."

Travis finally grinned. "That's true. All they're looking for is an excuse to celebrate."

Everyone turned out for the festive wedding celebration.

Chang Li was there. The loyal Chinaman who, thanks to Kate's generosity, was a five percent owner in the gold-rich Cavalry Blue Mine, was almost as happy as the bride. He sipped French champagne for the first time in his life and looked eagerly forward to the day his wife and child would arrive in Fortune.

Doc Ledet was there. The smiling physician had agreed to give the bride away, and he couldn't have been more proud if Kate had been his own daughter. He told anyone who would listen that he had known all along that the town sheriff and the new heiress were "meant for each other."

The deputy, Jiggs Gillespie, was there to stand up with Travis. The well-scrubbed best man almost held up the ceremony when he couldn't remember which pocket he had put the ring in.

Fortunately, Kate's glowing matron of honor, the reliable Alice Hester, remembered exactly where her shy beau had put the ring. She remembered because she had helped Jiggs dress, and she had placed the ring in the inside breast pocket of his dark frock coat. With an almost imperceptible nod of her head, Alice motioned to Jiggs, and saw the light of recollection appear in his eyes.

H. Q. Blankenship was one of the many guests. The old sourdough, whom Kate had contracted to oversee the restoration of the mansion, had a new lease on life. It had been so long since anyone had needed him or his services, he felt almost like a young, vibrant man again. He stayed busy these days drawing up plans to turn the run-down house back into a grand mansion.

Clifton Barton of Barton's Emporium was there, taking great delight in commenting on the weather. "Why, it's as cold as a whore's kiss," he was fond of exclaiming.

Everyone in Fortune had been invited to the 10:00 a.m. wedding, and a majority of the population had shown up. Once the brief ceremony was over, Travis kissed the bride and led her onto the dance floor. The happy newlyweds whirled about for a few minutes before pausing and inviting everyone to join them in the dance.

The liquor flowed in the Eldorado Hotel's large dining room and spacious lobby as the wedding crowd celebrated.

"Think they'd miss us if we leave?" Travis asked, his arms locked around Kate's narrow waist.

"We'd better slip away soon if we're to catch the noon riverboat," Kate replied.

The pair had booked a cabin on the *Golden Swan* to take them downriver to San Francisco. There they would honeymoon in the bridal suite of the city's finest hotel.

"Then let's go, sweetheart," Travis whispered.

"There's just one thing I need to know," Kate said, her arm looped around his neck.

"Anything, Kate."

"You don't mind being married to a rich woman, do you, Travis?"

"No, but I like being sheriff of Fortune. Rich wife or no, I don't want to give it up."

"Good," Kate said with a smile. "I like seeing that silver badge on your chest." She looked into his beautiful dark eyes and added, "Arrest me anytime you please, Marshal."

Travis grinned. "How about right now, baby?"

"I'll go peacefully, Sheriff McCloud."